The Darling of the Blackrock Desert

Also by Laura Newman

The Franklin Avenue Rookery for Wayward Babies

Parallel to Paradise

The Darling of the Blackrock Desert

Three novellas of the West

Laura Newmant

Delphinium Books

THE DARLING OF THE BLACKROCK DESERT

Printed in the United States of America

For information, address DELPHINIUM BOOKS, INC.,
1250 4th Street Suite 5th Floor
Santa Monica, California 90401

Library of Congress Cataloguing-in-Publication Data is available on request.
ISBN 978-1-953002-53-2

Jacket and interior design by Colin Dockrill, AIGA

Dedication:tk

CONTENTS

The Darling of the Black Rock Desert   01

City of Angels   122

The Saints of Death Valley 175

Mountain Bluebird, Nevada State Bird

The Great Basin of Nevada, together with the Sonoran, Chihuahuana, and Mojave, form the vast North American Desert. The Great Basin is the coldest of the four because it lacks the parka of humidity. It is a place where beauty comes in small pieces. In chips of topaz, white turquoise, and petrified wood. In snowflakes, and canyon groves of quaking aspen. Shifting mountains of singing sand, washes of borax, and twisty bristlecone pines four thousand years old. Animals that will only be wild. Its wealth is in gold and silver and history. In next-door California, beauty is the headliner. But a quiet mind can find beauty in the high desert.

THE DARLING OF THE BLACKROCK DESERT

Of course Julia knew not to pick up hitchhikers. Everyone knows that's how girls die with dirty knees, broken nails, and a two-inch headline. Something about the underwear, missing or ripped; always something about the underwear. There was that girl who had her arms severed below the elbow, pushed out of the van, down the ravine. She lived! And then fifteen years later, they let the carver out of jail. No good story comes out of hitchhiking. Not since after World War II, when damaged young men in fading uniforms crisscrossed the country looking for a place where the bullets in their heads quit ripping holes in their hearts. Everyone picked the soldiers up, moved them down the road. Bought them a Coke, ignored if dark whiskey was poured into cold bottles.

Julia wished it could still be like that. That she could belong to a country where anyone could hitch and know they would be that little bit closer to where they were going. Share a story. That's a place to live. Waiting for a bus is waiting.

It was 1964 and Julia knew not to pick up hitchhikers. But there he was. It was 100 degrees. She had just stopped in the reservation store to buy cigarettes. She had miles of desert to cross, and she liked to roll down the window and watch the tobacco smoke blow back. The visible exhale—a little piece of her on the loose. Julia took in the man's hair, his fringed moccasins. The hippies in San Francisco were starting to wear all-things-fringe, but for now, in Nevada, only Indians wore moccasins. Sometimes with colored beads that told a story on their feet—maybe *White Man Go Home*. A white person wouldn't be caught dead in them, or would be caught dead in them, for what would come to be known as *cultural appropriation*. Because that's how things sometimes go. When it's 100 degrees in a state that didn't yet use the term *Native American*.

The hitchhiker's skin was dark, but so was hers. She knew what it felt like to be out of place in the desert, in the West, although in truth he belonged. He looked about her age, early twenties. His jeans were that old blue color, almost as much white as blue, with soft frays around a hole on one thigh. Some women would want to patch that hole, others rip it wide open. Julia pulled over, against her better judgment.

Newspapermen just love a girl like Julia.

"Where you goin'?" Julia asked, rolling down her window the rest of the way, momentarily obscuring the man's face in smoke, immediately embarrassed. *Smoke signal. Peace pipe.*

"Empire." He stayed back from her window. Experience had taught him that some people tend to like their Indians wooden, carved more than alive. Painted and hanging in the National Portrait Gallery, more than alive. Indians belong to the past. He knew this. But the past is never past; he knew that too. "I work at the gypsum mine," he said. There are few reasonable destinations in the Northern Nevada desert. That's one.

"Hop in," said Julia, although Empire was 70 miles in the wrong direction, away from Reno, where she lived. He started to open the back door. If she had been white, he would have kept right on walking. White women are powder kegs. "Ride up front, it's okay," she said. He walked around the car.

"Thanks, name's Howi," said the young man, shifting his face away from Julia to reach for the door, pull it closed.

"Howard?" She hadn't quite heard.

"No, Howi. It's a Sioux name—Turtle Dove." He knew

women loved that; it would make her feel better about picking him up.

Julia thought it sounded like a fib, to make her feel better about picking him up. "Your dad went along with that name?" Julia countered, putting the car into gear.

Howi's dad did not go along with the name.

Julia's long fingers were already on the wheel, foot on the gas. Howi did the sideways peek at her. Noticed the way the straps of her summer dress skimmed her bare shoulders, the nearest one missing it's mark, ready to slide.

Julia didn't seem to notice that Howi ignored her question about his name. She was concentrating on trying to figure out what made her pick up a man in the middle of the Great Basin, where the dust and bighorn sheep would watch her murder with indifference. Snakes don't care. Jackrabbits stop for nothin'. Hadn't she just passed the carcass of a car shot to death in the 1920s? There are no good Samaritans in the desert.

"I'm Julia," she said, calming herself down by looking at the hole in his jeans, at his soft-soled moccasins. Surely men of poor intent wear steel-toed leather boots. "Want a cigarette?" She pushed the pack of Pall Malls his way. The cellophane over the pack crinkled under her hand, giving off a small, radio static sound.

Howi shook his head no. "Where you headed?"

Now Julia had to improvise. "Gerlach."

"Why?" He knew he didn't have any business asking, but it wasn't an odd question. There were few reasonable destinations in Gerlach—it was only about 10 miles from Empire.

But Julia was ready with an answer. She looked straight at him. He saw glints of gold in her dark eyes, whole little worlds in there. "I feel like eating at Bruno's."

"Raviolis?"

"Raviolis."

Common ground. Julia pushed the level of the fan up to bring her tension down. They headed east, Pyramid Lake to the left of the desolate road. The thing about Pyramid is that it can disappear if no one's looking at it. But really, what can be expected of a lake the Paiutes say is made of tears? The Paiutes would know. The mountains around the lake are beaten down, but there are streaks of garnet. Opals and crystals, silver. Every desert hides things of great beauty.

Julia was driving an old wood-sided Plymouth station wagon, a car big enough to raise a family in. Or start one in. The seats were like chesterfields. Howi kept as close to his window as he could. The faded emerald of the car, 60 miles an hour, the blur of it was the greenest thing for miles. The only green. But by the time they got to Gerlach, the car would be dusted down, blended.

There were far more Native Americans—Koso, Paiute, Panamint, Shoshoni, Washoe, Ute—than Black people in Northern Nevada. Howi had a history with the West; Julia didn't. Her family was from Louisiana; she knew how to cook the crayfish she and her father, Trautmann, caught in the Carson River. Trautmann liked to quote Shakespeare as he dropped the yabbies in the black pot of boiling water, *Double, double, toil and trouble.* They cracked the red shells with their teeth.

Trautmann moved his family out to Genoa, south of Reno, to work as a year-round ranch hand, foreman within two years. He looked good in a cowboy hat and he was bow-legged to start with—born to the job. Her mother was a nurse, but the Genoa *e-lites* didn't want a Negro woman to touch them, at that time in Nevada. So she worked as a school nurse, because while no one said it out loud, it was understood that Ruth's *kind* were good with tending kids.

Trautmann and Ruth were no fools. Their child would get a college degree. They bought their house on a good green piece of land, grew it into a small ranch of its own. Trautmann knew that if there were few Negroes around, they would not be a threat. Safety in a *lack* of numbers. Ruth knew they would be tolerated in town and welcomed into the church, the Coventry Cross Episcopal, with its white steeple and blue trim. It's easy to be godly when the full count is three. Thus Julia did not feel the urban brunt of her heritage. It was easy for her to believe things like she could become a school principal if she got the degree; to believe it when her father said she could be anything at all.

The fact was, when Julia picked up Howi, she had just been out for a Sunday drive. School started back up in about a week, her last year. Double major—art and education. She was already set up in the room she was renting from Mrs. Bennett by the university. She had time for a drive, but she had only planned as far as Pyramid Lake, to dip her legs in the hard water of the salt lake, walk on the shore of crunchy, broken shells. The beach looked the dark side of the moon. But now she was driving to Empire. It felt good. They didn't talk much. Just rolled down all the windows to catch the cool and listen to the whistling. The musical stylings of Nevada.

Gerlach. An Indin man and a Negro woman walk into a bar. They hesitated. It wouldn't have been any less ironic if the doors were saloon-style. Howi and Julia knew that everyone in the joint (five people) would turn and stare at them when they walked in. Bruno's Country Club. The place was a coffee shop, brown vinyl and speckled Formica. *Best raviolis in the West.* That part was true.

"What'll it be?" asked a young waitress in old cowboy boots, pulling a pencil from behind her ear. Julia noticed the pencil had bite marks, pictured the girl writing poetry on blue-lined paper. Shook the image loose. "Raviolis and garlic bread?" the waitress guessed.

"How'd you know?" asked Howi, smiling.

The girl sighed. Anytime a customer didn't open the menu up, she knew what the order would be. Just once she wished someone would order the clam sauce linguini so she could tell them clams were out of season. Bruno put the exotics on the menu just to fluff it out. Shrimp scampi. No one orders fish in the desert. It was always raviolis, lasagna, spaghetti and meatballs. "Lucky guess," she said, turning away, about as interested in the Injun and the nigger as she was a booger. Julia saw the look on her face and knew that girl couldn't write poetry.

No matter. Julia broke open her first ravioli with her fork and released a puff of pure oregano steam, as if a genie had escaped from a bottle. Magical. She ate the full order and one of Howi's. Girl could put it down. They drank Picon Punches—a drink so strong, the name's a double entendre.

"So's Howi your real name?" Julia asked, inhibitions splashing, drowning in grenadine and brandy. Swirl of lemon.

"My mom says it's *He Who Squawks Morning, Noon, and Night*." Julia smiled, butter—shine to her teeth. "Really, it's just John Ox, after my dad. Howi is my nickname, but I like it."

"Howi Ox. Howi Howi Ox. Sounds like *olly olly oxen free*," Julia sang in a child's cadence while thinking *I have to stop drinking*.

Somehow this made Howi feel less guarded, as if he *could* come out.

"My family lives on the Pyramid Reservation now, but I grew up in the Dakotas." Howi didn't want to talk about his dad. An Indian on an Indian motorcycle, knocked off the road by a brute of a Chevy, rifle rack in the back window. Kind of like how some people swerve to hit cats. Hit and run. Police didn't care, even with a witness, because the witness was a Blackfoot. His mom still wears her Black Hills gold ring with the twined leaves, soft pink and silvery green. There had been other men, but not until he was almost grown up. Boss, and now Matthew. Decent men. Build-a-fire-and-bank-it kind of men. "We came out to Nevada about three years ago."

"Why'd you go to work in Empire instead of something in Reno?" Julia might have considered Reno a bar fight town, but Empire looked like a gutter drunk in comparison.

Howi took a moment to answer. "I really like hitchhiking." Julia laughed; he could see all her teeth. White, little hard candies all in a row. Dime store candies, all in a row.

Julia and Howi left Bruno's, and instead of returning Howi to Empire, they headed out to the mineral flats of the Black Rock Desert. It wasn't far. And it was okay to drive Picon-Punched, because there was absolutely nothing to hit. As the sun went down, Empire and Gerlach twinkled behind them, two desert towns that look best in twilight.

The Black Rock is a gargantuan desert beach—the ancient remains of Lake Lahontan—although there are those who believe that the lake returns from time to time. A vengeance of water, when no one is looking, because sometimes there are new high tide marks on the serrated mountains that suffocated the lake. Who knows what goes on in a landscape of pale dust. They parked the Plymouth and left the headlights on so they could find their way back in the dark, wandered far onto the cracked playa. Nothing lived here. In a dry year, not even a bug. The white playa dust ghosted their skin. When the stars came out, there was no ambient light to compete. It was a showgirl of a sky.

"I've never seen a night so bright," whispered Julia, the Milky Way arching above. The air smelled of minerals. It was by now so dark, they could only see their bodies as shadow.

Julia put her hands up and felt she was swimming in stars, had stars on her fingers; if she ran, they would cascade her hair. Howi wanted to touch her, just her hand, her shoulder, something small. A temple. To feel the pulse of her. He didn't dare. Julia lit a cigarette and it was a firefly, following them, glowing brighter with her inhale.

There is a train track that crosses the east side of the Black Rock, transporting the gypsum, dislodged hunks of Nevada. A sort of midnight express, escaping with the goods in the dark. When the train passed through, all they could see was the moon of a headlight and a breath of smoke. When the whistle sounded, it gave a melancholy voice to the death of Lake Lahontan. Julia reached for Howi's hand. As they walked back to the car, Julia thought she might understand why Howi would choose Empire over Reno.

Empire is a company town for the United States Gypsum Corporation. All residents work for the company, live in company housing, buy goods at the company store. *I owe my soul to the company store*—Tennessee Ernie Ford sang about the coal mines, but mines is mines. Howi drove Julia's Plymouth back to his tiny house with the small front porch, squeaky steps, one, two, three to the front door. Julia followed him inside. Howi was a neat enough man; that part didn't worry him. Dishes in the sink, but rinsed. Clothes over a chair, but folded.

"Julia, you take the bed."

Julia looked into the little bedroom, walls clair de lune blue, old chenille coverlet. She knew the sheets would hold the scent of him and she didn't think she could resist it; she would call him to her if she took one more step toward that bed.

"I'll take the couch, I insist," she said, turning in such a way that there was no room for argument, kicking off her shoes. Howi brought her a blanket, scratchy, and a soft pillow.

He put a glass of water on the side table. The water caught the moonlight coming in the window and shone a cloudy silver. No one was keeping track of Julia. Mrs. Bennett would not call a posse on her behalf. Suddenly, Julia was exhausted. She lay down on the couch and fell asleep as if she were in her mother's home. Howi did not feel right sleeping in a bed when Julia was on the couch. He got his covers and slept on the floor next to the girl, who curled her hands up under her chin and snored, just a little bit.

When Julia awoke in the morning, Howi was up, the covers put away—she never knew he slept on the floor. She could hear that Howi was in the shower and she pictured that. Soapy skin. *What the hell's wrong with you?* She shook the image away like a dog shaking off water, her whole body moved. She shifted her clothes into place, put on her shoes, folded up the covers. Her fingers were nervous. Howi came out. Work clothes, jeans and a button-down blue shirt. His embroidered name tag said *John*.

"Well, John," said Julia, "it appears that I am still here." He smiled, handed her a washcloth and a new toothbrush. That made him look either the good host or a Casanova, but the truth was he had just bought the toothbrush for himself the week before. She closed the bathroom door and looked in the mirror. There was still playa dust on her face, in her hair. She did the best she could, gave up when she smelled coffee.

Howi poured her a cup that vaguely tasted of the mineral sediments of the hard Nevada water. Copper and things that are not good for you. "Back to Reno, then?" he asked. She nodded her head. *Yes.* This was it, then. The end or the beginning. They both knew it. Howi took the chance. Said those magical words, the words that would open every messy, wonderful thing there is to dream about in this world. "I'd like to see you again."

Julia walked over to him; she still had her cup of coffee. She placed her other hand on his chest, all five fingers pressing in to gain the measure of him. She reached up to kiss him, and he took the cup of coffee from her hand the instant before it spilled like good intentions, just before it scalded them both. Too late. The warning was averted. They kissed like the savages we all are; like the savages we want to be. And like every good first kiss, the world was new again.

Howi went to work and Julia drove back to Reno. The desert never looked so beautiful to her. She had the eyes of the curious coyote. On the lookout.

Autumn in Northern Nevada is a pot of gold. Through the alchemy of a cold night in late September, the aspen trees distill the last of summer into their sun-yellow leaves. The wind whittles and harries the leaves away, tosses them up like mad money and lays them down on a sure bet for winter.

Howi bought an old International Harvester pickup rimmed in rust with a two bullet holes in the tailgate. But he bought new tires and laid a wool blanket of stripy design over the blistered-leather seat. He made the trip to Reno to spend a few hours with Julia so many times, he knew where the dust devils were most likely to dervish, and what valleys the wild mustangs favored for late-growing wheat grass. The mustangs disdained his passing motor, but the devils were attracted to his cloudy wake, scouting for recruits.

Julia was busy with classes. She gave no thought to fashion, wore knee socks and sensible shoes. Her hair pulled into a pony that stuck straight out the back of her neck like a defense. She smelled of chalk and books long unopened and then cracked at last, or that might have just been in Howi's mind, she was so schoolish. One Friday, Howi called in to work, said he needed the afternoon off to take his mom to the city doctor. Bad luck, he knew that. So he told his mom and she laughed the luck back in her direction. He didn't have a way to contact Julia, but he liked the idea of a surprise. Howi waited for Julia on the university quad with its surround of noble elms. It was easy to pick Julia out of the shifting tides of students—she wore that plaid beret. Howi stood in the shade of tree. Most people did not see him there, just under the long elm limbs, but she did. "You're here," she said. He took her crooked stack of books.

"Where else would I be?" He bent down to feel the small heat come off her.

For a moment she looked very pleased, but then she started walking. "Look, I have to return those books to the library and then I promised Debbie we would study together." He nodded his agreement. "Midterms wait for no man." He smiled at her small joke. "No really, I . . ." Oh, she had a list. Howi just kept walking, making his way to his Harvester, and Julia was still counting down responsibilities when he shut the passenger door with her inside. A little pile of rust sifted down on his shoes, a kind of automobile ashes to ashes.

He walked around and got into the car. "It's Friday. Whatdaya say we go for a burger and shake?"

"Great. I'm famished."

He knew she would fold.

They went to Landrum's Hamburger System #1, eight swiveling stools at a sparkling counter, the tiny prefab building unloaded in 1948 from the Virginia & Truckee Railroad tracks right behind the property. Sue owned the place, and if you didn't want to sit next to a Negro or an Indian, or a Negro *with* an Indian, well, get out. *Plenty more behind ya.* She never said it out loud, but Howi and Julia could tell just by the way she placed their plates in front of them: burger in the middle, fries Lincoln Logged, pickle off to the side at a jaunty angle.

The disenfranchised know what it means when their food is served sloppy; if the lettuce is sliding out the side of the burger, don't think it just means lettuce.

They drove out to Windy Hill and watched the city twinkle and wink. There was ranch land at the bottom of the hill, the smell of hay and cattle and earth. It was the time of year for collecting. Julia tucked herself into Howi and they kissed. Howi had waited all day for this kiss. He could see the future so much more clearly with closed eyes.

Later, Howi parked on a dark side street, spent the night in his car. Twice he heard ambulances banking into emergency at the not-so-distant Saint Mary's Hospital. It was a lamenting sound, kin to foghorns and winter geese; it left that kind of feeling. But that's an easy feeling to fend off for a young man, so many days ahead he cannot count them, but he can count on them. In the morning he walked stiffly into the Cal Neva for 99 cent ham and eggs and scalding coffee the color of nothing. Then he drove to the YMCA for a shower, and over to pick up Julia.

"Let's take your car today and drive out to my place. I'll drive you back in tomorrow." He didn't even say good morning. Julia was not a frivolous girl—she knew what he was asking. She felt a nervousness electrify her body, something like that moment of letting go of the rope swing over the river, plunging down. "Howi, I'm not going to marry you." He knew she had other plans that involved big cities. "That's not what I'm asking for." He smiled and damn if that fine girl did not go back into her rented room, fill a small bag with clothes, and come back out to him.

It was a cold day. Pyramid was a flat sheet of gray, a deadmen-tell-no-tales sort of lake. Howi drove fast. Julia thought he should drive faster. They smiled more than talked. When they got to Howi's little house, Howi grabbed her, laughing, and carried her over the threshold, Julia kicking off her shoes, pulling off her schoolgirl socks, everything akimbo, Howi tumbling her onto the couch. They each took off their own clothes without preamble or coyness, or even self-consciousness. They appraised each other, standing in the light. Pieces of art.

Both were breathing hard. Howi wanted to slow it down, pull out the romance of it. But Julia said, "Now *that's* what I call a wooden Indian." And they raced for the bed, dove in as if it were a summer pond, the kind with dragonflies and wild daises.

Julia did not go home the next day and missed classes on Monday. By the time the long weekend was over, there was no going back.

Although Julia tried. To keep her heart out of the deal.

It was not an easy courtship. In honesty, although Julia truly liked Howi, she did not want to marry someone who worked at the Empire mine. She didn't want a man with a lunch pail, name embroidered on his shirt. Or a man on a horse who smelled of cows and spilt milk. Nor a janitor, a bartender, or a door-to-door salesman. She wanted a collar so white, it discriminated against blue. How could she fall in love with Howi? *Turtle Dove. Good Christ.* She tried to break up with him, two times, three times. "Howi, it's just not going to work. I'm going to get my teaching certificate and move to San Francisco or Chicago. I gotta go."

"I know it," he said. And then he would find a way to lay her down, to fill her up with the bristlecone smell that only came from his chest, the smell of his heart coming right off his body. She could feel it beating beneath her hand. He touched her soft and hard and in and out. She never knew such things. She was a cat in tiger skin. A woman intrigued with a man who knew if he pushed far enough inside her that she would always call his name. Could that be enough? Probably not.

But then, in spring, Julia realized she was pregnant.

Julia was furious. Incredulous. If she had a knitting needle, she might have used it. On Howi. *That asshole.* She felt derailed. If someone would have handed her a pot of blue cohosh tea at that moment, she would have asked for seconds. She didn't wait for the weekend; she drove out to Gerlach. But there is something about driving the wide-open, the uncluttered Nevada. By the time Julia got to Gerlach, she knew the pregnancy wasn't all Howi's fault. They had been careful in a sloppy way. Condoms but sometimes in his truck she was his bouncy cheerleader and she would say *pull out, pull out,* but how do you pull out when someone is sitting on you and all the words seem so far away? Later she did the vinegar rinse with a meat baster. *Good God. Idiots.* On the drive she had time to ask herself if she had been self-sabotaging. But it seemed more accurate that she had believed they were in a bubble. She would be gone by fall and none of this was really real, *was it?*

Julia let herself in to Howi's never-locked house, sat on the couch, waited. Full of fear. Men love a conquest and she had provided that, never agreeing to a future with him in it, never inviting him to come along. Never taking him home for a holiday. But now, she realized, she needed him more than he needed her. He could walk away. Men did.

When Howi got off work, he saw Julia's car on the street. Parked crooked. *Always making a statement, that girl.* He jumped the steps into the house assuming she was a midweek treat, a Hostess CupCake, but there was something brittle about her. No creamy center there. "What's up, baby?"

Baby. Yep, that's exactly what's up. She wanted to pounce and take him out. Leap. But she was just too tired. She knew it wasn't his fault, or her fault. It was terrifyingly their fault. "John Ox, you are going to be a daddy." Why wring it out?

Howi could have said a hundred things, all the words available for him to string together. He chose some. "Are you sure it's mine?" he said as seriously as every man who has ever played that opening gambit. But here's the thing. It's not the words, is it? It's the way the hand moves, the crinkle at the eye, the arms folding. Or reaching.

He was at her feet before she could even get the laugh out. He buried his head in her middle, pulled up her blouse and started blowing raspberries on her belly. She pulled his hair, pulled his face to her face. He looked into the eye of her hurricane. "Don't worry about this, Julia, I'm right here." She started to cry. He knew why. All her silver cities were turning to tin. "I know what you're thinking. You can't go to Chicago; we won't have any money." He tucked her wild hair behind her ears. It sprung right back out. "Maybe that's true. Maybe it's not. Let's just wait and see." It didn't make her want the baby, but it made her feel safer.

Julia was so tired that, if only for this moment, she let her worries fall asleep on the couch while Howi made her a cup of tea. Just Lipton.

Howi went to Roger's Jewelers, but the salesman treated him like an Indian, as if Howi had come in there wanting to trade for a ring. Made him feel like he should leave and go search for a wedding ring tossed into the Truckee River when the divorce decree was signed, under the bridge across from the courthouse—that old Reno legend. Lisa, that's what her name tag said, saw the look on Howi's face and took over, showing him slender silver bands with glinting chips, sliding them on her fingers for show, down her long, white fingers. In the end, Howi's mom gave him her Black Hills gold band with the silvery-green leaves. Julia cried at the beauty of the gesture, at what Howi's mom was giving away. But then, she was crying all the time.

They had the wedding reception out at Trautmann and Ruth's ranch in Genoa. Married in the Coventry Cross Episcopal Church, goddamnit. The Ladies Auxiliary had spent some time over Instant Folgers discussing if it was even legal for them to marry, but Mrs. Shelton put the matter to rest when she said, "Injuns and Negroes are kissin' cousins, so let 'em kiss." Ever the practical one, that Mrs. Shelton. No one noticed Mrs. McCreary, who suddenly blushed, illusioning a cover for a romance novel. *Darkest Love.*

If Julia's wedding dress was forgiving in the waist, the lace gathered gracefully full, who's to know? If Nia Ox came seven months later, eight pounds, five ounces, well, that Howi's a big man and Julia's pretty big herself. *Just look what a beautiful thing Nia is—dang, she looks like a buckskin pony!* That's what Trautmann said, proud of his granddaughter, never once looking at Julia like he was counting up months. *Don't ask what it won't help ya' to know.* Words to live by. Besides, the legitimacy of the child was hardly the biggest issue. But when Nia put her little arms on Trautmann's chest, he always told the child, "Nia's the prettiest girl at the ball."

Mrs. Hutton of the Ladies Auxiliary said more than once, "What do you expect when you mix them races?"

"They aren't horses," retorted Mrs. Shelton, but most nodded along with Mrs. Hutton.

History is that wily chunk of time that just won't stay under the bed. The Future is frivolous, always looking ahead, weaving daisy chains. Go on. Toil and plan. But don't expect it to work out. Not in the expected way. *Everyone knows the past is never past, but none could ever guess that Nia's birth-plight began in Gangsterland:*

19

There is something elegant in a cat burglar, soft paws and dia-
monds. And perhaps Baby Face Nelson was looking for some of
that type of elegance when he pulled his heists in a gray topcoat
and fine felt hat with a turned-down brim. No face mask for
him. He had the audacity, some say balls, *to rob Mary Thom-*
son, the wife of Big Bill Thomson, Mayor of Chicago, while she
was home. $18,000 worth of gems. Mrs. Thomson told the press,
flash bulbs exploding, "He was very good looking," so one might
imagine her heaving bosom while Nelson pulled the emeralds
from her very white neck. Oh my! It was 1930.

By October of 1934 when Baby Face hid out at Wally's Hot
Springs in Genoa, Nevada, he held the record for killing the most
FBI agents. His likeness hung in the National Gallery, post office
annex, Public Enemy #1. No doubt he spent some time in the
hard, hot water of Wally's springs, shrouds of steam pushed into
eddies by a Zephyr wind, Baby Face's trigger finger going pru-
nie. He must have been easily spooked by the rat-a-tat-tat of a
white-headed woodpecker. Jarred awake at night by the near-si-
ren sound of marauding coyotes, those bad-boys of the high des-
ert. Always alert for trouble, but there was nothing to do in Ge-
noa; the event of the year was the Candy Dance. Baby Face lit
out, back to Chicago, every gangster's glitter gulch. Within a
month he was dead. Bang bang.

But Baby Face Nelson wasn't really dead, was he? Now he
Lived in Infamy, he belonged to History. His real name was Les-
ter Joseph Gillis, and Gillis caused great damage to Julia and
John Ox, to their daughter Nia.

Wyatt Dillon Pacini, who would eventually be Julia Ox's ob-
stetrician, was born in 1926, successfully birthed at home in
his parents' Minneapolis, Minnesota, walk-up apartment.
Wyatt's father was fond of Louie L'Amour westerns, and he

branded his son with a western name and raised him on imag-es of purple sage and arroyos. Wyatt would grow to feel that Minneapolis was too cold a place, or the wrong kind of cold, brought on by steel and glass. As a young man he found him-self longing to set the spurs of his heart for the West. But he was equally influenced by his own times and place, pulled in by the shouts of the newsie boys and the gunshot headlines.

Chance, or fortune, sent the Pacini family north on a driving vacation to Little Star Lake in northern Wisconsin, to a log cabin rental with Adirondack rockers on the porch. Wyatt and his father stomped the woods. On Sunday night the family headed over to Little Bohemia Lodge for the $1 fried chicken special. The Pacinis were just beginning to drive away as a 1933 Chevrolet coupe skidded into the parking lot, guns a-blazin'. The FBI had word that the Dillinger Gang, in-cluding Baby Face Nelson, was staying at the lodge. His father yelled, *Get down, get down!* and threw himself over his moth-er. As Wyatt pulled his body into a round stone in the well of the backseat, his mother keened in fear. But Wyatt stilled himself by imagining it was the voice of the whippoorwill out on Little Star Lake—the cacophony outside their open car windows was only a sudden summer storm, thunderheads and hard hail. He pictured himself as taking cover from the storm by an old felled tree, fishing pole in hand, night crawler still on a cold hook down by the fat-trout deep.

When it was over, Wyatt saw dead people, pieces missing or squished up, and in the morning he saw two bullet holes in the fender of their rented Hertz car. "Thank God I bought the insurance," he heard his dad say, Wyatt putting his fingers in the bent metal, like the little Dutch boy, trying to hold back sooty memories. But my, what a fine story to tell! Baby Face escaped and stayed with a Chippewa family who didn't give a fuck for the FBI. It was the aftermath of the slaughter at Little

Bohemia that ultimately led Nelson to the backwater hideout of Wally's Hot Springs in Genoa, Nevada—where Julia's parents would eventually reside.

The aftermath of the slaughter of Little Bohemia for Wyatt was a found ability to transport himself into a *Wind in the Willows* frame of mind in any time of stress, something he never told anyone, but that served him well in World War II and for the rest of his life.

Years later when Wyatt had become Dr. Pacini, he and his new wife, Penelope of the Cincinnati Howards (who almost didn't marry him because she didn't especially care for the damsel-in-distress sound of *Penelope Pacini*), honeymooned by train, with tickets clear to San Francisco. At last, Wyatt had crossed the vast West. Because of his personal connection to Baby Face, he planned a stop in Reno with some days at Wally's Hot Springs, even reserving the room said to have been occupied by Nelson, small extra charge. But worth every penny! Because there's something about lying in the same bed as a famous gangster that makes a young man feel sturdy. It was a pleasantly romantic sojourn that turned into a Decision. Dr. Pacini cut the honeymoon trip short, bought the practice of retiring Dr. Carter and became the family doctor of the small western town of Genoa. Penelope again wondered if she had made a poor choice as the social whirlwinds of Cincinnati, Chicago, or at least Minneapolis turned to tumbleweeds and blew completely away.

Because Dr. Pacini had grown up on the poor side of a northern city, the color of Trautmann, Ruth, and their child Julia was of no consequence to him. When Mrs. Hutton asked him, "Isn't this the examination room Dr. Carter had only for them Negroes?" uncomfortably wondering if she wanted to even get up on the table, Dr. Pacini told her, "Negroes are people, Rosemary. Nurse Cindy changes out the paper on the table after everyone, even you."

Of course Dr. Pacini would be the doctor for Julia when she became pregnant, and he would tell the townspeople that babies come in all sizes when they asked, *Wasn't Julia big for only three months along?* because he was a gentleman. While Julia found it cumbersome to get to her monthly appointments in Genoa, it was also comforting. Medical journals peacocked his desk. He polished his diploma from the Chicago Medical School until he could see his face in the reflection. He was fascinated by new drugs and felt that a utopia of health was a laboratory experiment away. When the pharmaceutical company Richardson-Merrell sent him samples of the FDA approval-*pending* Kevadon, he gave it to Penelope to help her sleep. The four-color brochure said it was widely used in Europe. He prescribed it to Julia for her intense morning sickness. It helped. Julia found it helped the little body within her body quiet down.

Oh Fate, that night-carnival, patiently working through generations to get Wyatt and Julia in the same room, a bottle of little pills passing from doctor to patient. A swirl of chemicals, a shark released in the bloodstream, dead set against the growing limbs of little Nia—while Julia was weaving daisy chains of dreams.

Back from their short honeymoon in Yosemite, Howi and Julia sat drinking coffee in a back booth at Sambo's, trying to find their future in the bottom of a cup. Julia would have her teaching certificate, but no one hired pregnant women. And until Dr. Pacini's pills, she had been too wan to even think beyond the couch. But she was feeling better now—decisions needed to be made.

Julia threw out the opening gambit. "Let's take my parents up on the offer of a section of their land." She knew this involved living with her parents.

Howi was ready for that one. "It could take years to build our own place," he countered.

"But then we would have our own place!" Julia said.

"Years!" Years are so long when one is young. "And where would I work?" This was a more serious concern and Julia knew it. His tenor turned dismissive. "Ranch hand, migrant farm worker in the fall?"

"My dad is a ranch hand," Julia said, but Howi talked over her.

"We wouldn't fit in."

Julia twisted her wedding ring. "I see. You're afraid to live in Genoa because it's a small town and we'll stick out. Howi, we are going to stick out everywhere! Is this why you work at the land of misfits—so no one will notice you're an *Indian!?*" She was both starting to get mad and starting to understand the man she was tied to. She pulled in a breath to launch into some sort of power, don't-tread-on-me speech. But Howi didn't wait on the speech. He'd heard that one before.

"I'm not afraid for us, I don't care what people think of us. I'm afraid for our kid." That stopped her.

"I did okay. You did okay." she said.

"No I did not! I was always getting into fights, anytime I was off the reservation!"

"Boys fight."

"This will be worse. The little Black Indian. That's what they'll see."

"What will *you* see, Howi?"

"I will see our son someday making the mistake of deciding to carry a knife for his own defense, or our daughter without friends, having tea parties alone with her Velveteen

24

Rabbit." He got her with the Velveteen Rabbit. "I hate to say this, but I think we need to stick with our own kind. And since there aren't many of *your* kind around, what I mean is my kind."

Julia swallowed her coffee like it was whiskey, slapped the cup down. "Okay, but we're saving our money and moving to Chicago as fast as we can. No one will notice what our baby looks like there."

She was wrong about that. Everyone would always notice Nia.

They moved to the reservation at Elroy. Julia thought of it as the penal colony, but kept that to herself. Julia did get a job teaching; the principal was so happy to have an art teacher, he didn't care that Julia was pregnant. And Howi was right—no one commented on her color or what color their child might be.

Their little house was not far from Pyramid Lake and they saw vast sunsets over dusty mountains. Julia's skin glowed amethyst in the desert twilight. In March, gray clouds came in like the Ten Commandments and the deluge followed. Julia had hoped for skyscrapers, but was granted sky. She found her heart expanding with her pregnancy.

One Sunday, Julia was lying in bed reading Dr. Spock with a highlighter when Howi came into the room hoisting a tin tray laid out with Cheez Whiz and Ritz, two open cans of Busch with jaunty paper umbrellas. He was in his red-and-black buffalo print flannel pajama pants. Window-filtered sun golding his bare chest. God, he was solid. Julia smiled, shut the book, put it on the bed stand. But she was looking at Howi and the book fell to the floor. She was wearing his pajama top—he never wore it. Even with her exploding belly, it skimmed the top of her thighs.

These two were never shy. Julia unbuttoned her top.

"You look like a fertility fetish," Howi said, her skin magnificent.

"You look like a cabana boy," Julia said, reaching for him. But Howi shook his head no, putting the tray down. He dove beneath the mountain of her belly as if into an emerald bay and stayed there until Julia turned into a thousand rainforest birds and flew away. Then they lay in bed and ate little volcanos of Cheez Whiz and made up bad baby names like Agnes and Dick.

When the baby was just a few weeks out, Julia moved home to be near her mother and Dr. Pacini. Her water broke in the night, as so many things do. The nearest hospital was in Reno, an hour away, but they had plenty of time to get there. Dr. Pacini said he would meet them at Washoe Med.; Howi was on the way too. Julia liked the white hospital room, the white sheets, the white nurses' uniforms. The silver glinting railings. It felt cool and clean. The pain was primordial but her body seemed to know what to do with it, seemed to tell her mind to recede. Or maybe it was the drugs, did they give her something? She couldn't say, she thought she was in a cotton ball, who was screaming? Not her mother? It must be her own high-tossed voice she was hearing.

At last Dr. Pacini handed her the baby, a daughter!—body swaddled tightly. Nia, they had settled on Nia. Julia examined every detail of the dear face. Julia was still in the sway of the drugs and in the fancy state she thought Nia had the face of America: Her father's proud, Continental Divide of a nose. Cheekbones wide as the plains. A sweet-tea Southern mouth. Great Lake eyes to drown in when the storms come. Surely this child was the melting pot; surely she would melt all hearts.

Howi came in. "You're shaking," Julia said, handing him his daughter. "Don't drop her!" Howi started to cry, something Julia had never seen. "Howi, she's here. It's okay." Now they were alone in the room and Julia could hear the hand of the wall clock marking time. Howi unwrapped his little girl. Her torso, her legs and toes, her shoulders, all were perfect. But her arms stopped just below her elbows and there her little perfect hands, perfect fingers, extended, right out from her elbows. She looked a little like a baby seal—flipper hands. She had no forearms.

The parents held each other and cried for their daughter, but their daughter just looked at them as if they were silly, because this was her life, and here she was. *Ta-da!* And then Nia started crying too, but only because she was hungry. *Hunger, what is that?* She wanted to learn it all, if she could only stay awake.

Everyone knows mothers are braver than fathers. Julia said it first. "Doesn't matter, Howi. She's ours."

Howi shook his head yes. "And to think we spent all that time worrying people would be judging her skin."

Outside the room, Julia's mother heard the laughter. It was like a shattering of crystal, destructive, nothing would ever be the same, but what a beautiful sound. She went in and held her granddaughter and never even commented on her arms.

"We'll figure it out, Mom."

Ruth didn't dare to cry.

Dr. Pacini was horrified. Never had he seen such a being except in sideshow jars of formaldehyde. He was a man of science and would not bring God into the room. "Sometimes these things just happen," was all he could say, his brain already halfway to Toad Hollow. "Don't waste time looking for an answer, and certainly there is none to blame," meaning the parents were not to blame. It never occurred to him that he was to blame. His bitter comfort to the new parents was, "It's just the variances of life," then he jumped on a lily pad.

Well, Wyatt was wrong about his blame. But it was decades before he knew it. When he eventually read the medical articles about thalidomide babies, all the deformed children born in Europe, and some in the United States when Richardson-Merrell distributed pills to twelve hundred physicians before the FDA denied approval, he knew whose fault it was. Wyatt had put his fingers in the bullet holes of gangsters, had parachuted out of a nose-diving B52 bomber, but he wasn't brave enough to tell Julia and Howi about the part he'd played in Nia's destruction. But it is possible the knowledge contributed to his stroke shortly thereafter, and the subsequent closing of his office. Wyatt was left with a drool problem, and thus generally socially shunned.

Not only did Dr. Pacini sideswipe Nia, but he completely wiped out the probability of her siblings. What could their next child be missing? Dr. Pacini gave Howi a vasectomy three months after Nia's birth, agreeing it was for the best and at no charge. Howi felt he was less of a man; he knew he shouldn't but he did. Julia felt like they were drowning kittens in a burlap sack, to intentionally end the possibility of life, even if it was just a baby-in-waiting.

One of the pediatricians who did pro-bono work for Crippled Children at UC Davis suggested removing Nia's "extremities" and providing prosthetic arms. He was teasing Nia with a rattle just out of her short grasp. "It will make her look more normal, proper portions and not as . . . startling to look at." He didn't turn to Julia as he spoke to her; the child was fascinating him. Nia was doing her version of jazz hands.

"Cut her hands off?" Julia asked.

"Well . . . remove."

"That's the best you got? We're out." Julia scooped her toddler up off the table. The doctor looked like he was losing his new toy. "Why did we even bother?" she asked the baby, who sort of smiled at her, which Julia interpreted as *I told you so.*

That night Julia told Howi about the appointment, which she called *the dis-appointment*, while she ransacked for salvation in her second bottle of Blue Nun.

"That wine's gonna make you sick," Howi warned. Nia played in her father's lap, pulling on his leaned-in face. "Who's a happy girl?" Howi asked, blowing kisses.

"That's the thing, Howi. She is a happy girl, and right now is the happiest she will ever be. She's oblivious to her future. She doesn't know. Once she figures it out, kablam. Sadness."

"Well. At least she will still have her hands to wipe her eyes with. And two legs to walk away on, and a voice to scream with. Don't consign her to sadness." Suddenly Howi was picturing dinosaurs stuck in the La Brea Tar Pits, photos he had seen in *Life* magazine. That's what sadness feels like. Julia was seeing through the glass darkly, a cracked and murky future. It wasn't like her. But Nia was going to get to decide for herself. Howi put Nia in her crib, and Julia in their bed; both girls howled for a time, little lost coyotes. In the morning Howi found Julia on the floor by the open back door. He knew she wasn't trying to escape—fresh air was her antidote when she drank too much. She had desert dust in her eyes, grit in her teeth. The night wind had blasted her with minerals and ozone. She came into the kitchen and Howi handed her a cup of black coffee. "You're right," Julia said, as if the conversation from the night before was still continuing, "To quote my daddy, 'She got more than she don't got.' That idiot doctor just threw me off."

"Psycho fucker."

"Good name for a band. Make me some toast so I have something to throw up."

"Eggs?"

"Bring your feet over here so I can barf on 'em now."

Howi smiled, his strong wife back, that version of her. Nia started screaming from her crib, knowing she could summon titans with nothing more than her *will*. How powerful she was! Her father came into the room and lifted her out of her cage, as she had *commanded*, simply by raising her magical arms. "You look like a banshee," Howi said. Nia had inherited her mother's hot-tempered hair, always having to stick up for itself. If Nia had the words, she would have said, *You look like my sedan. Where's breakfast?*

Now here is the wonderful thing about small towns. Mining towns where all is dust and muscle, or the straight lines and squares of a farming town. Or a hard-pressed town of rusty cars and glass bottles shot to shatter: Familiarity breeds familiarity. In a short time no one sees the gimp, the drunk, the little girl with seal arms. They see Frank, Charlie, Nia. In a city the anonymity that Julia had previously planned to hide in might only serve to turn her daughter into, at best, a curio. At worst, the organ grinder's monkey or some Joseph Mengele's raw material. In Elroy, in Genoa, Nia would become unremarkable for her arms. In fact, it would be unkind to do otherwise in a small town. Like her father before her, Julia came to understand the safety of a backwater. She never brought up moving to Chicago, to San Francisco again.

But that is not to think that the little girl did not become self-aware. There came a night of sparkling starfall; Howi took Nia out onto the Black Rock Desert to watch the meteor shower. In the mostly dark, held up in her father's so-strong arms, the seven-year-old found her courage to ask her burning question: *Why me?* Howi and Julia knew this day would come, though Howi had not anticipated it would be asked beneath the silky Milky Way. He could have given the Sunday answer of *Jesus doesn't give you more than you can handle*. Or, *It makes you special*. Or what would be defined as New Age jargon in just a few years—*Don't let it define you, let it refine you*. He could have said, *Life's not fair*, his mother's favorite alibi. Or, *There's others worse off than you—children are starving in China*. All those stupid answers.

Instead, Howi said the one true thing a father can say to his child's questioning of personal unfairness and inequity: "Little Miss Chevious, I don't know why. But I wish it were me instead of you." Nia leaned into her father's bristlecone chest. They counted falling stars and made all the wishes. "Don't be sad," he encouraged.

"Sometimes the heartbeats are sad," his daughter sighed.

Nia did have a Velveteen Rabbit, and a donkey named Tingalayo, and a best friend named Wynona, who came to tea parties and built blanket forts and preferred making snow cones to snowballs, and who thought the color pink was just right for any occasion. Wynona tended to string four thoughts together before each breath, and thus exhausted most adults. But Nia loved her.

When the girls were ten, Wynona's auntie gave Wynona a waist-length fall of blond hair—a Barbie wig—for Christmas. Wynona's mother rolled her eyes at her sister. Wynona's skin was the color of a one-minute-overcooked sugar cookie but her hair was dark as peppercorns. Yet the auntie had nailed it. It was exactly what Wynona wanted to be—Barbie. To press the pedal of a pink Karmann Ghia with her high-heeled foot, floor it, never run out of sparkle.

At last, but not clear till February, Wynona let Nia wear the wig. Nia had to corral her hair into a tight pony. Polymer strands the color of oleo silked her shoulders, cascaded her back. Oh!, the glamour. She twirled. Ran her fingers through the long strands. But when Nia looked in the mirror and saw the contrast of her Made-in-America face against that California-gold-rush hair, she was flooded with discontent. She would never look like Barbie. Despite a cider-taste of shame, she kept that false idol on her head the entire day, feeling both inadequate and graced.

"What do you want to be when you grow up?" Wynona asked blond Nia.

"I don't know." What could she be? With her arms. "What about you?" Nia asked, deflecting.

"A princess," Wynona said. No hesitation.

"There are no princesses in America," said Nia, the girl who felt forced to face reality.

"Good," said her friend who was not. "Then I'll be the only one!"

Nia and Wynona made a pact to bleach their hair for their high school senior prom, "and wear matching pink dresses," Wynona threw in.

If Julia had seen that thing on her daughter's head, she would have burned it, a reverse KKK. Would have read her *By Any Means Necessary* as a bedtime story.

The shamrock plant on Nia's bedroom desk was in bloom—a good luck day for sure. Late July with an over-bright sun, the land dusting to shades of dun blue and low-value garnet. Every shade of brown, but no shade. Water in the cat's dish with a sheen of opal. Nothing to do. A *rural* nothing to do. Nia ran the hose just to watch the arc catch the sun, ran her fingers through the rainbows. She saw the line of boys heading off into the field of no-good grass, wheat tips like origami, tipsy in a small wind. Jimmy, Wonder, Robbie, and Hale. Her age, thereabout, thirteen. They were all in the same class as she. The boys went some ways out and then sat down in the grass and disappeared like ships over the horizon. Nia trailed; no need to track, the path was clear through the dry grass. It crunched under her feet but only gave off the smell of crumbling dirt.

Jimmy was her friend, reaching up to hang her watercolor paintings from the clothes pins on the string that crisscrossed the classroom. Trading an apple for an orange, because he knew Nia would rather eat the color orange than red.

Wonder was a little slow, but no one said it. It was his nickname because the same thing could surprise him twice.

Robbie was one year older, but held back a grade. He smoked, ashtray stubs from the Wash & Dry or pilfered whole ones. Robbie talked big, but his daddy was dead, run over by the midnight express out on the Black Rock. What was he doing out there? Walking the line, probably to keep from getting lost in the vast black. Parts of him went all the way to Idaho. Well, Robbie wasn't the only one without a dad. Parts of him went all the way to Idaho. Well, Robbie wasn't the only one on the res without a dad.

Hale liked dogs and swore his pit bull was a Rhodesian Ridgeback, which it wasn't because Nia looked it up at the library. When she told him, just him, not around any of their friends, he said, "What makes you the expert, Seal Girl," and she learned her lesson: It doesn't matter what is true, it matters what we need. She apologized, not because she didn't want to be called the behind-her-back nickname to her face, but because she realized that a Rhodesian Ridgeback gave Hale something a mutt pit bull couldn't: A vision. A peek of life beyond. A bigger life.

The four boys were in a loose circle, sitting cross-legged. A rogue wind blew Hale's untucked shirt up and Nia could see the back waistband of his underwear. Jimmy's hair flew off his head like a black crow, and it was when he put his hand up to tame it that he noticed Nia, off to the side. A face is a fast talker; Jimmy's gave a warning. Nia hesitated in her forward movement, but Robbie had seen Jimmy's silent soliloquy and followed Jimmy's gaze to Nia.

"Oh great—"

They all looked at her now. She pulled her hands into her body, minimizing. "Whatja doin' with that gun, Robbie?"

"It's mine. What's it to ya?"

"It's not yours. Maybe your dad's."

"Well, it's mine now, innit? I . . . inherited it, like."

"Whatja doing with it?"

"Shooting rabbits," Jimmy said quickly.

"No rabbits in this heat." Nia knew better.

"Whatsit to ya?" Robbie said again.

"Yeah, whatsit to ya? We're gonna play Russian roulette."

"Wonder! Shut your face!"

Nia snorted. "You call Russian roulette *playin'*?"

"Yeah, we do. You wanna play, smarty pants?"

"Don't let her play. She's a girl!"

"Wonder! Shut up!"

"I don't believe you guys. There's no bullets."

"Well, why don't you come find out—"

In that moment Nia still had all the options. It was that instant before placing fingers on the Ouija Board stylus, before everything was spelled out, or winnowed down to *Yes, No, Hello, Goodbye*. She could turn around and go back to spraying hose water at the sun and pretend she vanquished it at dusk. She could go find her mother, or any mother. If Wynona was with her, none of this would have even happened—they would not have bothered to follow the stupid boys. Nia's hair was loose and high and backlit; her summer dress wind-pressed against her thighs. If not for her misplaced hands, she looked like the Black Madonna. Or Aladdin come to grant three wishes, somehow managing to take more than give. Girls like that don't walk away.

She sat down next to Jimmy. "You don't have to do this, just 'cuz Robbie says so."

"All right then, who wants to go first?" Robbie interrupted, demanding their bravado. There were five of them, and presumably one bullet out of six chambers.

Nia had a fantasy with death, with the idea of dying. As soon as she was aware she owned that right, the possibility of suicide was a comfort to her. Something to put under her pillow at night, or in a locket. A savings bond, something to cash in on in the future. Because there's no fooling the crippled. There was no prom corsage, no flight attendant job, imagine—*exit here* with her half-arms! Why pretend she would ever have a kid. Who would chance it, with her?

So why not now? Take a wager on the Wheel of Fortune. On death.

"I'll go first." Jimmy reached for the gun.

"Jimmy! Whatja doin? Don't point that thing at your head!"

"Shut up, Wonder. Let the man play!"

Goddamn if the whole world didn't just halt. Nothing moved but a single digit.

The gun made the second most beautiful sound it can make, because really, the sound of an accelerated bullet is singular and arguably more beautiful than the sound of a hollow *click*. Nia knew Jimmy did it to stop her; she knew it clear as diamonds. She could see his soul like he was a lit-up firefly atremble.

"Jimmy, whatja do that for?" Wonder was crying. "I thought we was playing Russian roulette!"

"Whatja think Russian roulette is, stupid?" Robbie yelled.

"Like Spin the Bottle . . ."

35

"Good idea. Let's spin the gun in the center and see who it points to next."

Robbie put the gun in the dirt and gave it his best *Wheel of Fortune* spin. Nia didn't wait for one revolution. She hijacked the spinner and shot off five shots into the sky. Five clicks. No bullets.

"Robbie, you are a . . . fucker!" Nia screamed.

"What, ja rather I put the bullets in? Gimme back my gun!"

"Fucker, Robbie!" What a powerful word.

"Get off me, Jimmy, knock it off."

Nia kept the gun, turned and ran for home while Jimmy turned pugilist on Robbie. She did have the legs of a pony.

Alone, back at her house, Nia stirred sugar into the bottom of a glass of iced tea and watched the crystals disappear, but still be there. Transformation. She drank the cool tea and tried to understand her feelings. Really she just wanted to be different by being the same as everyone else. She sat at her desk and painted rabbits scattering through spent grass, just their ears sticking above the fringe, four sets in a dozen tones of washed gold. She would give it to Jimmy. He fought for her.

She gave the gun to her father because she knew better, but the only answer to his questions was, "I don't know. Ask around. It's an Indian reservation."

"My life is a Boston Molasses Disaster, I'm a bug trapped in spilled syrup." Nia entered the kitchen dramatically, cascading into her chair.

Julia looked up from her magazine. "Do you need a fainting lounge?"

"Imagine those Bostonians, 1919, swamped by a 30-foot wave of escaped industrial molasses! They say you could smell sugar on hot days for decades after."

"Imagine. And that's your life?"

"Trapped, Momma. Suffocated."

"But sweet?"

"Well, yes."

"And we can smell you decades after?"

"On hot summer days."

"Do you want to go to Pyramid today, Little Miss Dramatic?"

"You know I can't swim."

"But it's funny to watch you go in circles and then under," Julia teased.

"*So* funny."

"How about a couple of days out at Grandma's? Get you out of the desert."

"Packing."

What Julia really wanted was time in the car with Nia. Talking to a teenager was like shucking silver-lipped oysters in hopes of a pearl. Ruth and Trautmann had given Nia an *Encyclopedia Britannica* set, and Nia spent a great deal of time on random reading, throwing intellectual darts. (This made the girl exceptionally prepared for the eventual arrival of Trivial Pursuit or for yelling *Jeopardy* answers at the TV.) So when Nia described her emotional state as a *molasses disaster*, Julia got out her shucking tools.

Everyone knows everyone is damaged. Inside, outside. Both. Trace a scar to its source. Julia once had a dream when Nia was a baby that she pulled on her daughter's arms and they expanded like soft taffy. Would that she could make that confection.

They drove across Reno, City of Trembling Leaves, took the farm route over Windy Hill, past the peacocks who dared the road. Who knows how those stunners got from India to Nevada. "I wonder what they think when they see their ugly feet?" said Nia, but Julia knew all beauty has a counter. They traveled farther south through Washoe Valley toward the Genoa ranchlands bordered by the Sierra Nevada range. Every mile was as if they were crossing deeper into the color wheel of green.

"Your dad told me about the gun . . ."

"Yeah, scary. Who loses a gun?"

"Who finds a gun?"

That thought hung in the trapped air of the old car, dust motes following currents of optional replies. "Mom, remember that time we were at Park Lane Mall, I was maybe ten, and that kid, maybe he was seven, walked up to me? I think he was in love with *Journey to the Center of the Earth*. Do you remember what he asked?"

"He asked if you were part T. rex! His mother was mortified and so was I."

"Remember my answer?"

Easier to forget God. Julia clearly recalled that before the mother could grab her son away, Nia was reaching down her arms.

"You said *yes*! You said, 'Do you want to touch?'" It was a Godzilla meets Frankenstein moment for the kid. But it was something else entirely for Julia. "I was really proud of you."

"So you know, Mom, you don't always have to save me."

"I know. But I always have to try."

"I know. But don't."

Nia made a bologna sandwich and took a dusty book from Trautmann's collection of Louie L'Amour paperbacks—*High Lonesome*—and headed to the stream. Tiger lilies, some tiptoeing right into the eddies, nodded greetings like Anglican church ladies—pretty-faced but insincere; they weren't talking to her. She parted the filigreed curtain of a weeping willow and sat down within the sun-stripes, spine against the trunk. The book was just a prop to leave the house. She was accomplishing the magician's holy grail of being in two places at one time—she took herself back to the dry fields. She studied the gun fixed to Jimmy's temple, the blue-black metal. The way Jimmy squeezed his eyes closed right before he squeezed the trigger. She felt the excitement and the dread, two sides of the same coin—queen on the front, eagle, talons flexed on the back. She was no better than the boys, although it wasn't for bravado on her part.

Nia worried the wishbone of telling her mother. But then, sooner or later, it would all winnow down to one question; she played it out in her head:

Why did you sit down with them?

Mom, I ran away with the gun! Did you hear that part? I'm the hero. Where's my plaque?

Were you engraving that plaque when you sat down? Because it might have been Jimmy's headstone instead.

No bullets, no body!

You didn't know that. Same question: Why did you sit down?

She couldn't tell her mother that at times she wanted to die, because how was a girl like her going to live?

In the fall, their sophomore biology teacher, Mr. Smith, tasked his students with finding, identifying and pinning ten different species of insects to a sheet of cheese cloth–covered cardboard. Or bringing in a skeleton. Wynona was already thinking butterflies, wondering if it was too late in the season, when Mr. Smith started calling out names to assign random partners. Wynona got Wonder; Nia got Robbie. The four of them met up after school.

"Plenty of bugs in our backyards," Nia ventured.

"Nah. Let's do skeletons," Robbie said. "I know an easy place."

Nia sighed. Leave it to Robbie to know an *easy place* to find bones. She expected the three of them to overpower Robbie and take the fleshless route, but Wonder said, "Sounds good." Males sticking together, Nia assumed. But that wasn't it.

About three years ago, Wonder got a new stepdad—Luis. Luis was from Puerto Vallarta and he told Wonder about a jungle of wild orchids. As a young man, Luis fished a pale ocean and hunted in forests that knew no sense of time. He was used to the music of parrots. Wonder loved to listen to the stories, to Luis's voice and how he had his way with the English language.

Luis swore he saw Liz Taylor's big, creamy breasts shining in the Mexican moonlight on the pounding shores of La Jolla de Mismaloya, the starlet waiting for Richard Burton to finish an evening shoot of *Night of the Iguana*. Wonder's mother would laugh at that, so Wonder couldn't tell if it was true, or even what it really meant, but there was a *romance* to Luis; even as a boy, he felt it.

Luis thought the forests on Northern Nevada were too formal, the trees growing too far apart. He was used to a wildwood that would throw a vine around your neck. *You call this a forest!?* he would say and blow his lips. But he liked that the prey were easier to see.

When Wonder was twelve, Luis took him out at dusk to hunt for deer. He had never gone before—normally Luis went with a buddy from work. But Wonder had been persistent. *Bien, hombrecito. Let's go before your mamá get home and we have to ask permission.* She was at a Tupperware party.

Luis didn't buy a tag—he thought himself the Poncho

Villa sort. They needed the deer because winter was creeping the low horizon. For Luis, hunting was never for sport. They went at near nightfall, traveled an unpaved logging road beyond Verdi, up into Dog Valley, in his ancient, begging-to-be-put-out-to-pasture Bronco. There were no doors. *Saves tiempo! Seatbelts! What are you, a puto?* Wonder hung on to the saggy seat, hands between his legs.

A doe froze in their headlights. Why did that powerless light hold her? Wonder heard an owl sounding a too-late warning.

Luis was fast. Wonder thought of the Saturday morning cartoon, *Speedy Gonzales* in his yellow sombrero, how quickly Luis centered his rifle. The doe took the shot. Wonder swore she looked straight at him with her dark eyes. *How can you allow this?* she conveyed to Wonder, for surely if she spoke, it would be with eloquence.

The doe ran into the forest, but did not get far. They walked over to the fallen body. The scene was a car wreck to Wonder. He didn't want to look; couldn't look away. It was like that. They tried to lift the doe to put her on top of the truck. It was impossible. Wonder's body was immature for his age, and he could not lift the deer. Wonder felt embarrassed, but Luis said, *"No problema, hombrecito."*

Luis told Wonder to sit by the doe. He would come back with a friend. Wonder was in a yellow flannel; it would show up in the dark when Luis returned; otherwise Luis may never find the doe amid the camouflage of forest. As Luis drove away, Wonder wished one of them would have thought to just drape his shirt over the carcass. But Luis would not have had that thought—he was never afraid of nature. Nature was his darling.

But the doe was not a carcass. She was still alive. When Wonder sat down by her, he felt her breath, her tremble. She was warm and smelled raw and leathery. He saw the slow cascade of blood deserting her. He felt her heart stop; it was just a quietening. She died with Wonder's head on her breast, creamy as any Liz Taylor. Wonder closed her eyes on this magnificent world. Her tawny lashes stroked his finger. The forest in all its sounds admonished him.

Luis came back for Wonder; it didn't take too long and the moon avoided all clouds while Wonder was alone. Luis and his buddy hoisted the doe on to the top of the Bronco. Held her with rough ropes, as if she could escape. Wonder's mother never knew he was out in the forest alone. When Wonder thought back on the doe, the death of her, he saw blood the same color as apples and harvest leaves. Not such a scary color. He liked to think the doe taught him something of courage and acceptance. He did not yet truly know if he learned anything at all.

So when Robbie said *skeletons*, Wonder did not go along with him because Wonder was a follower. He agreed because the doe had changed Wonder.

Robbie, being a year older, had his driver's license, so on Saturday the four novice biologists headed south to Washoe Valley in his mom's sapphire Opal. On the west side of the valley, Slide Mountain pushes high into pine forests, creeks, and shade. On the east side, the land is parched, dotted with lowly pinions, sagebrush, and wind. In between, silty Washoe Lake alternates between shallow lake and marsh depending upon how long the draught lasts. The hourly workers, including Robbie's best aunt, live on the dry east side; the rich ranchers on the verdant west. Migrating birds live—and die—in the middle.

The kids rolled up their jeans, sacrificed their sneakers to the marsh-mud, and pushed through a cattail maze. Wonder carried his old Daisy Red Rider BB gun, which Robbie rolled his eyes at, but Wonder ignored the look. Robbie thought the low water levels might reveal ready-to-go skeletons of skirmishes past. They found blue feathers caught in the rose-gold tassels of switch grass, and a wrecked nest of spotted eggshells, broken, yellow embryos glossed to the insides. The air smelled of drying fish. They were intruders, and their bodies knew it. Nia watched a Robbie she was unfamiliar with, quiet and blending. But then, most children of the reservation know how to hunt—it will always only be a question of the quest.

Robbie found the mallard. Iridescent emerald outer feathers and bits of white down catching the tiniest of winds. Iridescent green flies creating the sound of decay. He picked the dead thing up, flies following. Nia felt a small sorrow, seeing the slender neck pour beyond his palm. The Indian summer golded over them as Robbie slid the mallard into his burlap bag. For once he knew to keep his mouth shut.

They walked farther into the marsh. Wonder took a bead on a pinyon jay, missed twice and then shot it dead. The bird fell like a shuttlecock, a little poof of indigo feathers weighted to earth by the lead in its heart.

They went back to Nia's house and boiled the bird heads in an old blue-and-white speckled enamelware pot. It was disgusting. Robbie picked the skulls clean, internally proud of being able to bear the feel of brains on his fingers. It was impressive. They all stared down at the bony white remains. Said and done, they were very small. "Cool," said Robbie. Wonder looked indifferent, although he felt stupid for killing something so beautiful as the jay for a high school biology class. He should have left his Daisy at home.

"I'm giving up meat," said Wynona.

"What, you eat a lot of blue jays at your house, do you?" said Robbie.

43

"Don't be a dick," said Wynona. "I feel sick. We should have done butterflies."

At last, senior year. Saturdays are best in September, in a small town. Football in a slanting afternoon sun, leaves blowing from the schoolyard trees onto the open field, drifting down, then drafting up in the wake of the running warriors. Cups of steaming apple cider. Parents and kids, all conflict confined to the game for a few hours.

On the final day of the football season, the Carson Senators played the Elroy Eagles on the Carson field. No one expected the Eagles to win, least of all the Eagles themselves. They could barely field a team. But win they did. The kids from Elroy loaded into their cars and trucks, perhaps with thoughts of a Dairy Queen celebration. But someone floated the idea of four-wheeling the dirt trail of Jumbo Grade, taking the party some twenty miles into the dry eastern hills to American Flats. The idea sparked. American Flats had long been a teenage siren and occasional vagabond motel. The crumbling structure was an isolated and abandoned, graphically graffitied 1922 cyanide plant.

How to evoke American Flats? Imagine a young woman: *She's got tats, full on, both sleeves done in vortex color swirls. A Chinese cherry blossom twining her spine, twisting 'round her exposed belly, jeans slipped low. Beautiful in structure, but she's at that point in her addictions, you can tell, it's too late for her; she's not going to make it back. She makes you feel so poignant that you want a piece of her, you want to tattoo the inside of her wrist, do a fashion shoot, buy her a drink, hasten the destruction.*

That's how the old cyanide plant made the vagabonds, the poets, and teenagers feel.

It wasn't a safe place to be. Entire exterior walls were gone, exposing crumbling steps, drops between floors. Footsteps echoed. Graffiti kaleidoscoped every wall: *Hope is Real, Shannon & David 4ever, Esther the Molester, Fag.* Robbie passed out the beers he stole from his cousin's fridge, pay that piper later. Nia and Wynona drank the beer that seemed to fall into their hands. One done, another appeared. Hale called out the stats of the game. Wonder was in Wonderland. There must have been fifteen kids, some out of high school, some too young to be there. Nia's group walked down to the old holding pond on the ground floor, the concrete pool filled with cloudy water. It was assumed that there was still cyanide in the pool and someone said that someone's little dog fell in there and the little dog disappeared in chunks, *like piranhas got 'em.*

The sun waned, long slants of light coming in the glassless windows, lighting up bits of graffiti as if it were pieces of art in a gallery. Nia stood by the cyanide pond, beer in hand—her third, fourth? Robbie was nearby, lighting a cigarette, face cupped in his hands. Hale was behind Robby, looking over Robbie's hunched shoulder. Hale saw Nia toss her half-full can of beer through a glassless window with surprising velocity. Outside, the can hit Wonder in the head. Wonder thought the building was collapsing, yelled *Look out!* The sharp cry startled Nia, who teetered on the edge of the opaque water. Forward, then back, forward again. Hard to keep her balance with her short arms. Wynona grasped Nia's danger and screamed, which frankly sealed the deal. Robbie began to turn in Nia's direction, but Hale had a line on Nia since the moment she threw the can. Hale knew he couldn't make it in time. He pushed Robbie into action. Robbie was no gentleman, but instinct made him pull Nia back, even though a part of him knew the *equal and opposite reaction* meant he was going in. He felt like a stop-motion cartoon, suspended over the murky water, held within the collective shock. He saw the falling star of his cigarette arch above him. Then he gracelessly went under the old water.

Robbie anticipated the cyanide-piranhas. He would not open his eyes for fear of corrosion. His feet touched bottom and he pushed for the surface like an Olympian, virtually propelled himself out of the wash. Snotty algae slimed his face, his body. Everyone was waiting for him to dissolve. But he didn't! It was just yucky water. Nothing happened. Except everyone saw Robbie, for the first time in his life, as a sort of knight. It was like a movie.

Hale was watching the movie from the cheap seats because no one saw that he was the one who animated the action hero. Even Robbie forgot Hale in the space of time it took him to understand that he was admired.

But nothing changed for Robbie. Not really. It was too late for substantial transformation; in that way, he was like American Flats. And if he was looking for a thank-you from Nia, he never got it. Nia still wasn't looking to be saved.

No one expected much of Wonder. He didn't learn to read until the fourth grade. Only the librarian knew that he now caromed his way through books, hard ones too, *The Magus* and *East of Eden*. Miss Margaret was borrowing books for him from the university library in Reno. She told no one. Neither did Wonder. He skimmed through the halls, closed his locker lightly while those around him slammed anything at hand. He ate his oranges in segments. Babysat the peripheral. He knew that it was Robbie who anonymously taped up the poster *The 10 Cheapest Licquors Every Student Should Know About*. (The English teacher corrected the spelling of *liquor*; the vice principal took the sign down.) He knew Hale planned to join the service to *get out of Nevada no matter what*. Wonder knew Jimmy liked boys.

So it wasn't hard for Wonder to notice that Nia had taken to carrying a notebook with lovely, thick watercolor paper, and a slim pack of colored pencils. He saw her write and sketch on the pages, her torso curved forward, the fact that she used the red pencil the most. Over one weekend Wonder produced a notebook of his own. He used different colors of ink and various pressures, gave the poems dates of up to two years prior. He spilled coffee on one page, smeared butter-prints on another. On the cover he applied half the rim of a wet wineglass stem and thought it sophisticated.

In a quiet moment he handed Nia his book. She read it carefully—it wasn't that long—spoke a few she really liked aloud:

TIME
The river I follow, it travels on.
It ran before me and it flow beyond.
And the river won't miss me when I'm gone.

MY FATHER
If Jesus turned water to whiskey
and faith to Copenhagen long cut straight—
then I'd line up for those pearly gates.
But as things stand,
I'll be the devil's handy man.

What Wonder didn't know was that he could write passable poetry; it was better than Nia's, and she knew it. To her honor, she told him so, and gave up poetry. To his honor, Wonder gave it up too. *Mission accomplished*. Although her praise did cause him to take on a Beat vibe, wearing a black turtleneck when the weather turned.

Well, despite her parents' worry, Nia did get asked to the senior prom. Someone broke into her locker and left a rolled-up parchment with match-burnt edges and ten pieces of Nia's favorite gum, Double Bubble, Bazooka Joe comic strip included. She unrolled the invitation. At first she thought it was from Wonder. But he wasn't the only poet.

A Cotillion Pas de Deux.
For two friends through-and-through.
Let's go together like pearls and a sweater.
And forget those boys with the varsity letters.

Res boys are gross and stupid. Let's just go on our own!

Wynona

P.S. Look behind your algebra book for a whole new YOU.

"For Christ's sake, Julia, what are those girls doing in there? That shower has run four times."

"Transformation, Howi. Transformation takes time."

"And apparently water . . ."

Prom night. Nia walked out the front door of her house with Wynona. She looked up. Nia liked to imagine the night sky as a prairie, farmhouse lamplight refracting behind old-glass windows, way up in the welkin. If only she could surrender her gravity, she could walk the dark dells. Wynona pulled her along, the movement of her pink tulle skirt whispering the repressed history of femininity. But Wynona wasn't ten anymore. Her top was a red-light-district bustier and she had stuffed it with Ziploc baggies of pine nuts for ballast, way better than tissue.

"Sweet Jesus!" Howi closed the door behind the girls and crumpled into the couch. Julia handed him the drink he hadn't known he wanted. "Did you see that?! Did you know they were dying their hair?"

"I did not. They were outside most of the day."

"Wynona's parents are going to kill us. She looks like she has streaks of Trix orange orange on her head."

"But she loves it! I think it was supposed to be blond." In the bathroom there were two plastic bottles of Sun In, castaways on an island of wet towels.

"But Nia . . ."

"I know! Howi, she looks so beautiful." Nia's highlights had turned out in twists of apricot, music box ballerinas twirling as she moved. Her plum dress skimming, almost a mirage, over her skin. Her bare shoulders, ballet slippers. Wynona was always a pretty girl, streaks or not, but Nia. Julia and Howi had been a desert waiting too long for a rain, waiting on their daughter to bloom. It wasn't that they didn't already know that Nia was pretty. It was that Nia didn't know.

"She looked confident, I think."

"She didn't cover up her arms."

"Did you pick out that dress?"

"Together. Joseph Magnin's. Overpaid."

"Did not."

"Thank you."

They sat side by side and drank themselves into melancholy. *How did time go by so fast?* The feeling propelled them into each other's bodies, that olde refuge, the reliable tavern, The White Hart, The Swan, The Plough. What better way out of the blues?

Not everyone fared so well. It is well known by small-town police that prom night is a bust-up night. Domestic violence; *she was asking for it*. Drunks headed to a hit- and-run.

Once a drowning out at Pyramid Lake, poor soul battered by cutthroat trout and something larger. Bar fights, lipstick exposés on the mirror of the Ladies, or on a shirt collar. The kids handled themselves pretty responsibly, but the parents took it hard, getting old. Most went to their own prom in the same gym, felt the power of seventeen. Where'd it take them—all that energy just a dust devil in the desert, cigarette smoke out the car window of life.

A school gym will ever be a place of great expectations. A young woman in a formal dress no less a gladiator than the wrestler in his singlet. That high-stakes potential for success and loss. The ritual of the school dance was manageable when kids were taught the bunny hop, the jive. But society jilted the rules in the '60s and left a new generation of teens without instructions. Figure out your own dance steps—Murray's retired. Yet there will always be that circlet of ornamental girls willing to lead the advance. Nia and Wynona held back, then worked their way in on the left flank, shimmied to the center. Jimmy, whom Nia thought was probably gay ("Hey, girls! Love the streaks!"), joined them, giving them some moves to mime.

Late in the evening, Nia found Wynona resting on the top row of the bleachers, tulle pulled above her knees, eating her pine nuts.

"I saw you out there slow dancin' with that nimrod Hale."

"He apologized for that time he insisted his pit was a Rhodesian Ridgeback."

Wynona snorted. "From when you were, like, seven?"

"Yeah. He likes my hair."

"Told you! You're gorgeous. But I tell you that all the time; it's not the hair."

"Really?"

"Shut up. Want some pine nuts?" She poured some into Nia's palm.

"Ooh, still warm."

The last dance was "Stairway to Heaven," a hundred silver balloons falling from the ceiling on the chairman of the planning committee's cue. Nia and Wynona watched from on high. Nia remembered her mother tying balloons to her little-girl wrist with curling ribbon. She felt the same way now: wonder, caused by something beautiful. And she wondered if she might be something beautiful too. Could she abandon her self-image? Forge a new one?

Here's something men in Elroy like to do: fix cars. There is an unspoken pact to hold on to old cars as long as possible, so there exists a sort of community pick-and-pull. They have an unspoken pact never to get rid of old cars, so everyone's yard on the reservation is a sort of pick-and-pull. It would be a stretch to call it yard art, although found-object artist Dobbie Williams, who had an affinity for rust, was known to buy this-and-that from incredulous homeowners. Husbands sometimes found themselves suddenly lax to sell when interest was shown in, say, a 1940 side view mirror that had sat so long, the reflection was a funhouse distort. But the wives always struck a deal.

Howi bought Nia a not-too-abused Pinto hatchback. He and his friends had no trouble finding the parts and figuring out how to extend the steering wheel so she could safely (or at least somewhat safely) drive the car. And the Nevada State Department of Motor Vehicles went for it! Possibly because Nia got the only Black instructor on staff when she went for her license.

From roller skates to luggage with casters, is there anything that represents freedom as much as a *wheel*? Even the word sounds fun. And if Nia couldn't use her arms for hand signals, no matter. There's turn signals for that now. Off she went.

On her eighteenth birthday, Nia drove into Reno. The new MGM Grand shattered the low-expectation skyline of the high desert city. It looked like the box Reno came out of. Nia avoided the casinos and headed to the wrong side of the tracks.

The chime of the tattoo parlor's entry door caused the young woman manning the counter to look up from *Infinite Jest*, which is impossible to read anyway. "Wow, I've never seen arms like that," she said, quickly coming forward. Nia took in the young woman's jean shorts, white pockets peeking out below soft fringe. The sacred heart of Jesus encircled by wicked thorns, protecting, or injuring one inner thigh, only partially visible when she walked. "Shit, I'm sorry," the young woman said, raising her arm to brush back her just-this-morning too-long bangs, revealing a Lilliputian schooner sailing the wave of her wrist; she felt awful for her insensitive words.

The room looked almost like a comic book store, tattoo designs in saturated colors tacked to the walls. Blown-glass bongs and Zig Zag rolling papers in the glass display box that made up the smudgy counter. A corner of the room was sublet to HEATHER'S FEATHERS & BEADS. The tattoo chair looked as if it belonged in a barber shop. Or an execution room, cracked black leather and salt.

"Don't worry about it," Nia said. "I'm used to it."

"Honestly, it was only because I was thinking how cool it would be to turn you into a design."

"Godzilla meets attack of the T. rex woman? Something like that?"

"Yes!"

"Go for it."

"Okay, I'll trade you the idea for a free tattoo if it's not too big." There was something about this short-armed girl that made Rebecca want to feel the ink altering her body. To control that. It wasn't sexual—Rebecca considered herself a connoisseur of skin. She would have said yes if the girl had asked for the burning of Atlanta.

"Tiger?" Nia asked. "Orange and black, but faded, almost pastel if that's possible on my skin color?"

"Cool. Where?"

"Where's most painful?"

Nia came out of the leather seat with her mascara seriously smeared, a ghosted Chinese tiger prowling the top of her left rib cage, a stylized cloud above the tiger, on the underpart of her small breast. She felt powerful and sexy. On the Heather's Feathers counter there was a Styrofoam head sporting a scarlet wig with a peacock headband. Nia slowed on her way toward the door, ran her fingers through the glossy strands of the fall, but it was the foam head that arrested her. It was hard for Nia to explain the beauty of that white and fragile mannequin. If anything pushed the foam in, the indent would be permanent. She felt a longing in the invisible face. "Can I buy this?" she asked.

"What, the peacock band? Sure." Rebecca removed it to look for the price tag.

"No, just the mannequin."

"Ah. Well, it comes with the peacock band," Rebecca improvised.

Rebecca followed Nia out the door to watch the strange girl walk off into the July heat, shimmering into the mirage of a day, holding the detached head under her arm. Rebecca never made the T. rex tattoo design, knew it would never sell, even as she had said the words to conceal her desire.

Julia had started mail ordering college brochures in Nia's

junior year. Ones from back East, ivy edged and top drawer. Pamphlets from out West that looked as if coeds could ride a palomino through the quad. Black campuses with pedigree.

"Mom, I know we can't afford these schools, even if Grandma and Grandpa chip in," Nia said, picking up the messy stack of brochures. "I'm going to cut these up and make a collage about disenfranchisement and the effects of media on today's youth."

"Oooh, great idea! We'll send it in with your application." Both of them smiled. "But really, Nia, you have to realize you are a poster child for a scholarship. You have good grades . . ."

"Anyone who shows up to class has good grades."

"Ha ha. But you do. SATs will show it. But more than that, these liberal schools are going to be falling all over themselves to get a Black, Native American . . ."

"Deformed girl."

"Stop it! You know what I mean."

"Yeah, I know. *Use my disadvantages to my advantage*."

"Sure, Nia! Why not?"

"Mom, you know how you didn't move to Chicago after I was born?" Nia had long recognized her parents had stayed in a small town to protect her. Julia certainly never said that her plans were trammeled by motherhood, but sooner or later, all children come to realize their cost.

"I know, I know. But maybe we made a mistake. You can't stay here."

"Well, I'm not staying in *Elroy*."

"Oh, thank you for that sarcasm."

"I just want to go to UNR. Reno's big enough. It's a start. I promise you if I want bigger horizons after that, I'll go."

Julia could barely look at her daughter. She so wanted her close to home, but did not want her own fears to narrow Nia's direction. "Really, that's what you want?"

Nia went over to the waste bin and let the brochures spill from her fingers in a high-speed glossy slideshow of so many paths not taken. But Julia was right about the poster child—Nia went to the University of Nevada on a full-ride scholarship. She took her potted shamrock with her and put it on the desk in her Nye Hall dorm room. Really, you can't kill that plant, it's just so lucky.

But Nia had underestimated the alienation. Discounted the comfort of her childhood bunting. She felt like a school dress hanging on a clothes line, a suggestion of a girl. It's not easy to be a sideshow—*Did you see that chick with the hands coming outta her elbows? That's fucked up.* She saw the surreptitious looks; she was probably the most recognized person on campus. Freaks and beauties, it's just the way it is. Her roommate from Boise asked for relocation after taking one look at Nia, and Nia became the only student with a private room in the dorm. "Good," Julia said. "Sleep in both beds—you only have to wash your sheets every other week."

In her art classes, Nia found other misfits. Ayn, a very white girl from Iowa whose real name was Anna Mae. Ayn's legs threatened a five o'clock shadow and she kept tweezers in her purse, ever-ready to pluck her eyebrows into submission. She said her watercolors, fields of flax in shades of bumblebee and honey, were of the Russian steppes. But they were just Iowa fields and the girl ordered rhubarb pie whenever they went to Marie Callender's. Ayn introduced Nia to Joe, whose paintings were violent. He liked to say springtime was painful for him, put his hand to his forehead—*all those pastels.*

Desperately desired visits with Wynona, who was getting her cosmetologist license, spending time with Ayn and Joe, the sheer beauty of the words that flew around campus like messenger pigeons delivering *ideas.* Nia wanted everything. What is growing up except a string of secrets kept? That transition from wanting your parents to *look at me!* to feeling they might not like what they see. Nia never told her parents about the tiger on her rib. That she smoked pot, Maui Wowi and red-threaded sticky Thai sticks. That sex had become a four-letter word. That she sometimes still thought about the short barrel of a cold revolver, that telescope, that kaleidoscope peek to the end of the universe.

She called home often, left funny messages on the new answering machine. *Hey, thinking of you. Thinking of you sending me money.* Julia took to calling back around bedtime and started reading to Nia over the phone. They were working their way through *The Madness of a Seduced Woman*, Julia's way of saying to her daughter that it's okay to grow up. No *Wind in the Willows*, that book. Julia told her how she had taken in a broken kid, Cole. Nia knew the family—his mom had died of breast cancer. Cole came over twice a week after school to work on art projects and homework, but it was just life skills, coping skills. "You miss me so much, you had to pick up an eight-year-old?" Nia teased.

"Yep. And he's way cuter than you."

"Well, he has those forearms and whatnot."

"I gave him your old school desk. He's putting wads of gum all over it. He made a Chiclet rainbow."

"Oh, you're killin' me now. I'm hanging up . . ."

They played a verbal cat's cradle, an ever-changing conversation pulled from the heart strings that really just said *I miss you.*

College days went on in a slip slide of words. An Etch A Sketch of equations. Shake the red frame and all the black lines sink into the subconscious. Start over again. Late nights in a back booth at IHOP drinking cups of philosophy, or when Joe got his monthly trust fund stipend, at the upscale Peppermill, where all the servers were pretty; career waitresses need not apply.

Over Christmas break Nia temped at Waldenbooks at Park Lane Mall, the mall anchored by a verdigris Victorian clock. She loved the smell of the books, clean and white, none of the acidy newspaper stink. All those new books locked up together, when the door was opened for the first time each day, those books pushed out a scent, a sigh of the forest from which they'd come. Nia sometimes thought about a tree surrendering to pulp and the press of letters.

Like all teenagers and young adults, Nia was on the verge.

Or in her case, Vergil.

Waldenbooks was a safehouse for Nia. Anyone who spends money on books can afford to be charitable, knew not to stare. Jennifer, her manager, a short woman who always seemed taller than those around her, put Nia in charge of window displays. That went well until Nia's display of sex books, including both *The Joy of Sex* and *The Joy of Gay Sex*. When Jennifer came back from lunch and saw the display, she walked into the store and right past Nia working the register. "Take it down," she said, without slowing her pace or even looking at Nia.

While Nia had been building the window (*Our Bodies Ourselves*, *The Sensuous Woman*, *The Happy Hooker)*, a young, Black troubadour was sitting out on a bench by the verdigris clock, watching the unique young woman build out the display. She walked in and out of the store, checking the arrangement for visual and color balance. When she cocked her head, her little ballerina curls performed their pirouettes. Vergil was styling himself in a fringed leather vest, jeans down low, beat-up guitar with the words *Ready Aim Fire* carved into the body of the Sitka spruce instrument. Scars on his wrists. But any young person living in the tiny town of Susanville, California, is going to try and kill themselves sooner or later. And he meant it only at the time.

Vergil's dad was a guard at the High Desert State Prison, which is a rather pretty name for a place encased in barbed wire. His mother worked at the library and Vergil figured he'd dodged a bullet by not being named Ovid, or her favorite, Euripides. It could have been worse. But she force-fed him books the way other moms forced vegetables. At his house, *You can't go to bed until you finish your broccoli* became *Why don't you go to bed and finish that story?*

His dad taught him how to shoot a tree, and if that didn't kill it, cut it down with an ax. "Tree's more useful dead than alive." And then figure out, actually write down, how many things he could do with that tree. Make it into a Christmas tree! "Pussy." Grind it down to pulp and make books. "Maggie, you're raising a pussy!"

The result of this bipolar upbringing was that Vergil wrote rather pretty love songs on his secondhand (or most probably fifth-or-sixth-hand guitar), and he could build just about anything that ever needed building and some that didn't. Like an igloo.

Vergil watched that girl with the little arms but foxy body build out that bookstore window on SEX. Now that was something to see.

Nia saw the boy—well, he was a man—enter the store, carrying a guitar like it was a mission statement. He browsed the shelves until her register was empty, then approached her. For a self-styled song writer, Vergil was surprisingly unromantic. "How's about it?" he said, like an idiot.

"What's that mean?" Nia asked. She was used to men thinking she might be desperate (she sometimes was) or available for a price (she never was). Freaks and beauties. But what to do when someone is both?

"Oh God, I'm sorry. I'm nervous," Vergil said, saving himself from her dismissal. "Let me rephrase." He cleared his throat, stood up straighter. "Would you consider having lunch with me over at the Black Angus?" He shrugged his shoulder out into the mall; the restaurant was just across the way. Dark, with individual booths surrounded by smoky glass, very 1970s. Lots of drug deals went down in that place. "My name's Vergil. Honest to God, you are the first Black woman I've seen since *Roots*."

Woman. Nia liked that word. Could she be that word?

"Sure, Vergil, but make it dinner and just know I'm gonna order the prime rib." And she did.

Vergil watched Nia eat; she was breaking all the girl rules of picking at a salad and milking a glass of wine. He tried to come up with things that would make him more interesting than the truth of him. Susanville is a kissing cousin to Elroy, not a reservation town, but a small town of agriculture— which is not culture—and a prison. But he liked books, and she liked books. Lots of conversation there. He worked in construction; she looked at his strong arms. He had recently rented his own place, just out of town, a Tom Thumb house, but his. It had a fireplace. Girls like that. Would she like to see it, what could he say to make her want to see it?

"I could build you an igloo. To sleep in, out in Susanville."

"Are you kidding?"

"Actually, I'm not kidding. Give me two days, come out this weekend." She was noncommittal but her fork slowed down. As Vergil was paying the bill, she surprised herself, passed a paper napkin and a pen over to Vergil, and told him to write down his address. She was off on Saturday; she would drive out.

"I could pick you up."

Reno to Susanville is about a 90-minute drive on a road so

straight, it almost disappears. Nia knew all about girls getting into strange men's cars. No way she was going to get in his car. His igloo maybe. But not his car. Crazy logic, but she was only twenty years old.

"It's okay. I like to drive," she said. Vergil didn't ask how she drove with those arms, and Nia liked that too. She walked herself out, knew he would watch. She looked pretty good from behind.

Northern Nevada is a high desert, windblown and pocked by sagebrush and tumbleweeds. The mountains are many but, until the snow comes, dull as dirt. But the snow does come. On nights of frost and pewter skies. Furious, or dreamy flakes. In the morning, the sky so blue it's Arctic, the white so enveloping it's hard to remember color. Nia set out for Susanville on a winter morning such as this, the roads clear but *sparkling*: the fair warning of ice.

Vergil had been working on his igloo. He cut the snow into blocks, established a circular perimeter and then overlapped each layer, tipping inward. The final block on the top of the small dome was purposely larger than the open space and he wedged it in, then used open hands to pack loose snow in the cracks over the whole of the structure. He cut out the door and air vents. Made a short doorway tunnel they would have to seriously stoop through. Not bad. He had some old Pendleton blankets—those things never wear out—and the stripy, primary colors looked great on the floor. He blew up an air mattress and covered it with his opened-up red plaid flannel sleeping bag and extra blankets on top. He brought in a lantern and knew the flicker would be just right. He had music on his Walkman—Lionel Richie, Diana Ross. And his guitar. Vergil stood back and assessed. *Yeah, Man*. He was bringing home the bacon.

Nia drove carefully, sipped from her mug of coffee. She had the sweet, thick feeling of anticipation. Nia wasn't a virgin; she had slept with Joe. Joe treated her as a canvas, had painted the suggestion of mountains on the spine of her back, a few pine trees, and a lone deer drinking from the pool of her sacrum. All of this in no more than twenty strokes of India ink, a haiku on her skin. He said he had never painted such a thing; she changed his art and he might hate her for it. They taught each other a lot, and while it wasn't love, it was lovely.

Nia stopped at Hallelujah Junction for more coffee and a stretch. Chilcoot to the west, Susanville straight ahead. The road marked the turnoff to the lowest pass over the Sierra Nevadas. There were ghosts there—the emigrants of the 1850s who risked it all for the oasis, or the mirage of California. Orville Stoy, who started Hallelujah Junction with a Richfield gas station, a diner, and a bar that refused Prohibition. *East Coast ladies—go fuck yourselves.* The West ever was for renegades. Hallelujah Junction sold lottery tickets now.

Nia stepped out of her car into the sparkling. She had entered the vast and wild land, mountains shouldering the white horizon, the crunch of pogonip beneath her feet. The Shoshone called the biting ice particles *payinappih*—cloud. Nia was walking on history and clouds.

She planned her arrival at Vergil's house for late in the afternoon; Nia wasn't counting on considerable conversation. The day had warmed up. She had on the Black Watch cape her grandmother Ruth had made for her, hood over her head, hands coming out of the slits, arms tucked in. Under green-and-black plaid, Nia's short arms were indiscernible. This cape was Nia's refuge in public. Ruth knew it would be when she sewed it, and Nia wore it often. Vergil opened his door and thought Nia looked like a piece of Scottish toffee, all wrapped up in tartan. *Yum yum.*

Who needs words when you have an igloo? Turned out, Nia was a woman, and she liked the way their two bodies looked together auraed in lantern light reflecting off the cold white walls. When her fingers found the welts on Vergil 's wrists, she whispered *Sweet Mary*, and touched the ridges as if they were a rosary.

They turned that ice palace into a sauna and slept on top of the flannel, as beautiful as anything this world has to offer.

Mornings are awkward when two people don't really know each other. Nia had no intention of carrying on this relationship; she knew her parents' story. In the past few years Nia had grown more comfortable with her *uniqueness*, and as much as she loved her father, there was no way she wanted to repeat her mother's decision and fall for a construction guy from Susanville because he was capable of building alternative housing.

Dressed, Nia stooped to exit the igloo. Yesterday's late afternoon heat had caused a melt off over the ledge of the low roof. The raw night froze the water and formed a wall of icicles that created prisms in the clear morning sun. There were little rainbows everywhere. But the curtain of ice was new and delicate; Nia broke through with her hands, releasing the wind chime voice of the icicles.

"Can I have your number?" Vergil asked, following her out, because Nia was clearly leaving. She looked back at him, considered her options.

"I've got yours. Let's leave it at that." She smiled, pulling her cape close around her body—the day was Siberian.

Vergil really was a pussy. He let her go.

Icicle is a word that is so cold, it chatters, repeats its opening letters. Says what it is. Announces the weather conditions, clearly.

Nia had to be at Walden's by 10 a.m.; she had enough time. After work, Wynona was going to try a Sugar Cookie frost on her hair. Nia couldn't wait to say the words *I spent the night with a man in an igloo!* Really, you can't make this stuff up. The highway was a dark ribbon of stars, a twinkling, earth-bound Milky Way running though the vast expanse of white. She felt a little star herself.

Their friend, Peace Officer Blue, said, "I'm going to try and be as honest with you as I can find words for." Julia heard the words but they floated around her like dust motes, uncatch-able and gray. Blue's voice was holding steady, but his tears were talking louder. Howi had felt lucky when he found the Pinto at a good price; rode hard, sure, but it was only six years old and cute as its name. He would never know it had a design fault Ford Motor Company admitted it could have fixed for $11 per car. Howi didn't read *Consumer Reports*.

Hit from behind by a skidding truck that smashed in the Pinto's rear end. Gas leak, vapors. Scraping the side of the road, probably caused sparks. The ice. She rolled one-and-a-half times, Pinto crumpled. Landed on its side. The fire. FIRE! She would have had to open the passenger side window to climb out. But her arms. Too short for such a thing? Her arms. Not enough time, all the time was gone.

And what of Nia in those slow-down minutes? The Rag-gedy Ann impact, flinging her forward, hitting her head against the too-close steering wheel. Confusion, metal crum-pling, sounding just like breaking ice. Wind chimes? The er-rant smell of gas. The car was fishtailing, sliding on the icy road, and she tried to control it but it was a roller coaster and then she did the loop-de-loop. The car landed on its side and both her shoulder and pelvis fractured on impact. Her head hit the metal steering wheel again, with its thin, dove gray pleather cover, covered in blood. Was that blood? She understood that she had to find a way to roll down the passenger side window and climb out. It was hard to concentrate. But then the golden orange, rippling, prowling TIGER. Her tiger? No, the FIRE.

Then she understood; here was her chance. To give in to the end of days, the very thing she had been known to so desire. The possibility she kept under her pillow. To be a tumbleweed, unmoored and skirting the desert.

But in the end, Nia knew the truth of herself and desire. She clawed, she roared, deep and snarly, raged from her very subterranean.

The mortuary gave Howi and Julia a box of ashes; who knew what was in there, metal and rust, bone and memory. They understood it was more so that they could have *something*. On the first night of the missing moon, Howi transferred a couple of big handfuls of that box into a plastic bag, and drove out to the Black Rock Desert, leaving Julia a short note on the kitchen table. It was past two in the morning, the road Hitchcock black, a film noir unspooling in his headlights. A band of mustangs watched the old truck fly by, but Howi couldn't see the wildings, the fog of their exhaled breath.

Howi parked the truck deep in the playa and walked out on the broken jigsaw flats. He breathed in more rime than air, it was so cold. He looked up at the fine arch of the Milky Way and allowed his memories. It took grit, like pounding on a new bruise because old wives say it turns the pain from blue to pale yellow. He kept getting stuck on the times when Nia was four or five, dressed up in her bubblegum-pink tutu, and she danced for him, round and round. Then she would hold out an empty Sucrets box for payment; she liked pennies best because copper is the prettiest money color, yes? It made him infinitely sad that he couldn't say which was the last dance, the exact moment she quit dancing for her father. When she was a little older, she would hold out the box and say *Please, sir, alms for the poor*, skip the dance. God knows where she learned such a phrase, must be that *Oliver* movie. He never let her Sucrets box be empty. Thank the Lord, he never did.

He thought on the time Julia sent Nia to bed without dinner; she was maybe nine and mouthy as a big bass. Half an hour later, Julia put Nia's dinner on a plate and sent Howi in with it, letting him take all the glory of the Forgiver. Both those girls had a fish hook in his heart.

Howi scattered the ashes; it was a real dust to dust because that's all the Black Rock is. The two of them loved this place. He pictured Nia riding on his shoulders, her little hands believing if he held her up, she *could* reach the stars. And why not? That's what daddies are for.

Julia wouldn't miss the handfuls of Nia he released to the cold night. Nor would she mind, but he was not of a state to share the Black Rock with her. As he drove home, a javelin of morning light came over the horizon, and there were those mustangs. They could represent beauty or freedom or incarnation. But Howi just saw dust and ponies.

When he got home, Howi said nothing. Julia remained silent, too, as she slowly stirred a tablespoon of Nia's ashes into her tea and drank it down like gritty medicine.

Julia knew she was never going to forgive herself for not being with her daughter when she died. It didn't matter that being with Nia at all times was an impossibility under the circumstances of Nia being an adult and moving alone through the world. Julia couldn't stop herself from feeling that she should have saved Nia, or burned with her.

When Nia died, Wynona died too. That part of Wynona that

believed she would always have a best friend who understood what it meant to grow up on a high desert reservation, who never needed to hear the backstory. Who didn't play the umpire when she said, *I shouldn't have slept with him,* or when she dyed some twit of a white girl's hair two shades too red (*Fuck, I look like a stripper!*) on purpose. Wynona felt as if her arms had been cut off at the elbows. She couldn't quite get a grip on herself. She wore a black armband until it weathered and fell away like a prayer flag.

Of course everyone went to the funeral. Tragedy attracts a crowd. Some came to help stitch the open wound of Julia and Howi, others just to watch the bloody mess. It was held in Genoa and it looked like a winter version of the Candy Dance, so many lasagnas, pineapple-baked hams, doily-edged plates of fudge laid out for the wake. The Ladies Auxiliary was pleased with the food, but a little unhinged by the Native American invasion.

Whenever Julia had the strength to look back on the day, it was like a jewel box. She would open the memories to the tinny sound of metal prongs vibrating on the revolving cylinder of her heart. Ruth fastened to her like a mother-of-pearl broach, Trautmann a chunk of solid turquoise set in silver. Howi a tarnished and broken promise ring, and Nia the little plastic ballerina spinning round it all. It was a box Julia buried beneath her bones.

Wynona had planned to tell Julia that she would become a fill-in daughter, a Sunday dinner daughter, but then she didn't. Julia looked like a black ghost, a negative space. Wynona was too young and unable to absorb that kind of emptiness. Instead, Wynona got drunk with the other kids from her high school class and ended up making out with that nimrod, Hale, who had grown some arresting muscles courtesy of Uncle Sam, *yes sir.*

Wonder would have liked to fill the space of a missing child. He watched Julia, empathy rolling through the deep of him, but language was never his wingman. Wonder did take her hand in the receiving line, but Julia was closed to his transmission, the little neon sign of him. It was a missed opportunity for them both; story of Wonder's life.

Jimmy brought the long-ago watercolor Nia had done of the four sets of golden bunny ears just above the wild wheat, and he gave it to Julia rolled up with a green ribbon his mother had added. Julia kept that.

Robbie, the Russian roulette jokester, the hero of American Flats, didn't attend. He was dead, shot by a hardcore survivalist in Idaho while Robbie was invading the man's property. Robbie had a tip that there was a cache of cash under the old oak tree, and he was stupid enough to believe he was the guy who was going to sneak in and dig it up. Really, his young death could have been anticipated from the day he was born, even his name a harbinger.

Robbie's funeral wasn't nearly as well attended as Nia's. He was buried in Idaho. Only his brother, Paul Sparks, ten years older and a licensed attorney in the State of California, attended. God, how Paul had hated his desert-dust childhood! God, how Paul hated his pinyon-pinenut-and-goat-milk family! But not his little brother. He had loved Robbie, the little boy had looked up to him. In Paul's hurry to get away from home, he had failed to protect Robbie; Paul had never gone back. Now it was too late.

Robbie could have been a little bug in a drop of amber, so precious to someone they made him into a necklace worn next to the heart. But Robbie never got that kind of love.

At the end of the wake, Wynona left with Hale and they got a room at the Carson Valley Inn, because if there's one thing the Grim Reaper can't stand to be around, it's romper room sex. Those kids tore the place apart. Then they went over to the J.T. Basque restaurant and ate platters of steak and French fries until there just wasn't any room left in Wynona for grief, and she fell all the way asleep for the first time since Nia went up in smoke.

Wynona woke up in the still-dark of morning. Her legs and arms were entangled in Hale's. For just a moment Wynona let herself pretend the body next to her was Nia's. The two girls had slept like that when they were kids in their soft flannel jammies, bellies popped out, skinned knees. But it wasn't Nia; they buried Nia yesterday, and Wynona ended up with Hale (Hale!) in a bunch of twisty sheets at the Carson Valley Inn. The mini fridge was ready for takeoff in the corner. The heater scented the air plastic. What was she doing here? She tried to disentangle herself—my God, the sleeping boy was solid as a war machine. She felt like she was under house arrest. But he did get the job done last night, she had to give him that. *The nimrod Hale.*

He was kind of beautiful.

Wynona left her phone number.

It was snowing. Big filigreed flakes on a slow fall, as if they were enjoying the ride down. Wynona sat in her car while it warmed up, the sun rising in a dim blue-gray band. Her car made the first tracks through the parking lot, but a fox had come before, little erratic prints, chasing mice. Wynona felt the unstoppable-ness of the earth, the crushing hand of time. Nia was *gone.* They had plans! Nia had just helped her pick out colors for the room she rented—paint chips peacocked on the kitchen table. Coventry Gray and Tanager—Wynona now thought they had been choosing names, how those names made them feel, more than the color. They were supposed to make fun of their husbands together, raise children. Grow old. They had barely grown up!

Suddenly Wynona couldn't construct her twenty-year-old self. She was a paper cutout. She saw herself walking into the forest, the Galena wind blowing her away, folding her in half and blowing her away.

Oh well. She had a shift at the Pink Puff to get to. She lit a cigarette and drove to Reno.

When Wynona walked in the door of the Puff, the chemical mix of perm solution and liquid acrylic was her personal smelling salts. She took a deep breath. *There's nothing like the smell of ammonia in the morning.* She tied her black plastic apron on over her black jeans and her Dead Kennedys T-shirt. The place was buzzing. Flo had started the Puff in the '60s and the sign was still a swirl of pink, Jackie Kennedy flips and bouffant posters, a wall of beehive dryers in faded pastels. The whole place looked as if it belonged in Palm Springs; in fact, Flo kept the radio tuned to KSRN, Wynona walking into Frank Sinatra doing it his way. But all that was now just a kitschy front and Flo knew it, because the young hairdressers she hired were Goth or Punk, or Flo didn't know what. She didn't understand it, but the cash register did. She thought the girls looked like horror-show widows, but of course she knew they were just girls trying not to look like their mothers while their double chins were coming in, all the same.

Wynona fell into the familiar. The hours between the funeral and *this moment* accumulated, and Wynona wondered if time could really scab a wound so deep. She thought alcohol might do a better job. So that night she decided she would live at the Blue Lamp. Or mostly live, because she wasn't really feeling like living anyway.

The Blue Lamp was a little bar on Sierra Street, just a storefront wedged between low-heeled professional offices. A small neon sign strobed like a blue heartbeat. There was a lighting to the bar, once the sun went down. The way it reflected off all the glass and the colors of the booze, the liqueurs. Wynona tried to name it. *That's it. Amaretto.* The lighting was amaretto. She didn't really fit in with her hot pink streaks and heavy eyeliner. It was a bar for gray suits and pencil skirts. There was a woman with those awful shoulder pads, cream silk blouse with high-collar bow, dancing on the bar.

"Try stuffing dollar bills into that," Jimmy said, shoulder flicking toward the dancer, passing Wynona a shot of something she looked like she needed.

Wynona glanced at the woman. "I don't know how she does that. I don't like but one set of eyes on me at a time."

Wynona went to the Blue Lamp because Jimmy worked the Monday through Friday 12p–8p shift, opening the bar for the daytime regulars, the old hardcore drunks who needed a stool as much as a drink. They were nice, or maybe just grateful. Then the after-work crowd, the attorneys, and the secretaries looking for a ring in the bottom of a Cosmo. They were better-than -average tippers. And he liked getting off at eight—he had places of his own to be after that. Wynona sat on the last stool, up against the wall.

"Who *are* these people?"

"Reno's E-lite." Three Republican lobbyists, legs spread, taking up as much space as possible at the back table, were talking shop. Dirty martinis and skinny ties. It was like this on workdays. But on the weekends, when they brought in the cello and saxophone bands, the atmosphere changed, the artists and the addicts came out. Well, everybody likes to drink.

"You doing okay?" Jimmy asked.

"No, not really."

"Yeah, it's tough . . . What was Nia even doing, driving *back* to Reno from, like, Susanville?"

No one could answer that, not the police, not Julia or Howi. Not Wynona. If Wynona had known that Nia had spent her last night melting the walls of an igloo—it would have at least made her laugh. "I don't know," was all Wynona could say. Jimmy moved away to hide his lack of words. It was an easily disguised diversion —someone always needed another pour. Wynona ate the curl of lemon peel Jimmy had put in her drink. Sour.

"Jimmy," Wynona said when her friend came back, "can I move in with you?"

Jimmy looked at her. He had a two-bedroom place and Wynona knew it. "You know I drink too much and bring home men?"

"Yep."

"It might not be the best place for you."

"I think it is the best place. Because I just don't want to be alone."

"You have a roommate."

"I never even remember her name."

"Yes you do."

"She sells Avon!"

"It's Jafra. You like it." Jimmy bought the Royal Jelly himself.

"She doesn't know me."

Jimmy sighed. "Yeah, okay." He got it. Wynona wanted to tuck her future into her past for a while.

Jimmy lived on Arlington Avenue in a small apartment on the second story of a subdivided and worn-out Victorian. He chose for his bedroom the tiny conservatory, thin windows on three sides and just enough room for a bed. In the summer, the room simmered and Jimmy misted the ivy plants fringing the glass so the leaves could sweat off the heat. In the winter, the windowpanes shrank in on themselves to escape the cold, allowing passage for the ice to creep inside. On the First Night of Winter, the ice became the windows and the moon the bedside lamp. When Jimmy brought a lover home to the icy room, the heat of their bodies would melt the windows clear.

Jimmy's house was directly across from Saint Mary's Hospital emergency entrance, and on a busy night, the sirens might shock him from his sleep, intensify an orgasm, herald his precarious health. Once a man was stabbed right below his window and in the morning he saw blood on the street.

Wynona moved in, painted Jimmy's kitchen Coventry Gray and Tanager, terms of the lease be damned. She took one good long look at Jimmy coming out of the bathroom in a surprisingly thick and creamy towel, at his long torso skinny as a cigarette, sexy yes, but way too thin. Magazine thin. She had already lived there for enough time to know the contents of Jimmy's food supply.

"Hey, loverboy," she called. "You gotta change out your four major food groups."

Jimmy shook his wet hair. Yes, sexy. "What do you mean?"

"Grease, Diet Coke, beer, and beer. I'm making you my mom's eggplant stew." For the entire time Wynona lived there, the purple stew was in a near-constant simmer on the stove. The apartment took on a vague compost smell, like a '70s hippie commune. Jimmy ate it—but it didn't work.

Jimmy took Wynona with him to the Chute and the Club 99, where AIDS was festering and no one yet knew it. He would break a little glass vial of amyl nitrate and inhale the fumes and dance the dance of the twelve dancing princesses, the dance of the seven vials. He would drink until his liver would painfully suggest he stop, and then he would go stir that earthy eggplant for a while. Wynona watched as so many stray-cat men wandered through his life, slept on Jimmy's couch, his crotch, shared his drugs, stole his things, titillated him, moved on.

Wynona brought home no one, woke up with no buddy but her memory of Nia. An after-vodka headache and a cloudy realization she had eaten Carl's Junior onion rings at 2 a.m., again. She always made it to work on time, but it was a good thing that jagged cuts were in demand because Wynona's work was looking as if it were done with pinking shears and a razor. Sometimes it was genius, but Flo knew a hangover when she saw one. "Girl," she said, "you gotta get a grip. Your friend died, sure it's sad, but Christ, you're looking like a drunk Indian on Sunday morning."

"It's Saturday," corrected Wynona. It was all she could think of. The drunk Indian part hurt; no one wants to fulfill their racial slurs.

"Saturday, Sunday, Monday, Tuesday, Wednesday, it's all starting to look the same on you. Look, you want to go to AA with me, just let me know." Flo had a tolerance level deep as magenta.

For Easter, for a joke because neither Wynona nor Jimmy was in a Jesus state of mind, Jimmy gave Wynona a bunny. Deep, pearl gray fur, they named the creature Pearl. They let Pearl run around the house (terms of the lease be dammed), hoping she would become potty-trained. But Pearl hopped right over their hopes and pooped under the bed, in the kitchen, everywhere. They fed Pearl pellets and lettuce, but Pearl's favorite was marijuana seeds culled of their stems and leaves, of which there was no shortage. Wynona found the sprouted pot plant growing out of rabbit poop, cradled in the shag carpet, just behind the toilet, watered by a slow leak. "That's what they get," said Jimmy when Wynona showed him, "putting carpet in a bathroom." They knew they needed to grow up and stop this behavior. Move out, give Pearl to a little kid, get better jobs, stop getting high, stop getting drunk. But, oh, the little Pearl-poop pot plant was just so divine!

A year slipped by, then another spring. Nothing had changed for Nia's friends. Their ruts had only deepened, threatening a name-change to trench.

For three weeks each May, Reno is the City of Lilacs. The flowers bloom so intently, there is a vague halo of color caught in the streetlamps at night. Women wear lavender eyeshadow and don't know why. The combined scent of the lilacs is reminiscent of old ladies sampling toilet water at Woolworth's. Jimmy and Wynona decided to throw the *First Annual Blue Lamp Lilac Bash*. They put posters in the windows. The requirement, of course, was to be dressed in white, green, or shades of lilac.

The night before the party, armed with Albertson's Grocery paper bags and Wynona's old sheers, they hit the established gardens of the old neighborhoods. After hours, at the deserted Blue Lamp, they spread out their petal booty, armfuls of spring, but just a few from each bush, so Wynona wouldn't feel guilty. Then they decorated. Leis and crowns. Flowers in every dime store vase, garlanded, and pinned over the door like mistletoe.

Everyone got drunk. Everyone got high. Quaaludes—that double *a*, the long *u*. Perfect spelling for how the drug made you feel. Snowy 8-balls of cocaine if you could afford it.

Tonight, Jimmy worked the bar. Wynona sat outside. It was a starry, starry night. A man, whom Wynona knew to be both an artist and a heroin addict, walked up to her and asked,

"How much?" Wynona was not insulted because really, how much simpler would life be if you could answer that question up front? She did, however, rethink her outfit.

Wynona went back into the bar, took up her recessed spot. Jimmy had abandoned post—and his shirt—to take a twirl; he moved so well, the music seemed to follow him. Lilacs were falling to the floor, no dancer as beautiful as the blooms sacrificed in their own honor. Wynona kept to the safety of the bar, where she could watch.

Wynona spied the room through the dream-distortion of her glass. The dream she got, or inherited, or sought out, was the Absolut dream. It's such a pretty dream in a martini glass, so elegant in hand. She found she preferred the reassuring sweat of the glass to the less-assuring glisten of human skin. She wouldn't dare the dance floor. She didn't know if the sweet, bitter vodka, tequila, gin, rum, absinthe, beer, wine, somebody give me a drink gave her all the confidence she had left, or took it all away.

How had she become this girl, this girl who wouldn't dance? This girl who didn't wear pink. How had she allowed it?

Wynona might have escaped the night intact had not Hale shown up, home on leave again. All muscles and military cut. He wasn't wearing purple. He saw her; the corner-doll. Black eyes.

"Why didn't you call me?" she said instead of hello.

"I did. You moved, no forwarding address." True. "You come here often?" It wasn't a pickup. Hale was examining her fracture lines.

"Oh, only just about every night. Since Nia." She didn't like to say the word *died*.

Jimmy came over, back behind the bar. But his shirt was still off. "Buy you drink, sailor?"

"No, I think we're leaving."

Jimmy leaned in, pulled Hale close. One part of Jimmy wondered what cologne Hale was wearing that smelled of foggy redwood, and *My, aren't his hands big?* The speaking part whispered, "Don't sleep with her. She's not herself, since, you know. Since Nia."

Nobody likes to say the word *died*.

"I can see that, fuck face. And I can see you're the one pouring the drinks. Give her a discount, do you?"

Wynona didn't note the exchange; getting her shoulder bag to stay on her shoulder was taking all her concentration. "I want some onion rings," she said, following Hale out the door, coronet of lilacs adorably a-bobble.

In the morning, Wynona was pregnant.

Technically, it was still night when the cells collided within the body-dark. But what does science know? Surely a rainbow arched, or stars exploded, or lilacs bloomed. *Possibility* should have a color.

Hale hadn't intended to intrude on Wynona's body. But he was just now twenty-two and so was she and she was sick. She had always been the strong one, brash and bright, helping Nia face her short-armed life. But now she knew, or was beginning to know, it was Nia who was the light and Wynona the reflection. While she was growing up, Wynona's parents were working, working, working, and when she graduated from high school, they moved to Alaska for her dad to work on the pipeline. It seemed to Wynona now that Nia had been the one to always turn her head when Wynona said, *Look at me.* Without Nia's attention, what was Wynona? *Apparently a drunk. How cliché.*

Hale took her home, carried her up the creaky exterior steps of the Victorian. An ambulance rushed by them, the revolving lights sweeping them red-blue. He felt like Godzilla, she was so small in his arms. She wanted him. Not him, he suspected that. Just someone familiar who wouldn't hurt her. Well, he would hurt her. Jimmy was right about that.

When Jimmy finally came home in the full-blaze of high noon, his fingernails were painted gold and he had no idea how that happened.

After Nia's funeral, Julia found she could not stand to touch Howi's body; even the smell of him was like corned beef and cabbage. Of course she knew he was hurting too; her grief was not paramount over his. He simply could not provide her solace, not in the flowers he brought home, not in the way he offered his chest as a wailing wall. She was having none of it. And she was sorry. It's just the way it was.

Like soldiers at war, they talked about anything except the bullets. They didn't even say her name. Maybe they would go ahead and leave Elroy. Move out to Genoa with Trautmann and Ruth, build a little place, like they had talked about way back in the beginning. Working with lumber is a solid thing to do. But Julia was stuck. She couldn't even box up Nia's things. Finally, Ruth came over. She ran her eyes up and down her daughter, gave her the tsk-tsk look. Julia was still wearing black. Julia caught the look, knew what it meant. "I'm wearing black until I find something darker." Ruth sighed and started collecting her granddaughter's clothes. Julia was agitated but Ruth said, *Trust me*. Ruth went after those clothes with her sharpest scissors and then sewed them back together in a crazy quilt, embroidered the seams with tiny-petaled daisies, rickrack, and bony French knots. She did it in a week, Luis Valdez spurring her on. When Julia saw the quilt, Ruth thought she had made a grave error, because Julia wrapped herself in the blanket as if it were a shroud. Slept under it every night. But Julia assured her mother it was her greatest gift.

In the empty hours, and there were so many, uncountable, Julia wandered their little house. She watched winter play paper rock scissors with spring until spring won. The daffodils bloomed—how can the color yellow still exist? Everything Julia did—pouring lavender fabric softener, spooning honey in her tea, setting the table for two instead of three—was loading a bullet for Russian roulette. Any action had the potential to trigger a memory and blow her away. But the ballistic missile was the answering machine. At the end of the tape, before it filled up, were a few awkward condolences, *I'm so sorry for your loss; I'm praying for you*, but the majority of the tape was a treasure of Nia's voice. Howi went back to work, but against everyone's better judgment, Julia refused. The only activity she continued was working with Cole Feather twice a week, and that was only because he still smelled like a kid. She spent hours wrapped up in the quilt, secretly listening to her daughter.

"Mom, all the kids' parents are delivering Marie Callender's pies to the dorms. I'm lookin' like an orphan here. Lemon meringue, please!"

She knew it was silliness, but oh, holding a photo of Nia in her hand, listening to her bluebird voice, it was a beautiful delusion. She kept it to herself, didn't want to share it with Howi.

When Cole came over, Julia assembled herself into something he would expect—brushed hair, mom makeup. But he saw the accumulation of dust on the furniture and really on Julia too; he wanted to quit coming. "I don't want to go to that dead girl's house." But his mother made him. He was twelve now and unimpressed by watercolors and pastels. He wanted to shoot guns and say the word *fuck*. He wanted primary colors. Cole had never been pliant; he was always looking for victims because he was one. In his simmering adolescent anger, Cole became a little thief of things he perceived as having little value. Just something, a dream catcher from the dead girl's room, a short-handled ax from the garage. An old, compact answering machine. Fit right under the sweatshirt, tucked in flat against his belly.

Didn't take long to figure out how to erase the tape and record his own voice. Narcissus, enchanted with his own reflection.

When Julia realized the tape was gone, she felt kin to the knife thrower's assistant, tied to the wheel, spinning round, knives thunking into the wood beside her face, her breasts, right between her spread legs. Barely surviving. And then one of the knives changed trajectory mid-throw and went straight into her heart.

Julia and Howi moved out to Trautmann and Ruth's property. Howi built the new house, an A-frame, pounded out his grief, turned it to nails. Everyone knows when someone you love dies, it makes you feel a little bit gone too. They both changed. But as year one entered year two, Julia took on a rag-doll look, something that sits on top of the bed with patchy hair and button eyes.

How can a thing as tiny as a snowflake accumulate into the avalanche? On a winter's night, Julia and Howi settled by the fire, Howi with a book. Julia peered out the window, icicles jailing her in. She recalled a long-ago snow day when Nia and Wynona, free from school, stayed outside until their eyelashes froze, then came in and thawed them in hot chocolate steam. When Howi got up to hunt a snack, Julia caped her crazy quilt around her shoulders, pulled on her rancher's boots, and made her way out to the Jeep. The quilt swept her footsteps away, filled the indentations with snow, but it would still be easy to follow her tracks. She was not hiding.

Julia sped down the county road as if it were a summer interstate. She didn't give a toss; she didn't even know where she was going, except away. A few miles down, someone left their ranch gate open, or the winter wind unlatched the lock, or the lock just froze and broke off, but all the sheep were loose and wandering the road like little lost sheep. But Julia could not see them because sheep are the color of snow and their eyes are bits of night. So Julia just plowed into two of those robust animals. The first one hit her front bumper, bounced up onto the windshield and flew over the top of her car to land behind her. The second one came right after, smack square into the windshield, this time crackling the shield like ice on a lake. Then the fluffer flew straight up in the air and fell back down, hard, on top of the Jeep. The heavy body crumpled the roof, making an indentation that held the sheep's carcass in place. The four legs stuck up into the air, but the head lolled off to Julia's side of the car, the long sheep face looking into Julia's window, smearing blood onto the glass. Gravity caused the dead sheep's mouth to open and the tongue to fall loose. Before the poor animal could actually appear to be licking its own blood off the window, Julia accelerated, then slammed on the breaks. The sheep came out of the roof dent and rolled back down the front of the car and off the hood.

Julia turned the Jeep around and went back home. Howi saw her headlights and came to the door, held it open while she retraced her faint tracks, held her quilt for her, that scattershot of memories in fabric, while she shook off her boots. For a moment, Julia thought she smelled wood fire and bristlecone instead of corned beef and cabbage. She almost rested her head against Howi's chest. She knew if she gave him the chance, Howi would turn the night to the absurd and goofy; it would end in laughter instead of feelings of sadness and loss. But she was used to those two suppressing emotions, dark angels on her shoulders. "There's a couple of sheep in the road by Engebritson's place. If they aren't dead, they wish they were. Will you please go look?" She took her Nia-quilt out of Howi's hands and started up the steps.

"You ought to throw that patchwork sarcophagus out," he said, slamming the door.

Julia lay down on the bed. She had to acknowledge the casualties of her life. It wasn't only Nia. Her life with Howi, living on the edge of the Black Rock was a hard memory. No one could survive out there; they shouldn't have tried. Spent their youth in a bed made lumpy by their own ins-and-outs, by their deep dives. By Nia's jumps and tumbles. That bed was Olympic, and held some of Julia's best-worst memories. Each hitting her as if she were a woman being stoned. Honestly, it was too difficult.

She fell asleep.

The second spring. The plum trees down by the far stream were in glorious petal. Early snowdrops sheltered between the roots. Julia sat on a mossy level and watched the stream encourage motion, babble the value of the moving on. She allowed herself the pain of thinking of her daughter, remembering the physical-ness of Nia, imagining her in an aura of radiating light. She never allowed herself to think of Nia in that car, in that fire. Always she put her daughter in a cool light. It is true that Julia was practically starved with pain and it was easy for her to slip into a half-world. So she watched with no surprise when the bouquet of hummingbirds arrived, fliting around Nia's aura, dipping in. Little spinning birds with raspberry throats and chartreuse bodies, some deeply blue and green, iridescent, like peacock feathers on the loose. Some gently pink and pearl gray. Julia watched the shimmer of hummingbirds pull her daughter apart, in tiny, backlit pieces; threads of rainbows in their mouths, they flew away.

Julia had known for quite some time now that she held the option to reclaim her life, whatever it might be, as solely her own. Howi could make the same claim for himself. Their love was knit from an unwanted pregnancy, a deformed daughter, and firecracker sex. And now, all that was truly unraveled.

When Julia got back home and told Howi that Nia had been *eaten by hummingbirds* and she, Julia, was leaving, Howi felt muffled and tired. John Ox was no pussy, but he simply did not possess the energy to parse that sentence.

He let her go.

Howi didn't wait on Julia's departure. He packed up his camping kit and lit out for the aspen canyons of Carson Pass into Hope Valley, and didn't plan to come back until after she was gone. He thought about getting some sage and smudging Julia out of the house when he got home, something his mother would have done. But really he would rather have just burned that place to ash. Smudge it to the ground. He would not be staying.

Hope Valley. Named so by Mormons coming home from the Mexican-American war in 1848, on their way to the promised land of Salt Lake City. Three of their scouts had been mutilated a few days before, at a place they then named Tragedy Springs. A broken arrow left by the bodies was as good as an old world stylus dipped in blood-ink for spelling out the tale. The deaths produced a general despondence among the troops, so that when they *discovered* the valley, hope returned to them. A lucent river twining through meadows of golden green, foothills of dark pine fringe and white bark aspens. Mountains, soaring without moving at all. Nature ever restores.

Later, the gold rush miners passed through Hope Valley on the original California Trail. The Pony Express followed—only ten days from St. Joseph, Missouri, to Sacramento, California! Hope in a saddlebag, perfumed paper, words from someone the heart already knows will never be seen again.

Howi knew the old stories. But he also knew history did not start in 1848. *Pewećeli Yeweš* is the first name the Washoe tribe gave their valley. Each year the Washoe crossed, laden with smoked salmon, heading east to overwinter in the clear-cold desert. History will always belong to the printing press, but the valley remained the same as it ever was.

Howi traversed the birdsong meadows and went into the pinewoods to set up camp. His fire smoked, then eventually burned blue and green as if the flames were burning colors alive. He made coffee. He hadn't said a word all day except to tell a stripy skunk *Don't even think about it!* He refused thought.

But the mind does wander when the body stops. Howi thought back to the four-day honeymoon he and Julia had in Yosemite. So many years ago now. Ruth and Trautmann had gifted them a room at the grand Ahwahnee Hotel as a wedding present. It was late winter, and they took a sleigh ride through the valley, the newlyweds covered in rabbit fur blankets, the smell of forest and ice lingering in the pelts. Howi remembered the horses had bells and the steam coming from their ice-sparkled noses created narrow clouds they passed through.

The mountains were an impossible 3,000 feet high on both sides of the valley, rising like Commandments in slate and gray and granite. Immovable. Although that was just an illusion. There were pieces of mountains all over the valley.

The next day they climbed up to the Devil's Bathtub following a locals' path from the Ahwahnee. The snow was not deep. They reached the high point just above the tree line, looked out over the dark and emerald valley. The small waterfall that fed the Bathtub was frozen and Howi could see the granite behind the water. There were flecks of mica in the stone, shining through the ice as if summer were trapped back there, waiting.

When they headed back down, Julia, balancing her pregnancy, took a misstep. She would have died. Actually died. Howi grabbed her, pulled her back in; she was already over the abyss. It was nothing for him. Julia was wearing those white boots of hers with the fur tops like a four-year-old. Howi put her on solid ground; she was shaking.

Howi couldn't type and he didn't own a suit, but he could throw the knife and hit the mark.

Howi put away his memories, rested in his sleeping bag. He was tired of trying to figure out what it was that Julia wanted. He began to wonder what it was he wanted.

When they were first dating, marriage was not presumed by Howi. Yes, he was careful with Julia's feelings, never forced anything on her. He did love her; he still felt sure of that. But she made it clear he was not cut from a cloth that interested her. She never took him home for a holiday, never made long-distance plans. Later, when Julia told their love story to friends, she made him out to be the great pursuer, wooing her to stay. He never contradicted her; what difference did it make now? But his truth was, throughout that first year he accepted that Julia was determined to exchange honking geese for honking cars as soon as she got her degree. Her golden egg. He never actually asked her to stay. He wasn't going to try and talk someone out of their ambitions. Or into loving him.

Julia seemed to think that a piece of paper written in highfalutin calligraphy elevated her above him. But Howi knew there were a thousand things he could do that she could not. And he knew about peace—not the kind that the hippies announced in a fractured circle necklace around their necks—but the kind that comes from a still heart and thighs that can run up a mountain. He never considered himself below her, but he never fought to correct her vision of him; he had always believed deeds spoke loudly. If she was feeling superior to him because her name was printed on embossed paper while his was embroidered on his shirt, well, he was happy to put her on that pedestal. Isn't that what love is—giving people what they need? And, let's face it, if a beautiful woman is willing to have sex with you, again and again, who cares if she thinks she's God's gift, because goddamn, *she is!*

Howi never told Julia he had intended to get his general contractor's license. He was going to call his company Oxbow Brothers because he liked the sound of it, the strength of it. He would hire Native Americans, and if it wouldn't work in the whitewaters of Reno, Nevada, he would move to Oklahoma, where the Osage still had all that oil money—they would trust to work with someone who looked like him. Or to Alaska, where on the side he could learn to make totem poles that told a story on a tree.

Nia, the pregnancy of Nia, changed it all. He *would not* be the kind of man who left a woman who was pregnant with his child. He would never let Julia see his freefall heart, his stillborn future hanging on cold-storage meat hooks. Then, when Nia was born with her little arms and her awkward hands, all he cared about was his little girl. And his big girl too. He did his best by them; he knew he did. After Nia was born, what was the point of expressing his desires? He just wanted to take care of them.

But it seemed to him now, lying in the darkening, the embers turning red as if to manifest his anger, that he had lived an unchosen life in reaction to other people's needs. And despite that, he still was not good enough for Julia. Even his grief over the death of his daughter wasn't good enough. She made hers an Everest of grief. And now Nia was *eaten by hummingbirds!? Pfft.* Nia was bone and ash and rust. But also memory. Julia never listened. The forest could have taught her about the seasons—that because something is past, it isn't gone. Just mulching.

The next day, Howi continued to climb through the chattering woods. He reached an alpine pond edged with water lilies, the pads like flat faces. The flowers were just starting to form, but Howi knew the color yellow was inside. He caught two trout. Wrapped them in lily pads to keep the flesh cool.

He felt an old longing as he traversed a granite scree—thoughts of his long-gone dad and Dakota childhood passed through him. Howi thought about The Trip they took to see Crazy Horse turn mountain king. Riding on the front of his dad's Indian motorcycle, the solidness of his dad's chest backing him up, the guardrail surrounding arms encompassed him in safety. He was eleven years old.

It was a four-hour trip from the reservation to the Crazy Horse monument. His dad paid their 75 cents each and they went in. The Lakota revered Crazy Horse, and Howi loved the chief's original name—Čháŋ Óhaŋ—*Among the Trees.* Howi once went as the warrior hero for Halloween—single white feather, lightening on his face, small stone round his neck. The feather flew away in the night, but Howi still had the stone. Of course he knew the story of the Battle of the Greasy Grass. Custer's Last Stand. It was a campfire favorite. Oh, the glory of it! Hatchets smacking white bone.

Howi and his dad looked up at the monument. All that had yet been carved was the huge face. The warrior's body and his horse still remained within the mountain. "What do you think of this?" Howi's father asked him.

Howi contemplated the emerging monument. Wasn't it playing to the White Man's rules to make such a stab at immortality? Grandiosity? Didn't the mountain already have a face, its own face? But of course Howi was proud of Crazy Horse. And the carving would be bigger than Mount Rushmore! So the boy was conflicted, and he couldn't put this thoughts to words.

They went on to Sturgis—not during the annual motorcycle rally—only a moron would take a kid to that cacophony. Lunch at The Last Stand Saloon. Over the bar was a large, old print of the Anheuser-Busch painting titled *Custer's Last Fight*. The artist, Otto F. Becker, a name Howi would never know, used faded earth tones, the combatants almost more part of the vast landscape, obscured in dust and smoke, then in a great battle. As if they were already passing into legend. Perhaps because if Otto had painted in the true red-white-and-blue of life, it would have been too horrifying. Better to be in memory-shades. What struck young Howi most was the Lakota who knelt next to a white man in the foreground. Those two were not fighting each other; they seemed invincible. The Indian wore a standout-red shirt. The only red on a field of wounds. Why was he fighting on Custer's side?

"You want to know something funny?" his dad asked. "It was a woman who killed Custer—Buffalo Calf Road Woman. She's not even in the painting."

It was less than a year later that Howi's dad was murdered. No retribution, no justice. Security is that space, that little puff of air, that exists between the joining of your parents' hands. That's what Howi lost.

His dad. Nia. Julia. He had learned young the comfort of

memory—that no one is really gone—but today, the accumulated loss just made him mad.

Howi got out his hatchet to splinter wood for a fire. There were no feathers or tied-on rawhide fringe decorating the tool—he had bought it at Ace Hardware. But suddenly Howi threw the hatchet, just the way his father had taught him, into the trunk of a fallen tree. The blade sank into the soft bark, a fluff of decomposed wood sent airborne.

The skin of the trout charred, and the flesh was like eating the peat of the alpine pond. Howi made himself a sludgy coffee and then hiked on. Eventually his anger gave way to the meditative state of the long-distance walker. When his legs went buttery, he at last set up camp.

Nature would always give Howi something to hold on to, his bedroll a warm frontier.

Howi was forty-four years old. He saw that some of the older women in the Genoa Ladies Auxiliary remained startled every time they saw *that Native* walking into the feed store or the bank, but there were other women who appreciated the way he wore his cowboy boots. No, Howi wasn't going to let his past, or allow Julia, to push him out of *his* life. He decided to spend a few weeks in the mountains; he had his rifle and his fishing gear. He was going to listen to the sounds brought in on the Zephyr wind, the warble and the hoot, the coyote concerts. Walk all the way to Chickadee Ridge, where the little birds chatter. That was all he was in the mood to hear right now. It was enough.

Julia didn't get far when she left Howi. She headed toward Reno and made it only to the Carson Valley Inn before all her emotions drained the strength out of her and she couldn't hold her arms up to drive the car. She rented a room, in fact the same room Wynona and Hale had *destroyed* after Nia's funeral, because Fate does love a funny. The sheets were white, the blanket cream. No colors to demand response. She fell immediately asleep. She slept for eighteen hours.

When Julia was a child, she ate her blanket. Thread by pink, blue, yellow thread until there was just a small plaid square left, which her mother saved, as you would save a lock of hair for remembrance.

If we could save our days, could they be like thread? Spools of silky-fine summer days. Childhood days of apron strings. Rough days of lumpy hemp macramé, chunky with driftwood and shockingly bright feathers. Days of anger, reeling spirals of red. Lanky nights of sex running in inky blue skeins. Workdays of wool. Bobbins, coils, whorls of floss, loomed together; if each day were a thread.

When she woke up, an odd memory came to mind. She pictured their old house out at Elroy, always filled with dusty sun. In the yard, the clothesline where she hung the laundry out to dry. Pink-flowered panties with a ruffle-bottom and a matching tiny dress hanging by wooden pins. The pinks next to battered blue jeans stiffening. A work shirt with the name *John* next to a blouse with seed buttons. Six pairs of socks in three different sizes. The littlest ones, heartbreakers. Look at the whole, you can assemble the family.

Julia was forty-three years old—what were the tangible products of her life? What had she spent her time accomplishing? Howi was behind her, Nia was with the hummingbirds. She decided she needed a job. If she spent any more time thinking, her head would explode.

But first, she might just stay another day in the white sheets with the two-inch bottles of booze in the mini fridge and that basket of M&M's and half-size tubes of Pringles. Sour cream and onion.

*   *   *

A few weeks after the First Annual Lilac Bash, while Howi was hiking and Julia was sleeping, Jimmy and Wynona took a sunrise drive out to Grover Hot Springs, south of Genoa. Grover's wasn't chichi like Wally's Hot Springs, no gangster past, no Harrah's Ranch beef steakhouse restaurant. Just a murky pool surrounded by a high wood fence and cheap entrance fees. They had not gone to sleep at all that night, so they were the first swimmers to arrive. The mineral deposits on the bottom of the pool refracted the morning sunshine, the water a clear green and honey-golden, like some lucky people's eyes. The temperature of the springs was 104 degrees, fever hot. But the morning was cold and there were Chanticleer pear trees in a nearby grove, the Zephyr lofting white petals their way.

In they went. Jimmy pulled a thermos of coffee-flavored vodka laced with steamy coffee from his backpack. Poured two plastic mugs full. Life was good.

Except heat from a hot springs will naturally expand blood vessels, swell body temperature. As does alcohol. If something can be used as fuel or an industrial solvent, you got to know, it comes with some inherent problems. Put high heat and alcohol together and you can shoot all the way for a stroke or a heart attack.

Jimmy pulled himself from the pool, feeling light-headed. Mica stuck all over his body in little gold flecks. "I look like a shot of Goldschlager!" he said, pleased with himself, doing a little spin. And then he fainted, the concrete breaking his nose and knocking out his two front teeth.

Wynona missed the whole thing, was sinking under, was she sinking under? It felt so good and warm. Like peeing the bed half on purpose when she was little.

The South Lake Tahoe High School Bike Club—a Schwinn rainbow—arrived at Grover's having just navigated the not untreacherous Kingsbury Grade. The payoff for risking their lives on the razor's edge of a road was the hot springs. It was there they found the young man with a damn bloody face and the young woman just about to slip into the green-gold of forever.

When Wynona woke up, everything was white and silver. Oh—it was a hospital room. There was a privacy curtain hung from silver rings, and it made her feel claustrophobic. The covers were too tight and a machine was beeping. There was a needle, and not the good kind, in her arm. She wasn't high at all. In fact, her body was shaking. *Fucking saline*, she thought, looking at the clear plastic bag.

"Jimmy, are you over there?" she asked the room beyond the curtain.

"Yep," he said.

"Are you okay?"

"Yep. All I want for Christmas is my two front teeth." It came out a lisp. He got out of his bed, limped over, and got into hers. Apparently he didn't need any more saline.

Wynona whistled, looking at his swollen lips, his black eyes. The ragged edges of his front teeth that would need to be removed. He looked so skinny in the faded-print hospital gown. "Fuck. What'd we do?"

Jimmy had already talked to the doctor. He told Wynona the science of the thing. "Plus she knows we're drunks." Wynona winced to hear that label.

"I like drugs too," she said to counter.

"Look, she's going to keep us here three days for withdrawal and some state-sponsored lectures." He paused. Next was the frightening part. Wynona could feel his fear and she wondered what could be worse than drying out in a hospital. "She told me she's checking us both for AIDS."

AIDS. So bad it had to be in caps. Of course they had

heard of it, but that was a New York, a barrio, a bath house plague. Things like that don't happen in Nevada, where the air was sterilized by sagebrush and pine. It was too much to face. But in that moment, really for the first time, they both fully faced the concept of death delivered in an orgasm. Absurd! Unfair.

Jimmy said, "If I die, don't think of me as dead. Think of me as shopping in San Francisco."

Wynonna laughed. "You're not going to die of AIDS. You're going to meet a U.S. senator at the Gay Rodeo and he's going to move you to a bungalow in Florida. You're going to die a silver fox, reaching up for oranges in your own backyard tree. Picking oranges in the hot, hot sun. That's how you're going to die."

Jimmy liked that image. *You're words to God's ears.*

Dr. Malone pushed back the curtain; it made that screeching sound, a predator bird with its talons extended. Their hearts leapt. Dr. Malone took in the sight of the two of them together in the bed, made some assumptions. "Is it okay with the two of you to discuss your medical issues together?"

Medical issues. They nodded their heads, dread a dark syrup in their veins.

"Okay! Good news, good news! Neither of you has AIDS," Dr. Malone quickly said. "But I want you to read these, and read 'em good." She handed them pamphlets with two men on the cover, whom Jimmy could tell, were obviously not gay. "It's important."

They took the brochures, relief sun-shining through their bodies.

Then Dr. Malone looked at Wynona. The doctor was pretty, Wynona thought, with a spectacular French chignon. "Honey, did you know you are pregnant?"

"Holy Christ!" Jimmy all but shouted, sitting up straight-er. "Ho-ly *Christ!*"

"It's not immaculate," snapped Wynona.

"Wynona, you have to stop drinking right now if you want to keep your baby. And no more hot tubs." Dr. Malone handed Wynona a plethora of additional pamphlets, all with white babies on the bright covers. "Well, I'll leave you two to talk things through."

Julia rented an apartment of dubious reputation on Saint Lawrence Avenue in Reno. Right around the corner from a dry cleaners. It was that kind of street. But there were old-growth trees lining the neighborhood, and her apartment had a tiny balcony with a needlepoint ivy fringe. What else does anyone need? She found her corner store, owned by a Mexican family, paper-thin tortillas hot and blistered, tacos instead of footlongs, and a curated salsa selection. Basket of dinosaur-skinned avocados sitting by the register. Home-rolled cigarettes for sale by the single. She ended up buying most of her food there.

The apartment was the first place Julia had ever lived alone. But she had been living alone, really, since Nia died. She just didn't have to pretend anymore.

Julia went to work at the St. Thomas Aquinas parochial school, attached to the downtown cathedral, close to the Truckee River. All the teachers were nuns, and it was made clear to her that she was not being hired to *teach*. She was a roving art assistant, more of a sous-chef, setting out the paints, rolling out white butcher paper. She was never asked her opinion for a project. Favorite themes were Noah's Ark and Saint of the Day. But it was a lovely atmosphere in the old brick building, the children in their tartan uniforms, the way the whole place smelled of moss. She started to do private lessons again in her home, for kids who wanted to paint beyond the halo. She was moving forward.

Howi was too. The chickadees drove him nuts, little buggers. They were convinced he was holding out on the birdseed and they kept talking to him about it. Losing his solitude, he walked back home. Trautmann told Howi that Julia had rented a place in Reno, and it was fine with him if Howi moved back onto the ranch. Howi had built the house, for God's sake! Trautmann was mad at his daughter. Ruth disagreed with her husband's offer, because maybe it would keep Julia from coming to visit. "Well, we'll go visit her, then. Just because she left, it's no reason to kick a man out of his home!" Trautmann said. Ruth didn't rise to the bait; he was right, they could go to Julia, and besides, Howi had taken over running their ranch. As far as Ruth was concerned—at least in this moment of parental turmoil—all Trautmann did anymore was ride his spotted horse about like a dandy in a 10-gallon hat. *Bowlegged idiot!* But Ruth would let Julia know.

People got to get along.

When Jimmy and Wynona were released from Washoe Med, they went home and Wynona started on a fresh pot of eggplant stew while Jimmy poured their table booze down the drain. The splashy sound was painful to hear. He licked his fingers. "I'm not flushing the pot," he said, placing the bottle back on the table to turn vase or memento.

Wynona was in a shaky state. She held an eggplant in her hand. Far-fetched, she knew it, but the weight and shape was babyish. The thin, deep purple, flawless skin, and the thick cream-and-brown-spotted, bruise-able interior. The texture was almost human. She ran the blade through, chopped the long slices into squares. She felt as if she were cutting up a fetus. She barely made the toilet, nothing to heave, just dry chokes.

She'd been thinking hard about abortion. It was probably the better way to go. Hale was supposed to come to town next week. She turned the eggplant back into the nightshade vegetable it was and set her mind to wait on Hale. He would help her decide. Thanks to *Roe v. Wade*, she had time. She was only about four weeks gone.

When Wynona told him she was pregnant, Hale could have said a hundred things, all the words available for him to string together. He chose some. "Are you sure it's mine?" he said as seriously as every man who has ever played that opening gambit. But here's the thing. It's not the words, is it? It's the way the hand moves, the crinkle at the eye, the arms reaching. Or folding.

Hale's arms folded around his clenched body. He reached for nothing but himself.

It wasn't that Wynona expected him to be happy or excited. *She* certainly was not. But Wynona might have hoped for a *we're in this together* attitude. Some sympathy. Some touch. But Hale held himself aloof. *Are you sure it's mine?* Pfft. She was sure.

"No. It's not yours." *Fucker.*

Hale exhaled. As if it were the first breath of his life. He sat beside her on the nubby couch, now ready to help. Not as the *father*, but as the friend. He put his hand on her leg; in fact, he was starting to feel a little aroused, thinking of her body lushed up.

"So, anyway," Wynona said, shifting her thigh away from his. "I wanted to let you know I will no longer be requiring your services." She stood up. Held open the door. Hale bewilderedly walked toward her, suddenly wanting so badly to put his mouth on her breasts, it was overpowering how much he wanted to be inside her simply because she was pregnant. He wasn't self-aware enough (who is?) to know that the fact that he was the eldest of five siblings, his mother almost always pregnant or breastfeeding when he was young, most likely accounted for his newly acknowledged fetish. He squeezed Wynona's breast, felt his body slip-slide into a little rush of ecstasy. It was unbearable how much he wanted her; she must want it too. He was in a glaze of desire. She resisted slapping him, simply moved away and pushed him, hard, out the door she locked behind him. *Fuckin' nimrod Hale.*

Julia had grown up going to Sunday service at the Coventry Cross Episcopal in Genoa with its white steeple and blue trim. So she was quickly comfortable at St. Thomas Aquinas. It was bigger by far, a cathedral, but it held the same quiet. She liked the way a space smells when it's almost a hundred years old and the windows had never been opened. The air held on to the candle wax and the Lemon Pledge. The sanctuary mural was Edith and Isabel Piczek's *Adoration of the Lamb of God*, painted by sisters who had escaped Stalin's Hungary. It pleased Julia that the art was done by women, in a religion that sidelined her sex.

Julia had once been to a Baptist church during her college days, thinking she might fit in better. Perhaps thinking it rebellious. Now she came to feel that the Baptists were quiet in their architecture and loud of voice, while the Catholics let their highly accessorized, voluminous, bedazzled, art gallery churches speak for them. The Baptists were just too noisy for Julia. All their hootin' 'n' hollerin'. Julia thought Jesus would prefer the tinkling of the altar bell, that little pull of His attention over the demanding outbursts of the Baptists. The service suited her, and sometimes she attended.

The one thing at St. Thomas Aquinas that Julia did not

like was the votive stand. She never lit a candle for Nia, avoided the flickering wicks within the blue glass. Think of the sound a match makes when it strikes the powdered glass and the red phosphorus. That scratchy sound and the wee whoosh of air. Then the smell of the blown-out match, the momentary, sulphury ghost. All the candles gathered together looked like little burning souls to Julia, not a bit like an intention for a prayer.

Flo took Wynona to her first AA meeting in an auxiliary room at St. Thomas Aquinas Cathedral. The room was mostly belowground, concrete and cool on the hot summer day. Fringe of grass greening the windows. The metal of the folding chairs felt blessedly chilled, if only for a moment. Wynona said not a word, not even *Hi, I'm Wynona and I'm an alcoholic.* Because what would follow? *I'm pregnant, the father is a nimrod, and does anyone know where I can get a cheap abortion, because* (and this was the part that she absolutely could not say out loud) *I've probably already pickled my baby.* No. She kept her mouth shut. The cookies, oatmeal raison, were good. Homemade and she ate four.

As she and Flo were walking across the parking lot, back to Flo's car, Wynona heard someone call her name. She looked up, startled.

Julia wouldn't have seen Wynona, because of course we do not look at every passing person, and further, do not expect to see people out of context. Why would Wynona be at a church? But Flo had recently colored her own hair Ruby Fusion; hard *not to* look at that flamboyant bird. And then Julia's eyes had flowed to the redhead's companion . . .

"Wynona!" Julia called again.

Wynona looked for the voice, recognized Nia's mom. Mrs. Ox! Mrs. Ox, who was like her second mom, but Wynona hadn't even called her since Nia died. Nia died! It all just crashed over Wynona. She ran to Julia and collapsed crying in her arms. Julia cried, too, and Flo joined in just for support. Julia took Wynona home, and Wynona stayed for quite some time.

Good thing Julia got the place with the second bedroom.

Wynona lay in bed, hands over her still-flat belly. She pictured matching mother-daughter dresses. Mother-son shirts. Hawaiian print. Hope is a lovely thing, a trumpet flower, night-blooming jasmine. And fear is shit. So much stronger. Wynona recalled the summer she had a high fever, 105 and rising, her father resting ice cubes on her eyelids, one step away from pennies on the dead. She pictured the news story about the mother and her two kids—Cuban refugees taking the E-ticket ride from Havana to Miami—washed up on the beautiful beach, wreaths of seaweed in the black-and-white photo. The strength of that woman to get in that boat. Oh, the risk of parenthood! And Wynona had read the pamphlets Dr. Malone gave her, learned all about fetal alcohol syndrome. The effects were irreversible.

But still. *Bad little kittens lost their mittens.* Bassinettes and onesies, bottles and binkies. And Jimmy had pointed out that she *drank like an Indian, two drinks in and falling down.* It was true. Her tolerance levels, possibly her genetics, might have played to her service.

She had gone to the consultation at the West End Women's Clinic. They had explained to her how they would start the procedure with a drug to relax her and then Electrolux her uterus. Those weren't their exact words. In her mind, she started singing *One pill makes you larger, and one pill makes you small* while the nurse showed her diagrams. And then the image of the chopped-up eggplant came to her, and she wasn't sure she could go through with it at all.

A baby! Someone to soften the blow of Nia. She was so lonely. Ridiculous, she knew it, to expect a little howler to replace her best friend, but there it was. Wynona's thoughts blew through the room on the swirl of the fan. She wanted a doughnut. She fell asleep.

The pain came, that nocturnal beast. It jumped up on her belly and pussyfooted around, then—little claws everywhere. Wynona woke up confused and thought that she had the fever again, instantly returning to a straitjacket of panic. Her bedroom was limned pale with moonlight, a film noir but for the spreading red on her sheets. She started to call out for Julia, and then stopped herself. She'd read all the pamphlets. One had talked about if a body spontaneously aborts, it most likely means that the fetus wasn't viable. Nature takes care of itself. She had reason to believe the baby might be damaged; she wouldn't interfere. And the pain was decreasing, just a backwash of cramps, not much blood really. She had read about that too—spotting in the early months. She fell back asleep. What will be will be. This was the answer she was looking for. Something to tip the scales.

In the morning, Julia was making a smoothie of oranges, flaxseed, and ginger. There was toast and slices of avocado. Of course, Wynona had asked Julia her opinion on the pregnancy, and Julia had discussed the options, but said repeatedly the decision was Wynona's alone. Some stones we pick up stay in our pocket forever. But it had caused Julia some contemplation. Would she have aborted Nia if she had had that option? Not even told Howi, just continued on with her big-city plans? She thought she probably would have. Well, it was way too late in life to bother with that scenario now.

"Mrs. O," Wynona said, coming into the room, starting to

set the table. Wynona couldn't bring herself to call her Julia, but Julia didn't want to hear the name *Ox* all day long, so O was the compromise. Julia O! "I'm so fucked up since Nia." Died. She started to cry.

"Me too," said Julia, hugging her.

Wynona found her voice, said into Julia's *Gee Your Hair Smells Terrific* head, "Let's go shopping for some looser clothes. I can't fit into anything anymore."

Julia pulled back, looked into Wynona's eyes, her young face still uncreased. Her tentative smile. Julia nodded, matched the smile. The decision was made.

Late one afternoon, Wynona at the Pink Puff, Julia opened the doors to her tiny balcony. She refilled her two hummingbird feeders with sugar water. She kept a dogeared bird book on the coffee table; there were over three hundred species of hummingbirds. Mostly it was Annas who came to her feeders with their raspberry-ringed necks. But today a single black-chinned male hovered above the dissolving sugar. The bird had gray-black feathers beneath a dark head with a ring of plum below his chin—the exact shade of Nia's prom dress. It didn't matter to Julia that the bird was male. She knew Nia when she saw her.

Julia sat out on her balcony. The needlepoint ivy offered a softhearted fringe for her view, but Julia's focus was interior. Everything she and Howi had done to protect their damaged child was worthless. Up in smoke. Her daughter was a book burned, a story good and lost. Well. That was a pain Julia worked to push as far away from her mind as possible. But never was it out of her body.

Once again she hoped her daughter had died from the impact of the somersaulting car and not the flames. *Somersaulting*. Always Julia tried to soft-sell Nia's death. *Somersault* is too fine a word, evoking grassy-kneed children tossing themselves down a dandelion hill. No. Nia's car was her coffin. Sometimes Julia just had to look the thing in the face.

Hummingbirds, hummingbirds.

Julia strove to exchange fire for feathers. Let Nia fly.

Grief is a gray ribbon on a black box. Inside—a mixed assortment of bitter bonbons. Oh, sure, always the five favs: denial, anger, bargaining, depression, and acceptance. But the hardest one for Julia to swallow was remorse. There was never a moment of no self-rebuke. She could not forgive herself for not being with her daughter when she died.

Surely Julia had spent herself trying to winnow loss into something that would puff and scatter. She went back into the house, wished she hadn't got rid of all the alcohol for Wynona's sake. She slowly felt her rage and sorrow distill into melancholy. She wondered what Wynona's child would work on her. Salve or savage.

Howi moved back into the house he'd built out of grief. The house was an A-frame, something he had privately chosen because it recalled a teepee. All the weather came right up to the glass wall and tried every trick up its sleeve to get inside. Howi could keep an eye on the ranch from his easy chair.

Julia had taken very little. But Howi wanted less, or just fewer touchstones. He loaded a haul to take to Goodwill. Ruth came out and stopped him, reclaiming the wedding china, some of the art, things she thought he, or Julia, would later regret losing. She stored them in the barn—what's the harm in waiting a little while longer? There was that watercolor of the bunny ears coming out of the September field grass.

Howi splurged and covered up a large part of his wide-planked floor with a Navajo-style rug he found in an antique shop in Markleeville. He ended up smudging the house after all, with sagebrush he just went outside and picked. The smoke was peppery and it made him cough. He felt a little stupid.

Howi understood that Julia was trying to leave her hopelessness over Nia as much as she was leaving him. He wasn't sure Julia realized that. Of course there was no reparation for the loss of Nia, but it seemed to Howi that time had worked a kind of slow miracle on him. The surprise came when he realized he was remembering Nia without a straight shot of burning grief, because somehow he was managing to detach the good memories from the bitch-slap of knowing Nia's ending.

That is the trick to tricking grief—Howi suddenly thought—make each memory a View-Master soft-edged still. Animate the grandeur of the oak barrel poised on the brink of Niagara Falls without ever thinking about what happens next. Hold time still. It's a burial site after all.

Howi wondered how long it would take to feel that way about Julia, to think of her without a sour poke. Sitting in his house set up to suit himself, he wanted to mark this day for the potential that exists in a made-up new beginning, like New Year's Eve, as if the past were gone. Howi knew the past is never past, but he was determined toward happiness.

The Sierra mountains disallow California from Northern Nevada, although a river of silver did flow from Virginia City to San Francisco. Lowly pinyon pines, and tumbleweeds on the blow. Far horizons always miles from home. Coyotes, golden bears asleep in winter, and jackalopes mounted over the bar. Valleys in the shadow of the mountains where the snow burrowed in 'til June, then ran so pure, it was near invisible but for its voice.

The Midwesterner, corn tassels over his head, the Texan with his Chisholm Trail of cattle—they could not guess at Nevada's number of sheep and cattle ranches, the acres of hay, alfalfa, onions, and potatoes. Hearts of Gold cantaloupes. Garlic, barley, and mint.

Wonder saw it all from the cockpit of his Piper Pawnee Brave, red stripe down the white body of the plane, as he dusted the crops. He loved the way the earth looked from the plane, the quilted sections of agriculture and the red-willow-lined rivers. It cleared his head of any earthbound thought.

Wonder had worked hard since high school. Miss Margaret, the librarian who changed his life, helped him apply for Pell and Native American Grants. She edited his application letter, but Wonder got the ACT score of 27 all on his own. UC Davis on a full ride of scholarships and grants. He took extra classes every semester, and summer school. Flying lessons for free from a generous soul. He graduated in three heavy years and now he was back in Nevada. Crop dusting and musing his future.

He was renting the attic of a 1930s farmhouse on Old Virginia Road on the southern outskirts of Reno. Wonder knew the farmhouse was haunted. On the night the ghost came to Wonder's room and sat on his chest, it felt like a sack of oranges. Wonder reached for his bedside gun and shot a hole in the roof of the house to startle the ghost, and after that, Wonder would watch for the North Star, or any twinkler to line up in the bullet hole in the ceiling so he could sleep in stardust.

The wonder of it all!

In September, the pines stay exactly the same. But the aspen trees that crowd the banks of any whisper of water turn to gold, and the Zephyr and Galena winds worry the leaves free and throw them up in the air like pieces of eight. The long-legged heron looks at the sky and thinks of movement. And Genoa throws a Candy Dance.

The first Candy Dance was held in 1919, brainchild of

Lillian Virgin Finnegan to raise money for a streetlamp in Genoa; the dance goes on still. Every September, the tents rise, a miniature mountain range lining Jack's Valley Road. Under the snowy canvas, so much confection, the air smells spun from sugar.

Julia picked up Ruth, as was their tradition, and Wynona, belly popped, came along, just as she used to do when she and Nia were kids. In the car, the three women talked about how it would feel to be at the Candy Dance without Nia. "The best thing to do is eat a lot of candy," Wynona concluded. She intended to eat it all and headed right to first stall and bought some rock candy, because it was pink and on a stick, and caught the sun. Such a pretty thing to eat. It was one of Nia's favorites, too.

The crowds were thick as molasses. Julia saw Howi before he saw her. He was talking to Molly Milton; Molly had been ahead of Julia at school, maybe four years older. Molly stood behind a table of red candy apples, that Cadillac convertible of sweets, hard and glossy. Molly had her dark hair in a long braid down her back, veins of early silver, and an easy way she moved in her stonewashed overalls. Probably stoned them herself. Julia couldn't see her feet, but she suspected Birkenstock's. Julia watched as Howi handed Molly some sort of sandwich or boxed lunch. Molly took it as if she was expecting the delivery. They leaned toward each other, and in that small, too familiar gesture, Julie knew they were sleeping together. *Molly!* Julia felt a rogue wave of jealously.

Howi then noticed Julia, or felt her gaze. He stopped his body's movement toward Molly and straightened. *Caugh!* A riptide of guilt, but what was he caught doing? Julia had left him. He nodded at her. Julia nodded back, dropped contact.

Howi turned back to Molly, her warm eyes, her skin lightly freckled like each dot was a little joke. From the beginning,

Howi wanted to touch her, as much for her ability to make peach cobbler as anything else. He wanted to touch the autumn sun on her hair, the sun, more so than her hair. Molly was a happy woman, and that was irresistible to Howi.

Julia, intent on Howi, had not noticed the young man next to him, nor had the young man noticed her. Wonder was too busy taking in Wynona—*was she pregnant?!* He told Howi he would see him later and made his way through the crowd, calling "Wynona!"

Wynona had just taken a big bite of a gooey brownie. "Wonder! Hi. What are you doing here?" It was a stupid question; they all used to come as kids. She felt embarrassed both by her pregnancy and her brownie-face. *God, what a dork I am.*

"Let's go find a place to sit." He let her off the hook. They made for the benches placed under a grove of maple trees, leaves turned last-call red. Of course, they had seen each other at Nia's funeral, but Wynona had been rolling in grief and then rolling in bed with Hale. She hadn't much paid attention to Wonder. Story of his life. She took in his black hair grown to his shoulders and his German grandmother's blue eyes. Wonder took in her lack of a wedding ring. She wasn't so pregnant that it was beyond possible that she had just gained weight, and Wonder knew it was bad manners to ask. He waited.

"Yeah, I'm pregnant," Wynona said. She smiled, and Wonder could see that she was happy about it and that's all he really needed to know. Wonder trusted emotions over words.

"Where you been?" Wynona asked, thinking his eyes were the color of a huskie, that darker ring of navy circling the iced blue.

"I got my pilot's license and I've been doing some crop dusting. I just finished a job for Mr. Ox." He held back telling about his degree; he didn't really know why. Just didn't want to be show-offie. He wasn't using it for anything yet anyway.

"That's funny, because I'm living with Mrs. O in Reno."

Mrs. O? Nia's mom, sure. So she wasn't living with the baby's dad.

Well, it always was a small, small world.

Wynona wasn't interested in men—even one with huskie eyes—*what a bunch of troublemakers*. You'd be surprised how much money she made at the Puff, especially when sober. Hair just keeps on growing. She didn't have to live with Julia from a financial standpoint, but they both liked it. It was comfortable and the chores seemed cut in half rather than multiplied. They were both neat, which was saying something for Wynona because her room growing up was a pink tornado. She had already reserved daycare at St. Thomas Aquinas. Julia would drive the baby there and home, and they both knew she would peek in on her lunch break. The Blue Lamp flickered out for Wynona and she didn't even miss it. Sometimes she and Julia would go for dinner at Simon's, where it was mostly old people playing dominos in the bar, and liver and onions was on the menu. Wynona was waiting on the baby and she refused to be anything but fine. *Hand me those bonbons!*

But worry is a creeper. What kind of mother would she be? "I don't even know how to cook!" she told Julia on an anxious night.

"Oh, I don't know," said Julia. "You made that three-shrimps-and-a-mango thing last week."

"I don't want to do, like, PTA, or go on field trips. Kids on a bus smell like cheeseballs. How do you even play with a kid!?"

"You can throw a ball from your bed and make your kid

chase it while you lie there and read your soft-porn novels one paragraph at a time."

"They aren't that soft."

"Look, it's not so hard. You're looking too far ahead. Just don't let the boy ride his bike off the roof of the house on to the trampoline and you'll be okay."

"I'm not having a boy!"

Wynona went to JC Penney because Julia told her she was looking like a Pop-Tart in her too-tight tops. Emphasis on *tart*. Maternity was relegated to the back corner. *Fucking smocks*—Wynona was losing her mind just thinking about florals with strategic folds. *Ugh.* Of course the store floor plan first led her through Women's, past round racks of pants with waists, tops with buttons. It was cruel really. Partway through she saw a woman about her age looking into a full-length mirror, holding a tight black dress up to her body, changing angles, neck on a slant. Posing. Imagining where that little knit thing might take her. That alone wouldn't have stopped Wynona. It was the boy seated in the woman's cart, maybe two or two-and-a-half, soft giraffe in his dimpled fist. The boy was looking at his mother like there were hearts coming out of his eyes—he was so in love with her. But the mother might as well have been climbing onto a stool at the Blue Lamp, nylon dress sliding over shiny red vinyl. Wynona knew that lure, the sound of the vinyl trilling like it was calling her name. *Wynona, come sit on my face!*

She felt a kind of dread. On some level Wynona understood that she was a voyeur of the mother and son. It was just a moment. The woman was probably a Hallmark card of a mother. But Wynona saw herself in the mirror's reflection. Understood that she would still rather be the girl in the black dress than the woman with a child. So what kind of mother could she be? Would her child look at her with exploding hearts and would Wynona remain Narcissus before the mirror? She felt defeated and shallow. And hungry. She turned around and headed to the food court.

Sometimes Wynona, and even Wonder would accompany Julia to Sunday mass at St. Thomas Aquinas. In fact, the closer her due date got, the more often Wynona went. One dreary Sunday, Jimmy joined. He ignored the sermon but appreciated the building, especially the stained glass. It reminded him of the shelf of bright liqueurs behind the bar at the Blue Lamp. He liked the smell of the smoke pouring from the priest's thurible, a mix of musk and wine cellar. The cathedral did make his feel something, but he was unwilling to admit it. After all, he wasn't really welcome there, was he? When Julia asked him what he thought afterwards, he fell back into his usual self: "I liked the priest's dress, but his purse was on fire."

Wonder came over to the Saint. Lawrence Avenue apartment sporadically. He usually brought tacos from the corner store and every time some little baby thing to add to the layette, although that word was beyond him. The three of them had an ongoing Scrabble game where Wynona insisted the word *Nia* was legal tender. As the months collected, maybe Wonder was stopping by a little more frequently. Keeping at least a half tank of gas. So it wasn't a complete surprise that he was there when Wynona's water broke and the baby started looking for the illuminated THIS WAY exit signs. Wynona had been in the early stages of labor all day.

"This is it!" Wynona said as her first true contraction waved through her. She suddenly imaged a boxing match, the ring girl in her hot pants carrying the square sign with the #1 printed bold. *Round one, here we go.* Wynona got ready for the fight. Baby was already throwing punches.

It was the night of December 31. All the bunnies were burrowed, the mice in the church. The hoot owls tucked inside their own downy brown wings. Too far from spring to believe in it. Wonder drove down icy streets that glittered in circles beneath frosted streetlamps. He had to go so slow. The car heater was cold and Wynona's increasing breath came out in clouds. The baby was three weeks early, the baby was pounding on the door.

Julia went in the delivery room with Wynona, who wouldn't let go of her hand. Julia was her Lamaze coach, but Julia didn't think much of Fernand Lamaze, that French sadist who told women to just *breathe! Pfft, as if he'd ever had a baby*. Julia said Wonder should go home, it would be a long night, but Wonder wandered around. He looked in at the babies through the glass wall, little acorns how mighty they would grow. He settled in the waiting room. He was the only one there and the nurses assumed he was the father or the brother, brought him updates, showed him the coffee station.

Wonder thought to call Jimmy, caught him at home because it was still early evening. A nurse was passing by the waiting room when Jimmy flew in, rose velvet pants, tight black lamé shirt that spangled—dressed for New Year's Eve. He grabbed her arm. "I'm the fairy godmother!" he announced to the delighted nurse, "How's our Cinderella?"

"You look like a sparkle pony," said Wonder.

"Thank you." Jimmy took a slight bow.

Wynona crowned at midnight and down the hall the night nurses blew their coiled paper noisemakers of harlequin print. The tinny sound reached Wynona's ears, and in her pain she thought it was a celebration for her. When she gave the final push, she saw confetti falling, but it was only phosphene, the infinite lights behind our closed eyes.

When the baby was wrapped in the pink cloud of a blanket Ruth had knit from angora, (there was a blue one in Wynona's labor bag too), and settled into the crook of Wynona's thin arm, Julia went and got Wonder. Jimmy had stayed too. He had given up New Year's Eve for Wynona.

"Ouch, girl, you look a mess," said Jimmy. "No wonder that baby's got no father." Wynona knew he was saying she was beautiful and the baby was perfect. Wonder was gobsmacked just looking at the five little fingers poking over the pink. The three friends gathered around Wynona and her child, and Wynona was sure that Ionia had all the family she would need. Her daughter would be a one-child united nations, keeping them all together.

"I told you I would have a girl," Wynona said, transfixed.

The *Reno Gazette Journal* announced Ionia Julia Fox, five pounds, three ounces, as the first baby born in Northern Nevada in 1986. The grainy photo showed an infant with tufty dark hair sticking up in all directions and eyes as big as a lemur's, wide open. Wynona got a case of Pampers.

Of course there was no reparation for the loss of Nia; Julia knew that. But it seemed to her that Ionia worked a kind of miracle for her. Certainly Julia often thought of Nia, even though every memory was risking open-heart surgery—just so painful. But somehow in the circus that was Ionia, memories of Nia emerged in a different way. When she held Ionia, she was holding baby Nia too. When Ionia took her faltering steps, it triggered Julia's memory of Nia's. But it didn't hurt, or it didn't hurt as much.

One night Julia zipped Ionia into her fuzzy pink footie jams and carried her to bed, patting her back as they headed toward the bedroom. In that moment she remembered Nia in just such jammies—hers were yellow—Nia maybe a year old. As Julia patted her daughter's back, Nia mimicked her mother, patting Julia with her chubby hand. Julia had forgotten that memory! Ionia returned a piece of Nia to Julia. This type of quiet excavation happened almost every day.

Ionia was her solace.

A year later, on the night that Julia fell to the floor trying to get out of bed for help, there was a pile of *Life* magazines, checked out from the library for old-timey reading spread across her crazy quilt. One of them from 1962 fell with her, open to a story on the thalidomide babies, 5,000 deformed. *Nia! How could I have never known?* She remembered the pills Dr. Pacini gave her for morning sickness. He must have learned about the birth defects, should have confessed his mistake to her and to Howi. Her heart constricted, emptied out remembering Howi having the vasectomy, snipping off any chance of future children. *Oh, Howi!* They believed it was their fault; even after Dr. Pacini must have known, he let them believe it was their fault. *Nia!*

The misery in her heart was visceral, a clenched fist. If Nia had been born with regular arms, she could have climbed out of the Pinto. *She could have lived!* Julia tried to get out of bed. Her body didn't fully belong to her. She rolled and her head hit the nightstand as she fell. As the jolt rolled through her, she pictured Nia's head hitting the steering wheel, and in that dislocated moment, Julia thought she was in the car with Nia. Where she had sometimes longed to be.

Julia's body lay on the ground. Her final, merciful thought was not of the awful wreck. It was of her toddler daughter in yellow footie jams, Julia carrying her, the weight of the infant so sweetly heavy in her arms. Then the footie jams expanded into a medallion light and Julia stepped through the gold of this world and into the rainbow-auraed arms of her child, Nia.

*   *   *

Trautman knocked on the door of the A-frame. When Julia and Howi lived there together, he used to give a quick rap and then enter; now he waited for the door the open. Howi never asked that of him, but sometimes things just feel like they needed to change. Trautman told Howi about Julia as quickly as he could; Ruth was already waiting in the car, praying on her old rosary of garnets and gold. Howi pulled on his boots while walking, which despite the situation, Trautman, an old man now, couldn't help but admire. Molly leaned against the kitchen entry, cup of coffee steaming, robe pulled close. Howi didn't even say goodbye. She wouldn't hold it against him.

There was an enamel vase filled with dried prairie smoke—those flowers that looked as if they were made out of circles of loose yarn—and sprigs of lavender faded winter gray. Julia knew the vase. She realized she was in a hospital bed, turned her head. Howi was there. She started to cry. Howi did too.

"Did you see the article?" she asked, taking his presence for granted, somehow assuming Wynona would have shown him the magazine.

"I did," Howi said. When he read the thalidomide article, his heart took a nose dive from the high dive, straight into an empty pool. Imagine the sound. And the fury. Lucky for Dr. Pacini, the doctor was already bones. Ruth had taken control, shooed everyone home. *You stay, Howi.* When Julia woke up, it would be Howi that she needed, and they should be alone. Nia was their daughter.

"We could have had more children," Julia said, and they both pictured the Elroy house a little more crowded.

"It would have been fun."

"Oh, Howi, I blamed so much on you."

It was true, but it was no longer important. The past cannot be changed. "We were just young, that's our fault." He took her hand. "Don't you want to know what happened to you?"

"I died. And Nia, *baby Nia,* gave me a pat on the back and pushed me back out."

"Yep. And you had a mild heart attack probably brought on by the shock of the magazine article."

"And all the doughnuts."

"Yes, the doughnuts."

Julia and Howi played *remember when* until they softened the shock into just another part of the story. Her death, yes, but they loved Nia too much to turn her life into a tragedy. *Better to have loved and lost.* Howi kissed Julia on the forehead and left the hospital, Julia so close to sleep, she missed the pressure of his lips. Or thought she'd dreamed it.

Reconciliation is a long word, longer than marriage or divorce, and probably harder to accomplish. How is it that two people can live together for most of their lives and forget how to talk? Howi found himself losing track of the newspaper article he was reading, his mind a wander. He thought he would plant sunflowers on the side of the house this year; Julia loved the sunny faces. He wondered how she was doing, but hesitated to pick up the phone. He had worked to build an anger up against her, those weeks he had hiked the mountains. Why was he bothering to think of her at all? He shook out the paper, put his mind back into the story. *Or was it black-eyed Susans?* He could never remember the flower names.

Julia was not as self-delusional. She was beginning to understand that she had turned on Howi out of her grief. Maybe she had desired pain, or felt that she deserved it. But after her heart attack, she found herself missing him. She didn't know if she missed him as a husband, or just as someone who shared her past. Validated her past? She couldn't quite figure out her emotions.

Well, only one way to find out, and everyone knows women are braver than men.

It took until spring for Julia to get up her nerve, and a little snooping, asking her mother if Molly came 'round the place. "Yeah, she did a while back, but not since your heart attack. I wonder if there could be any connection?" Ruth asked, spreading irony over her delivery. Ruth was nobody's fool.

Julia drove out. There was a small scaffolding on their house; evidently Howi was scraping the siding in preparation for new paint. The old periwinkle-blue exterior was peeling away, paint chips collecting by the foundations as if the house sat in a surround of decomposing petals. She hesitated at the split Dutch door. She had walked through that door a thousand times, but it was the first time she rang the bell.

Howi answered, glass of water in hand; he had just come in for a break. He was overlaid in periwinkle paint chips, and Julia momentarily thought he could pass for a mosaic, or a Gustaf Klimt painting. Or Krishna cracking up.

Howi thought Julia looked like a Coca-Cola.

Neither spoke. Words are for the soft hours, words are for the undecided. She had to make the first move, she knew it. Julia's hands rode over Howi's tall shoulders, curved his familiar neck, pulled him to her. Julia thought she had come over to discuss the possibility of reconciliation, but apparently she had come for this. Maybe it was the same thing. She realized she had wanted to touch Howi for some time. Howi kissed her with the passion of a man long gone to the desert. She kissed him with the passion of a childless mother who wants to lay her grief to rest. Holding hands, practically running across the front room, Julia said, "I like the new rug." *What a dork!*

They made up in wild what they lacked in finesse. Howi's jeans stayed bunched around one ankle. Julia hoped he hadn't noticed when she launched herself naked onto the bed and her boob lobbed into the space between her arm and her armpit and made a little farty sound. None of that mattered. They knew who they were.

Later, Howi ran his fingers over Julia's skin, silently naming the rivers of blood and the low and high lands of her body, a whole new country across the Plains of Julia. He thought the emerging silver in her hair a motherload. An unearthing of something valuable to come.

Two winters later, Wonder and Wynona got married in the snow. Wonder went out early in the morning and beat a crooked path through cedar pines to an arbor he had made of brambles. Julia followed with a tinkling bunch of clear glass wind chimes to hang from the branches like icicles. They stood back and admired the scene. They were ready.

The bride wore a winter white parka, fur hood haloing her face, sprigs of winter berries in her mittened hands. Ionia and her brother, Everest, sat in a red wagon and tried to eat the birdseed. The chickadees came and stole the seeds right from their little hands, and a small breeze obliged the chimes.

Wynona would always say that Wonder fell in love with Ionia before he fell in love with her. But it wasn't true. He remembered Wynona sticking up for Nia on the playground when Robbie was bullying her. Wynona had wedged herself between Nia and Robbie and shouted, "You wanna try picking on somebody your own size!?" Ridiculous!—she was at least a half foot shorter than Nia or Robbie. And then she smacked him with a Barbie doll. Wonder remembered Wynona was wearing some pink coat that could have stood in for a toilet rug. Wonder thought he might have fallen in love with her right then.

In the following summer, Trautmann left this earth sitting on his spotted horse, eyes to the wavery horizon. He thought the aneurysm was the sun exploding in his head and measured the pain worth the glory. His family gave him a cowboy funeral, barbeque and crawdads, corn on the cob. They left the seat at the head of the table empty, his Stetson in place of a plate. Everyone who attended went home with a yellowed Louie L'Amour paperback—*Silver Canyon*, *How the West Was Won*, *Beyond the Great Snow Mountains*.

Ruth buried him on their own property, down by the weeping willow. It was strictly illegal, but in Genoa those things can happen. Howi dug the grave, would bear no help. Julia sat under the willow and wept.

Julia and Howi shifted into the bigger house with Ruth. Wynona and Wonder moved into the A-frame. The kids had beds in both houses and Ionia liked to sleep under the Nia quilt with its tiny-petaled daisies, rickrack, and bony French knots.

Wonder's agricultural degree sowed the seeds for a career at the Nevada State Farm Bureau. Brass nameplate on his black walnut desk, but he still freelanced crop dusting. For Wonder, the world would always be Turtles All the Way Down, the idea of the flat earth riding on the turtle's back. He could not hope to understand the kaleidoscope, but from the sky, how beautiful the colliding patterns. He loved Nevada, and he hoped the mustangs of his soul ever listened when he called *Rise up, Silver and Blue*.

Wynona went through a gold phase. She spray-painted everything she could get her hands on. Pine cones, picture frames. The toilet seat.

One night Wynona saw Hale on the evening news. It was a story about the Keystone Pipeline, and Hale was protesting with the Standing Rock Sioux. Ionia walked through the room while the story was still on. Wynona half expected her to slow and stop, to see the man on the side of the screen who was, and certainly was not, her father. Ionia kept on going. And so did Wynona; she changed the channel and the past pixelated anew.

Jimmy did go shopping in San Francisco. But only because he moved there. Every day he felt like he was living in a misty postcard. He and his ludicrously handsome partner, Hal, bought a lavender Victorian on Russian Hill and opened up a yoga studio and juice bar on the ground floor called *The Downward Dog*. Occasionally the cherry-headed wild parrots of Telegraph Hill landed in their backyard Chinese magnolia trees for a delightfully one-sided chitchat. Jimmy tells the parrots that he loves Hal best out of all the men in all the bars, in all the beds, in all the world. When he goes shopping, he sends Wynona gifts from Gumps—Asian chinoiserie and Bavarian crystal—*So fab!*

In the fall of 1987, the year that Ionia was born, President Reagan was yelling *tear down that wall*. Baby Jessica was falling down a well, and Freddie Mercury was on his way to becoming a square on a very large quilt. And on Baker Beach in San Francisco, Larry Harvey was burning a man.

Larry Harvey might have personally missed out on the height of the Height, but he was hosting an after-party and he was doing it annually. Inviting all the little Flower Children. In 1990, he brought the party to Nevada. Burning Man moved to the Black Rock Desert.

Eventually Howi decided to go see what kind of ruckus

was going on out at the playa. It irked him something awful to have to pay to enter what he considered his backyard. A bunch of girls in tutus and sunburns were trying to get him to bang a gong because he was a Burner virgin. *Bullshit.* He kept right on going. Some of the girls were topless, though. That was nice.

When he got into the actual festival, he thought he had entered a comic book. He could not see artistry in the cars made into floating ships and roving musicals, the golf carts turned mutant vehicles. To Howi, the art installations placed around the playa were ugly-fantastical, a dark circus. The people all drunk clowns in their round-eyed goggles and pelts. It wasn't that Howi couldn't see the fractured beauty and understand that it was a collective *fuck you* to the conscripts of society. It was that they doing it on *the playa*, and to Howi, the playa was ever meant to only be a place of dust and quiet. A place for Reverence, not to man—silly creature—but to Nature.

In the middle of the festival grounds was the Man—a giant stick effigy built to burn, symbolizing release of past pain. Letting go. *Good luck with that.*

When night fell, the stars were not invited. Guess they didn't buy a ticket. The Black Rock lit up with mad neon and minor fires, people wrapped and roving in glowsticks. Music came and went. Howi walked until he was so far out in the playa, the festival reduced to nothing but a glowstick itself. The whole thing hurt his soul.

He sat down; he was tired. The star-tapestry of the Milky Way had emerged. Wall-to-wall. Howi had walked his anger and self-righteousness out. He knew the playa would remain the same as it ever was. Burning Man couldn't change it. Nia's ashes were somewhere at the festival, and Howi admitted to himself that Nia would have loved it. The anarchy and—he had to say it—the art. The spirituality. She would have loved the colors. In that moment of near-physical and emotional exhaustion, Howi wondered if the loud hubbub and audacity of the whole thing might not call his daughter down from the welkin. Might Nia be out there tonight—and for one week each year!—might she come join in the merry?

Long ago, Julia chose to picture Nia as eaten by hummingbirds, and now, Howi chose to think of Nia attending Burning Man on the Black Rock Desert. Darling dancer in the dark.

As the years collected, Julia sometimes reflected on the person she once was. Everything that had spooled for her because she stopped for a flint-haired boy in ripped jeans in the heat of 100 degrees. The pain it had cost her to stay in Nevada. When she was young, she didn't believed she could ever be happy in the high desert. Autumns so gold, you can bank on it. The way snow falls from pine branches like a leap of faith. Spring weather that can't make up its mind. Summers without rain and then it rains and the air smells of hay, wildflowers bloom overnight, and the heron stands on one leg. Blue feathers and a sharp black eye.

Julia had found her peace.

Blue-Throated Jungle Barbet

It is hard to mark the change of the seasons in Los Angeles, they slip so one into the other. Spring is the jacaranda tree, that drama queen in full violet petal. Summer is night-blooming jasmine, best paired with champagne. Fall is the pink-and-silvery-white plumes of pampas grass. Winter is Christmas trees in department store windows. But all year long the bird-of-paradise reprises its role as the official flower of L.A., and stars sparkle on the Walk of Fame. Oleander- and ivy-banked roads, a city on the brink of oranges. Breathe the dry on the Santa Ana winds, sense the drought in the clipped language of the brown-edged lawns. It is a city of mirrors, as they all are—but only the City of Angels has the stellar Los Angeles Central Library.

CITY OF ANGELS

When Lenny Henri was released from the West Los Angeles Veteran's Hospital (all charges dropped—the bus driver was a veteran himself), he was fortified with new antidepressants, counseling, and disability checks. But he was no longer employed at LASAN—the Department of Sanitation. Well, Lenny never really wanted to be a garbageman. He took to sitting out on the shared front porch of the subdivided house he lived in. To pass the time, Lenny dug out his chisels and started work on his personal Rosetta Stone. Wood shavings scuttered around him like rolly-polly bugs. He was whittling the surface of an oak end table into a haiku of jungle war stories—tiger in the bamboo, akimbo warriors with knives in both hands like tiny blades of grass. It was looking pretty good. He ran his fingers over the braille of the grooves.

Sometimes his landlady, Ruby, or her twin sister, Garnet—he couldn't tell them apart—brought him a lemonade, heavy on the sugar. The sisters had a double set of rooms with a view out the parlor windows. *That's real nice, son, real nice.* The old gals smelled like they were one day past their expiration date, but Lenny wasn't one to judge.

He tried not to dream, but how does one accomplish that, exactly?

It was Ruby who told Lenny about the Los Angeles Central Library, that excellent haven for both intellect and body. "You outta get out more often," she said—the sisters knew the outlines of his situation. "Go to the beach." Lenny just looked at her, imagining more sun, more heat. Ruby saw his deadpan, tried to think of other free places. "How about a library. Ooh! You ever been to the Central?!"

Everyone who enters a library knows to *Be Quiet*, but most fail to understand the instruction is for life, not just for the library. Lenny Henri chose to fully follow this cardinal rule. It was as close to sanctuary as he could hope for.

But—oh!—what a library. Built in the 1920s, the Los Angeles Central Library was Bertram Goodhue's swan song as the architect died before the books were shelved. The exterior seemed at first to presage Stalinist architecture; it is a brute of a building. But then it isn't. The buff-colored concrete is a foundation for the soaring statues, warbling fountains, and lofty quotes—IN BOOKS IS LIBERTY—that make the exterior as literary and eloquent as a cathedral with its rose window. Lenny didn't really set out to virtually live in a library. But once inside, it no longer mattered that his meager rental was a soup kitchen, because the Central Library was a buffet.

Lenny walked through the hushed rotunda with its soaring, Moorish-flair stenciled dome. From the center of the dome hung the Zodiac Chandelier, illuminating the history of Los Angeles, told in clear-eyed murals of industry and glory. He spent his time wandering the privacy of the book stacks, and in the reading room with its long, wood tables. Walls throughout the old sections of the library told stories in earth-toned murals under tole-painted, beamed ceilings. Lenny thought to himself, *If you had to take one building with you to a deserted island*, smiling at his own joke. There was plenty to read, to do. To watch.

While the library certainly had its fair share of elbow-patched academics and tired women in mom jeans herding their ducklings to story hour, Lenny found that a lot of the patrons of the Los Angeles Central Library were his people—the loony and the broke. He came to anticipate their trajectories, like trash pushed along street gutters. The homeless began to clutter the gates about half an hour before opening, especially on colder days, anxious to get in. Well, Lenny was used to poor. He avoided everyone, hunted out the smaller places, so it was somewhat of a surprise that he took particular note of the young punk woman who walked into his aisle. Her ripped jeans were held together by enough safety pins to diaper an orphanage. There was no end to the buckles and chains bandoliering her black leather jacket; Lenny thought it must have been an aerobic workout just to walk around. She stopped—not so very far from him—and swung a culturally appropriated army duffel bag off her shoulder, took of her jacket off, and stuffed it into the duffel. Lenny had little choice but to read her Sex Pistols T-shirt. *God Save the Queen*. She had skin the color of bone. Blond hair, black glasses. She started walking toward him, and Lenny thought her jacket sounded like the Ghost of Christmas Past.

Lenny knew he was in Fiction HA–HO. What he didn't know was why he opened his mouth: "You'd think it was the comedy aisle," he said to the young woman. Now he saw that the last two inches of her blond hair were dyed dipped-in-the-inkwell black.

Simone (he didn't yet know her name yet, of course) didn't notice Lenny at first. She was seeking Hemingway, his shot-of-whiskey writing an assignment for her American Lit class. She glanced at him and Lenny saw Simone didn't understand his joke. "HA through HO? Well, if you have to explain it . . ." He took in the sketch book—Strathmore 400—she had tucked under her arm. There was graphite on her fingers, a Picasso-esque smudge over one eyebrow.

Simone gave him a smile meant for anyone, scooted past him, smelled the eucalyptus leaves Lenny kept crushed in his pockets, a kind of dry-cleaning trick he was trying out. She turned around, just before she left the aisle. Lenny was reversing a book so that instead of the spine, the pale pages faced out from the stack. Simone had seen this a few times before in other aisles. "What are you doing?" she couldn't help herself from asking.

Lenny stopped, turned toward the young woman. "Reversing the ones I've read. Saves time later." Lenny thought there was something about her that said *outcast by design*. He knew that sometimes that just means it's hard to relate to people and you don't want anyone to know it. It reminded him of when he transferred to a new high school mid-year; he briskly walked the halls at lunch as if he had somewhere to be, just so he wouldn't look like he had no one to sit with. That's how the young punked-up woman felt to Lenny. She didn't look poor, but she sure was skinny. Was she hungry? Lenny hated to see people go hungry.

Still he could not believe the boldness of his mouth. "Hey," Lenny said, "if you want some lunch, I went to the day-old and I've got some good salami." He motioned to his book bag. "I keep a jar of Grey Poupon and some Goldfish hidden behind Melville—nobody goes there." He hesitated, but then kept going. Her eyes were meeting his eyes. Blinking. "Name's Lenny Henri. Henri with an *i*. We could go out in the garden. . ." Too bold. He knew it.

Lenny didn't know why he'd even asked. He remembered that people don't much like him, and the woman just gave a little shake of her head and continued out the far end of the aisle, as good a no as he expected. Why would a woman like that spend time with a clown like him?

But the next day Simone came and found Lenny. He was sitting in a chair tucked close to a potted bamboo palm. Very literary. If she discounted the stretched-neck T-shirt and the so-faded jeans they could pass for trompe l'oeil. Tall and thin, with skin something less than American Standard. Simone knew, after all, that the United States is a country that carries a color chart in its hip pocket. Well, she had a color chart too. *Biscuit.* She remembered his last name: Henri with an *i. French Creole?* Reading a paperback edition of *The Grapes of Wrath,* Simone liked the way the light knighted Lenny's shoulders.

"Lenny?" she said tentatively.

He looked up from his book. "Nope." He smiled. Nice teeth but for one uncivilized, snaggle-toothed incisor gone wild. Thirty pieces of silver in his dark, circa 1970s hair. He looked to be in the well-worn eclipse of his '30s. A little younger than her dad.

"Get up, joker. I want that free lunch." She turned and walked away, expecting him to follow. He did. They stopped by Melville and then headed outside.

It was a cool day. Simone chose a grassy spot in the sun, sat down with the vertical drop of youth. Lenny silently admired the collapse of her knees. His put up a fight. Out of her duffle bag Simone pulled sugar cookies with pink icing that she had made the night before, just right for Los Angeles. Then an ancient red plaid throw blanket, and a matching old-school thermos. She looked like she was camping out.

"Where's your harmonica?"

Simone ignored the implication. "I'm an artist." She showed Lenny her hands to prove it. "Watercolorist. Name's Simone Bouchard. Have you heard of me?" Simone asked.

"Did you make that name up?" Lenny asked back.

"Yes."

Lenny gave a half smile. "Pleased to meet you, Simone," he said, laying out the hard salami to be dipped in haughty Grey Poupon, and a few slices of now one-day-older Wonder Bread.

"Lenny, why are you homeless?" Simone asked, reaching for Lenny's pocket knife. The paper around the salami left a dusting on her fingers and the scent of fennel.

She's a forward one, Lenny thought. But Lenny didn't care. He knew pussyfooting was for pussies. One thing he'd learned in the Army—don't count tomorrow. The future can be blown to bone. "Oh, I'm not homeless," he answered.

"Well, you sure dress the part. Are you an understudy for a new production of *Bleak House*?"

"Ha! You're funny," Lenny said. "I'm one of Reagan's little orphans. I'm cuckoo for Cocoa Puffs, but they ran out of funds at the looney bin, so now I live on disability. I got a place over by Anthony Quinn, but I bus it over here because . . . well, because of the building."

Simone nodded. She didn't know that Anthony Quinn was the library closest to Lenny's house, but she understood the lure of the Central. The place is a work of art.

"And Mrs. Ressel," Lenny continued, "she's the reference librarian with the Elton John specs—she's really good at picking out titles." Mrs. Ressel recognized in Lenny the need to distract himself from the hazards of his own consciousness. In the time Simone had spent doing artwork at the library, Simone had already begun to understand that inner-city librarians were underpaid social workers with a deep understanding of the Dewey decimal system. Simone shook her head yes, she understood.

"What about you?" Lenny asked. "Why are you here two days in a row? You look pretty homeless yourself." He indicated her old duffle, but still made sure no part of his body touched the olive drab. He hated that color.

"Yeah!" Simone said. "That's my mom, the thrift store queen. Every time I visit, she sends me home with stuff I *just gotta have.* Turns out, she's usually right."

Lenny thought for a moment about how nice it would be to have a mom who did that. Shook it off. "How do you even get past security with that bag that size?"

"I'm an artist in residence." She pronounced it *artiste.*

"Is that so?

"Well, I made the *official* designation up. I'm an art student studying at USC Roski School of Art and Design." Lenny could tell she liked to say those words. "I couldn't believe it when I got in. With some scholarships! I thought I would have to go to Chico State with all the other little pot smokers." It wasn't her watercolors that got her in, so much as her portraits. A little wonky, a little smudged. By now, Simone knew she was legally blind—20/200. Her glasses gave her perfect (or perfectly good) vision, but Simone rather liked that she could soft-edge the world at will by taking them off. Turn people rainy day, star everything like it was Christmas. She tried to bring that feeling into her work. Sometimes she painted with her glasses off.

"You working on your art, then?" Lenny asked, shrugging toward her pad, sticking out of the bag.

"I got clearance from the library to copy the murals, so they know what I'm up to. Security goes through my bag when I arrive and leave. I started with copying the murals, but now I'm doing people sketches. You get all kinds in a library." Simone loved *all kinds*, that was true. She pulled out her sketch book, showed him. The drawings were part exacting pencil replicas, part painful LSD melts. Twisted limbs. She worked them into watercolors later.

Lenny let out a low whistle. "Don't do me."

"I'm so gonna' do you."

That's why, Lenny thought. No one would want to talk to him, just to talk to him. He licked pink frosting off his fingers, felt like a four-year-old at a birthday party where he just found out *he* was tail on the donkey. *Oh well. What else is new?* "Where's home for you, Simone?" Lenny asked to shift his thoughts.

"Lake Tahoe. I have to take the Greyhound to visit my mom. It's like seventeen hours. An actual greyhound could do it faster." Lenny laughed. "I've been in L.A. for almost two years now," she added. Simone thought back to when she'd first left for school. It had scared her to leave her home. She couldn't put it to words, but at Lake Tahoe, she knew her way over the mountain. Could count on the scent of pine and a sky so blue, cold water in a creek. Fighting blue jays and short summers. She wasn't really ready to go to *the big city*. But she would see new colors in L.A. She knew a lot about brown and green and blue. It was time to go over the rainbow.

They were quiet for a minute. "What do you do when you go Fruit Loops?" asked Simone.

"Cocoa Puffs. Depends. They got a name for it now— *post-traumatic stress disorder*—isn't that fancy? Means I might stay in bed all day keening or beat the livin' shit out of a local bus driver because I am certain the gook's gonna attack *me*. Either way, not so good. Especially since he was Chinese, born in San Francisco." *And it wasn't the first time.* Lenny didn't tell her that he had gone straight from a hospital in Saigon to Walter Reed, then into a long-term institution.

"Oops" said Simone. No sense in being judgy when she was fishing for Goldfish in a grubby paper box. "Everybody's got a burden," she said, licking orange crumbs off her fingers.

She rooted around the bottom of her duffle and pulled out a glass bottle of Log Cabin syrup.

"It's like Mary Poppins in there," said Lenny.

"Want some?" offered Simone, holding up the bottle.

"Thanks, but I'm more of a Hungry Jack man, myself."

"What? Guy like you says no to free booze? What's the world coming to?"

"You first," Lenny said.

Simone and Lenny threw back a few shots of what tasted like a bottle of maple-flavored kerosene, and then Lenny fell asleep in an afternoon that was set on collecting clouds. He only slept some fifteen minutes. He awoke to find Simone had placed her plaid blanket across both their legs. She had his Steinbeck paperback and was eating more Goldfish, leaving orange fingerprints over the print.

"You're reading my book now?" he asked.

"Only the wraths parts."

The clouds looked like they were planning some wrath themselves. Thunder. "I don't think it's going to rain here," Simone said, tracking Lenny. "That thunder's out over the ocean. Cool feels kind of good."

But thunder was a trigger; his counselor told him thunder, loud noises might always be a trigger. Lenny pulled the blanket off and put it back on Simone, crossed his arms, and tried to think about anything but the way the jungle looked in the rain, the green smear of it and the rot. The ambush, when they were trying to take a hill that didn't even have a name, just a number to equal its height.

Dear Mrs. Boyer, The United States Army regrets to inform you that your son, Private First Class Whitt Boyer, was blown to fuckin' shit on Hill #482. His friend Lenny Henri, who wasn't a very good shot, didn't help the situation. Yours truly, Uncle Sam

How many times, in how many different ways, was Lenny

going to mentally write this letter? Lenny could feel himself slip-sliding away. He knew that by this point he was looking the junkie, shaking. *Good God! Stop it!*

"Hey, Lenny," Simone called, and it sounded to Lenny as if she were far away. But she just had her face in her bag. She emerged with a portable cribbage board. She reached for her red plaid thermos of still-warm coffee. She poured him a cup and said, "Let's play."

Lenny spilled only a little of the coffee on his jeans, and he won the game. She might have let him. She was right, though, the thunder was far off as Cambodia. Not his war. He felt better. Lenny got up to go to the bathroom. When he came back, Simone had broken down camp and apparently headed out. Against the tree was a half sheet of paper, decent stock, with a pencil portrait. It was good—she got the eyes right. He didn't even want to think what the LSD version would look like. He turned it over:

Lenny,

I really like you. But man, you got Nam written all over you. I see it in my older cousin. That war's over and nobody's coming for you. Maybe see you around?!

Love, Simone

P.S. I stole your book. Fucker can write.

P.S.S.Keep this drawing because I'm going to be famous. Wish it was on a cocktail napkin, because that would be way cooler.

Oh, and the Log Cabin is behind the tree. You're welcome.

Lenny picked up the bottle, put the note in his back pocket, and headed home. Simone was right about the storm. The rain fell over the ocean and never made it to shore, because L.A. does not like to smear its makeup.

Talking to Simone about his past had put Lenny into a retrospective state. He lay in bed and thought about the last few years of his life. When he was released (*kicked out*) from the mental institution (*loony bin*), thanks more to Reagan's deinstitutionalization than to personal stability, he had twirled the atlas of his mind. Lenny had left his ability to think too far ahead in Vietnam, so he made a metaphorical choice: Los Angeles. *City of Angels*. Surely there will be some comfort there. Of course, Lenny realized the only thing he would be changing was his location. He knew he couldn't lose his past. Memory can contract or expand but it can't be stuffed into a suitcase and left at the station. Or the battlefield.

When Lenny arrived in L.A., he spent some days riding around on the local buses. He could see the beauty of the city in its architecture and showgirl palm trees, in cultivated flowerpots and hard-candy convertibles. But he found it too sunny, the sun as unnuanced as a child's yellow crayon. And there seemed to Lenny a heartlessness to the city—L.A. doesn't want to hear about your boo-boos. Well, that part was fine with him.

Lenny rented rooms from Ruby and Garnet in East L.A., the 1930s house separated into apartments, no credit checks needed, pay by the week in advance. The government paid for six months' rent. The place looked like it needed a walker just to stand up, and the plumbing let out murderous screams, apparently scalded by the hot water. But the house was good at catching the breeze, and the front porch looked out to a large magnolia that, come spring, would giftwrap the treetop. A little present for everyone.

Lenny hardly knew what to do with the expanse of freedom. He always liked mornings best; the true magic of dawn lies in the possibility of a fresh start. An eternal Mulligan. He imagined the morning air as released from the burden of everyone's feelings, purged by the passing of night. As the day progressed, the air would suffer, not only from the pugilistic Southern California sun, but from the auras of emotions that passed through it. Love, anger—it's all hot. By 2 p.m. it's a war zone.

Lenny knew he needed to get a job; he was thinking too much. It was safest for him to nap through the worst of the heat, ensconced in the whirly air of a fan set on high. But even so, sometimes that fan sounded kin to the far-off approach of choppers, the approach of his personal war.

He found his corner store, footlongs with a curated mustard selection. Fried chicken with stacks of waffles. The cashier smoked a hand-rolled by the front door when the store was empty. Lenny sometimes saw her leaning there and found himself wanting to cook the kid a homemade steak dinner, she was so skinny. But he never offered; knew he looked homeless. Or worse, might strike her as a predator. And he didn't have the funds for steak anyway.

Lenny avoided Venice Beach, Rodeo Drive, Sunset Boulevard. The Bird Streets. Magically delicious Tinseltown. Well, he knew those places would reject him, so he did it first. L.A. is a hard place to meet people, though. Story of his life. Lenny got some come-ons from street corner pharmacists looking for new customers. *What you want? I got it. I'll be your friend.* He bought some weed, but lucky for Lenny, his one true friend was Lynette at the unemployment agency.

Lynette with her save-the-world voice, her feed-the-world bosom. "Oh, Lenny, honey, I'm glad you came in today. I got just the thing for you!" She sold it like gold. Lenny got a little excited, but then she said, "Garbageman!"

"Seriously, Lynette? Come on!"

"Oh, no, no, no, honey. This is the good job. I'm telling you. It's got retirement. You don't know, but retirement, that's what you want. Plus it's good pay."

Lynette was right. Garbageman was good clean work with a pension waiting at the end like a cherrywood rocking chair. Lenny found it wasn't too hard working for the LSAN. He hung from the back of the truck cable-car style, and when they drove up Topanga Canyon, the coastal sage and chaparral beat back the exhaust and the used-up smell escaping from the truck. But it turned out to be a lonely job. Too noisy, too much movement to even really make friends with his shift mates, most of whom were already family men and not looking for a new buddy. And the truth is everyone knows garbageman is one step away from sin eater. That's why the pay is better than average. Lenny probably smelled mulchy, even on Sundays.

Lenny tried to envision going to a bar. Over loud music he would tell a dirty-martini woman that he worked at *La San*, leading her to imagine a French restaurant over on Wilshire—it would have to do with his delivery, the arch of his brow. Certainly it would get him farther than *garbageman*, at least for one night. But he felt he was too old to go to bars, lost confidence in the plan. Stayed home and played Scrabble with Ruby and Garnet. (Garnet tended to invent words, mostly three letters.)

Lenny knew he was drinking too much, walking on the wrong side of the street. He could feel poor decisions coming his way. Join the Crips, or buy a gun just to remember the weight of it in his hand. Or on an unusual night of heavy artillery-sounding rain, take out the gook bus driver, beat the shit out of the little fucker before he beats the shit out of you.

Now, the library was his safest place. And that was that.

Simone kept coming to the Los Angeles Central Library. She had expected to finish her sketches and move on, but the work was coming together. She tossed the murals, but the combined portraits were starting to make a story. Really it was the watercolor backgrounds she did later that entranced her. She attended her classes and found herself spending an hour or more at the library three or so days a week. It was so peaceful a place to do her homework. At her apartment building, her neighbor Elena, who was only about forty and not at all hard of hearing, liked to play KWKW mariachi music at full blast.

Simone kept mostly to her work, but usually throughout the course of any day, she and Lenny would meet up in the aisles for a whisper. Lenny filled her in on some of the regulars, most of whom he did not actually know, but for which he devised names and stories. The Cat Woman, who hissed at any man who invaded her territory:

"She scratched me! I had to get iodine."

"Well, why'd you go near her, you idiot!"

Lenny told her about the Jehovah's Witness couple, who scattered *Watchtower* pamphlets around the reading desks like travel brochures for your final destination. Or poor Buddy, who kept shooting up in the kid's room, Simone suggesting perhaps he liked the rainbow spines of the children's books. Hobo José, who stole yesterday's newspapers to put into his worn-down shoes. Or to use as a pillow. Lenny swore one time José's cheek said THREE DEAD, backward. They had a giggle and Simone got an *Excellent!!* on the portrait she created just from the image Lenny created with his words.

Simone did sketch Lenny. She saw the trenches on his face, the ghosts that made his fingers shake when he lifted up his hand in greeting. He could not camouflage his past. Ten sketches in, she had him down. Those eyes.

Every time they parted, Lenny never really expected to see Simone again; figured one day she just wouldn't come back. Maybe at the end of her semester. It couldn't be a real friendship. He didn't know that Simone was finding in Lenny her own personal missing link. Drawing it. Drawing it out.

Lenny and Simone played Scrabble in the gardens on Lenny's portable plastic set. The set was missing two A squares, a Y, and a K. The K was a problem. On a day when the warm weather shooed almost the whole city outdoors, Lenny and Simone met up by the Italian cypress. The high sun gave the concrete exterior of the library a porcelain sheen. Lenny pulled two peanut butter and honey sandwiches out of his pack. "Yum, chunky," said Simone. Backs against the trees, Simone asked, "Lenny, don't you have any family?" Simone had not said much about her family, and Lenny wasn't one to push. But Simone didn't have that filter. She wondered why Lenny was alone, or seemed so. As they were both facing out—away from each other—maybe it felt safer to ask. She could not see what Lenny was remembering play across his face.

Lenny's mind spooled to a scalloped-edged photo he kept in his wallet. He pulled it out and handed the black-and-white shot to Simone, easily replicating the image in his head. "That's my parents, Reggie and Alice, in Sarasota, Florida." In the portrait, wind was blowing his mother's dress up against her body, creating a sort a flower-print x-ray of her thin form. His father's olive drab uniform looked a size too big, and new. Reaching up to catch his just-now windblown field cap, Reggie's face blurred as his eyes followed the cap's trajectory. This was the only photo Lenny had of his dad; it seemed prophetic that Reggie's face was a smudge.

Simone knew something about blurry dads. She turned the photo over; there was a date, 1950, on the back. "Your dad was in the service," she said.

Lenny glanced over at the photo, remembering the family lore: An artic front from Siberia shivered through Korea, delivering frostbite to the U.S. soldiers, to the tips of Reggie's fingers. Freezing his weapon. Ice crystals caused a rifle jam. But when the bullet sent from the People's Army entered his chest, his heart wasn't frozen at all. The U.S. Army was severely underequipped for the harsh winter of 1950, and it could easily be argued that Uncle Sam set Reggie up, but his death certificate said *Killed in action.* Alice learned the story of the chattering death in a letter that followed sometime later from a war buddy of Reggie's who thought she should know the cold truth.

"I never met my dad," Lenny told Simone. "He died in Korea."

"Oh, that's sad," Simone said, looking closer at the forsaken man in the photograph. It wasn't just words for her; there was a warble in her voice. "You know you telling me this is going to make me call home tonight." They both thought about the ability of a wallet-wrinkled photo effecting an action over thirty years later. Life is strange that way. Simone realized that Lenny must be in the photo too. "Your mom was pregnant when he left?"

"Yeah."

"Your poor mom," Simone said.

"My mom," continued Lenny, "she was *The Little Engine That Could,* you remember that book?" Simone nodded, conjuring up bedtime stories. Lenny pencil-sketched his childhood, told Simone that before the service, Reggie worked on the fishing boats in Sarasota Bay, Alice at Walt's Fish Market. But his mom didn't work at the checkout counter where filets were laid out on beds of ice with lemon wedge and parsley accents. She met the fishermen unloading their catch on the backside of the market (including the man she would marry). She slung those fish right along with the men, on to the long tables, and then she magicked those fish from bloody, silvery monsters into something that looked civilized and good for dinner. So it might not have been a complete surprise when Alice used Reggie's death benefit on a somewhat hurricane-battered Boston Whaler—that boat can break into three pieces and still float—and started fishing for herself. "It was an odd thing for a woman in the '50s to do, but it seemed normal to me."

Lenny took the photo back from Simone. Ran a finger over it. "My mom's passed too," Lenny said. He put the photo away, pulled out the Scrabble game, and Simone knew that Memory Lane was closed to through traffic. But Simone pushed one more question: "Lenny, why did you join the Army?"

Lenny fell quiet, then said, "I was lonely." Simone didn't respond. What could she say to that? Lenny filled the space—"Enough about me. I'm boring." He wasn't. "Tell me something about you—you said you grew up at Lake Tahoe?"

"Yep," Simone said, picturing the lake. The water is nothing but melted ice, flawlessly clear in shades bright to shadow. Simone believed every bit of turquoise and sapphire in existence would trade it all to be that alpine water. Hopelessly deep—1,645 feet—Simone's mother thought they could Davy-Jones's-locker their blues into a lake like that. Scuttle it.

What are your parents' names?" Lenny asked.

"Vivi and James," Simone said. "My mom and I moved from Pasadena to the South Shore of Tahoe in 1970 when my mom's identity changed from wife to single mom. I don't have a lot of memories before Tahoe." Simone was still called Staci then. Staci was barely six, and she might have retained clearer memories of her father if her mom hadn't have been so sad. Vivi packed James into a box and didn't unpack him at the new house. *Move forward* was Vivi's mantra.

"In Pasadena, my mom had been a court stenographer,"

said Simone. "But at Tahoe, the available jobs were at the casinos." Waitress, change girl, dealer if you could shuffle the cards sharp. "My mom had to take a job as hostess at Harvey's Casino. It was kind of embarrassing for her. She wore this low-cut, hibiscus print halter dress. The restaurant was called The Top of the Wheel—Polynesian theme on the highest floor of the highest building in town." Nonstop views of the showgirl lake.

"Tiki drinks and orchids?" Lenny guessed.

"Yeah. It was okay for me. I got leftovers. Once, I remember, I ate slices of kiwi. Kiwi! Dipped in sour cream and brown sugar. I felt like I was eating a whole new color. Honestly, I thought my mother was beautiful in her uniform, flowers in her hair. But she hated it. On her days off, we went to thrift stores. It was fun, really. I didn't know old from new. I had a collection of the rattiest-haired Barbies you've ever seen."

Vivi hunted the thrift stores for castaways and she remade those cloth orphans into the stuff of hippie dreams. Her long patchwork skirts were era-defining, and she knew it. She sold them to Olive & Peach in San Francisco, the boutique on Union Street catering to the type of woman who wanted *the look*, but certainly wasn't going to Haight Ashbury to find it. The money was good for Vivi because her overhead was quarters, and she put most of the profit in a college fund for Staci.

"Really, my mom was a hippie," Simone told Lenny. "She was always making us these matching long skirts and peasant tops. We looked like *Little House on the Prairie*."

"I don't exactly see you as a flower child," Lenny said. Simone was wearing a yellow plaid skirt—quite short—and ripped fishnets. She had two pencils sticking out of her blond ponytail with the dyed-black tips. She was skinny as a paintbrush.

"Ha! No." (Although she did really like flowers.) Simone was no follower of Twiggy, or *Seventeen* magazine, or the native Tahoe snow bunnies in their tight stirrup ski pants. "I was punk from the minute bad boy Kurt-the-glue-sniffer introduced me to The Pogues and Patti Smith." She could still hear the scratchy voices on the scratchy vinyl. Glue was for ripped-paper collages, but oh, the music! And that tartan, ripped-tee-heroin look! By high school, Staci wanted to dress like an artist. Because she wanted to be an artist. She wanted to change her name.

It seemed like a pretty good upbringing to Lenny. And here Simone was, going to art school. But Lenny took note of what was missing. Simone had said almost nothing about her dad. In Lenny's experience, what isn't said might be what matters most. Or is missed most.

That evening, sitting on the porch, Lenny thought about the concept that we are all victims or victors to our times. Of course his dad joined the Army—*Uncle Sam Wants You*. Lenny grew up proud of his father for serving. For a long time he wanted to know Reggie's war stories; surely he did more than hold still for a bullet. He tried to talk to other old vets he sometimes met. But most of those who endured active duty won't talk; don't bother asking. Now that Lenny had experienced Vietnam, he understood. How could a man tell a child how it feels to slide steel into flesh? How to describe the singular whistle of a bullet or the mad cacophony of a bomb? A building, or a man, collapsing down to the earth once and for all? Lenny didn't want to talk etiher.

But as Lenny felt the sun go down, Simone's question of *Why did you join the Army?* stalked him.

Of course, Lenny was not aware of the full story of his past; none of us are, for certainly the past does not require our cognizance to have its way with us. When Lenny's father died in Korea and the protection his wide shoulders had promised his mother was replaced by a blue field of stars on a tricorn-folded flag, Alice knew she was in trouble. Alice had Reggie's death benefit nesting in the bank, allowing her a shake at the Magic 8 Ball of life. But she put off decisions, waited on the baby. Labor was a Twilight Sleep chemical mix of morphine and scopolamine, cracked leather restraints on her wrists and ankles as she thrashed through drug-induced hallucinations. She remembered none of it. It was when the nurse placed her son into Alice's hesitant arms that Alice decided on the Boston Whaler. She knew Reggie's fishing routes: night fishing in Sarasota Bay by the Ringling Brothers' Ca' d'Zan winter mansion, and in Siesta Key. Grouper and snapper around Vamo Road and Blackburn Point. Alice would buy the boat and hire a local salty until she knew enough to do for herself.

By the time Lenny was a teenager, he wordlessly knew he lived on the border of meager, with a quizzical mother who worked most mornings on the Whaler and most afternoons at Walt's slinging the day's trawl. It was around this time that desire began to erode into discontent. Lenny wanted a bike and wondered if he could steal one. Maybe if Alice remarried, they would have more money, and he a dad, although Lenny had heard some stepdad horror stories. But his mother never went on dates; if she had time to go out at all, it was with her best friend, Mary. "All the good ones died in the war," was what his mother said if she spoke of men at all.

On the last day, the one that would delineate *before* and *after*, Alice was cleaning fish at Walt's. The new hire, Gilbert—God, what a mess he was, leaving entrails on the table to slime off the edge and land in a bloody snot on the cement floor—accidentally slapped Alice in the face with a good-size speckled trout. The cold fish left sparkly scales on her cheek. "Oh, sorry," said Gilbert, and Alice was just about to whack him back with a grouper, she was so irritated by his inefficiency, but the effort caused her to slip on the bloody snot. She fell and hit her head.

Gilbert helped Alice up. "Sorry, sorry. I'm so sorry."

You sure are, thought Alice as Gilbert helped her out back to the smoking table. Gilbert left her there, beneath the Japanese paper lanterns someone had strung between two palms, lighting a cigarette she pulled from the front pocket of her gray rubber apron. When he came out for his own break, Alice was dead.

In the last moments of Alice's life, her still-racing mind left the splintery picnic table and went back home. *Hurry, hurry!* She illusioned herself opening the door, balancing two full bags of groceries. Alice started a load of laundry, then into the kitchen to cook up lasagna, tuna casserole, dish after dish that she put in the freezer under starry tinfoil lids. She changed the sheets on her son's bed, put Lenny's old stuffy bear on his pillow, even though Lenny was way too old to admit attachment to the one-eyed fellow. Then she hung the laundry out to dry—she would *just die* if someone found her unwashed underwear.

Chores done, everything she could think of doing for her child in advance of her absence *(and done so quickly!)*, Alice ran a bath for herself. Hot, and she added soft rose petals *(where did these come from?)* and then lowered her tired, tired body into the water. It felt like Heaven.

It was Heaven.

Mary, Alice's best friend, delivered the news of his mother's death, promised Lenny he would live with her. That first night they slept together in Alice's bed. But Social Services did a background check and found Mary *morally unfit to raise children*. In fact, she was not allowed to get near Lenny under threat of arrest.

Lenny moved in with his estranged grandfather, who was courting the bottle like it wore a polka dot dress. He wasn't a bad guy, but Pop lost most of his monthly pension betting greyhounds at the Sarasota Kennel Club, reducing their late-in-the-month dinners to butter beans and bacon, and earning Lenny the nickname *Stinky Farts* at his new school. Always Lenny would fight. He didn't care about winning. A fading bruise is a Purple Heart.

To a child, even on the brink of adulthood, the death of a parent is kin to being lost in the beating heart of the Okeefenokee Swamp. At sunset, all the beasties coming out. How to paddle out of that feeling?

Lenny worked on a fishing boat, but even after high school, he still had a hard time making friends, or even getting a second date—except with La Lique and he had to pay for her. (Worth every penny—that girl was all cinnamon and ginger.) What could a damaged young man do? Join the Army!

It might have been a good idea, but Lenny's timing was not. Jane Fonda was vacationing at the Hanoi Hilton. Ho Chi Minh was hiking his trail. The Napalm Girl was running away, while Kent State was becoming a Neil Young song. And Nixon was playing hopscotch on the Vietnam/Cambodian border—deploying his secret agent man, Orange.

On the morning Lenny was leaving for basic training at Fort Jackson, South Carolina, he called La Lique. He knew she would be home—it was her bedtime. "I'm leaving for Vietnam, come down to the bus stop and see me off." That's how it was in the movies—departing soldiers always had a girl at the station, hankie in hand.

"Sugar, you goin' to Nam?!"

"Well, just South Carolina first."

"Whoa. Pigs be bad there. Be careful. I got a cousin, she

got a kissin' cousin in my line of work, got *roughed* up real bad in the elevator goin' up to the booking, you know, where no one could see what they do."

La Lique couldn't see Lenny shake his head. "Just come kiss me off to war, La Lique."

God bless the girl forever, she did it. Showed up at the bus stop in church clothes, if you don't count the stilettos. Kissed him, full body, her breasts pushed into him, and the pressure atomized the cinnamon smell of her with just the tiniest undercurrent of jizz, which Lenny could ignore, because let's face it, we are what we are. La Lique waved him off, and even if he never saw her again, he would never forget her. Girl like La Lique (née Jackie) knew that, and they were both better off for the memory.

At Fort Jackson, Lenny got in line with the other enlisted men to get his duffle bag with his fatigues, underwear, and socks. Two pairs of boots—one with white dots on the back and the other without—the boots meant to be switched every other day to break them in evenly. Lenny had never had two new pairs of shoes at the same time. It felt like generosity, Lenny forgetting what he was giving in exchange. An officer came into the room, clipboard in hand, and the man behind the desk saluted. In a ripple effect the new enlisted men followed suit, Lenny included. But the G.I. behind Lenny whose accent hollered Kentucky *holler*, just looked confused.

"Boy," the officer shouted, pointing at his captain bars, "you got any of these?"

"I don't know," Kentucky said. "Let me look in my bag."

Oh, Lenny liked that boy immediately. He was either hilarious or hilariously ignorant, either being likable traits.

That night in the barracks, it could have been the first day of school. Everyone talking at once:

"Where you from?! Why'd you join up?!"

"To get out of the city."

"To get off the farm—fucking cows!"

"To get the G.I. Bill."

"To kill Gooks."

"Gooks?" asked Kentucky, whose name was Whitt—*oh the irony,* thought Lenny."Orientals," enlightened Bob, who was raised on moonshine-laced Kool-Aid.

"To learn a trade"—lots of nodding heads there, as if shooting people was a marketable experience.

"To get away from Karen."

"Susan."

"Darlene."

"She pregnant?"

"Maybe. Got to get out before she says it's mine!"

And yes, "To see the world!" Lots of nodding heads there. Although many of them were unsure of exactly where Vietnam was.

"Didn't it used to be called Siam?"

"No, that's Laos."

"Jesus, who'd want to live in a place called Louse?" asked Whitt.

"Siam is Thailand, you dumb shits!"

Lenny kept quiet through most of this, paying attention, catching names. When Whitt asked him what he did before joining up, Lenny said, "Nothin', I'm nothin' but an orphan." The room quieted.

"You want to know why I joined *this man's army*? I'll tell you why," Lenny continued, looking around the room. He pointed his finger at each man—counted each man silently—lips moving. When he'd finished with the count, he said, "I've been in the Army exactly one day. And I have twenty new friends."

Whitt whistled. "Yes, sir."

"Yes, you do, Brother."

"Amen."

Twelve of those boys would end up part of a long black wall in Washington D.C. Mothers and fathers, sons and daughters they never met, would rub over their engraved names with rice paper and pencil. Eight would come home, seven of them with two feet. None without scars, addictions. Black clouds.

Lenny liked the PX with its cheap 3.2 beer, a holdover compromise with the Prohibition gals from before World War II. He liked the men. But it ended there. What the fuck had he been thinking? It was plantation hot in South Carolina, sugarcane hot, and *Massa* Sargent was relentless; they were his slaves. The heat didn't matter so much until Lenny put 80 pounds on his back. "You think this is hot, you little cunts, wait till you hit the rice paddies! We humping 30 miles today. Load up!"

"I thought we was going to the cotillion today," whispered Whitt to Lenny.

Whitt could shoot; that's one thing a boy in Kentucky learns. It was another thing for Lenny. The only thing he had ever killed was a fish.

"Son, you're going to have to do better than that," said Sargent, watching Lenny miss targets, so appalled he dropped his martinet persona.

"It's not me, it's the gun," said Lenny.

"That's an M1 rifle," said Whitt, leaning over, shooting all of Lenny's marks. *Bull's eye.*

"You might best stick by your buddy," said Sargent. "Although myself, I'd ditch ya."

"Don't worry, Lenny, I got you," Whitt said. "But keep practicing."

And then those boys went to Vietnam and found out that shit was real.

When Lenny remembered it—oh Lord, he doesn't want to remember it—the heat, the dead-set-on-being-green jungle, the feeling that he was breathing more water than air. The villages with thatched roofs, bamboo walls. Only take a Zippo to light the fire. The kids. That one he accidentally shot, because all the gooks are fuckin' small, and the ones that aren't gooks look like gooks. *Because he was on acid.* Oh Lord.

When Lenny remembered it, mostly what he remembered were the sounds. The sucker punch of the grenades, the artillery coming in like the voice of God, the whap-whap of the savior choppers. The library silence when the attack ended, that moment before the birds started back up again, asking each other *You okay? You okay?*—and the soldiers on the ground asking the same thing.

Lenny almost made it a year. But each mission his original friends peeled away from him like paperbark, one, two at a time. Something he tried to make unimportant, like paperbark. He couldn't afford to feel; that would be a bamboo pit to lance his heart upon. So when Bob flew out in an open-sided Huey—one defiant fist up in the air, one foot left in Vietnam, but not in the grave—Lenny just got high and watched a grove of bamboo wave goodbye for him.

Less than two weeks later, Lenny woke up in a hospital in Saigon. His hip and his spirit were fairly mangled and he didn't want to listen to anything either of them had to say. Lenny couldn't even *think* of what he did to Whitt, Whitt who had always looked out for him.

The hospital was overcrowded. Lenny's cot was outside

on the veranda of the single-story yellow building, the covered galley open to a garden of peacock topiary. When he first saw the green-leaf birds, he assumed it was the painkillers taking him for a ride. But there they were. It was impossible for Lenny to imagine a groundskeeper keeping up the peacocks during a war. What an audacious statement! Lenny couldn't decide if it was a declaration of faith in the future, a solace for the wounded and staff, or an administrative oversight—*Why are we still paying the gardener when we don't have enough money for morphine?!*

Well, many things about this war were incongruous.

Past the menagerie, on the far side of the garden, was a single *hopea odorato* tree. The fat trunk of the giant fig had been bound with a rainbow of ribbons by the expat Thai gardener, and Lenny did not know that it was an offering to Nang Ta-khian—the spirit lady of the tree. It reminded him of maypoles and of the yellow ribbons he had heard people were tying around trees back home for those missing in action. *I am missing in action*, Lenny thought, lying on his cot. *We all are.*

If Lenny recalled the day he was shot, all he really felt was heat. The sweat of the gun in his hand, the pulse of the jungle, the bird-twitter of bullets. Humidity without humanity.

Steam coming off guts.

Soldiers, both sides, and admit it—civilians too, children—eaten by flies. The shiny shimmering, moving wings. Heat would always take Lenny back to Vietnam. He came to believe that he was fighting the cruel cold hand of the heartless Heat, more than the Viet Cong. He was fighting the visible breath of the jungle. He never forgave God for unleashing the charred and crimson fury of it all.

Lenny could not think of his friend Whitt Boyer. In the hospital, he took up whittling, trying to copy the topiary. He made a sort of friend with a visiting blue-throated barbet jungle bird, green body feathers losing their camouflage to a riotous red crest. Lenny fed the bird crumbs of *banh mi*, and the bird sang the notes that earned her species the soldiers' nickname of the *Re-Up* bird. But Lenny was having none of that. That bird could sing herself blue; Lenny would never re-up.

The U.S. Army gave Sargent Lenny Henri a Purple Heart, the exact and really rather beautiful shade of his visible scars. All in all, his hip came out fine, but, thank God, the Army said his shooting days were over. There was no one waiting for him in Sarasota. No yellow ribbons. No *Welcome Home* banner stretched between front porch sentry trees, the wind making it wave *hello*. The way he might have imagined it. The Myakka River looked too much like the Mekong. His grandfather had passed. The only souvenirs Lenny brought home from Vietnam were a pack of Ruby Queen cigarettes pilfered from the pocket of a dead Viet Cong, and a cane he carved from teak to use until his hip finished healing. The wood exhaled the scent of black tea when it rained.

Lenny came to believe he had made a bad exchange, joining the Army for friendship. Friendship, Lenny learned, can be blown to bits. By the time he was discharged, Lenny was certain that if the Army did a DNA test on him, he would be 24% lunatic and 38% unraveled. And the Army agreed. Sent him to Walter Reed and kept him in the mental system. Something about his attacking an orderly at the Saigon hospital, and he couldn't even remember it.

After the war, the worst day of the year for Lenny would forever be the Fourth of July. He fought for the essence of that holiday, but the fireworks, the concussion of that bright artillery, buggered his brain. But then it wasn't only the Fourth of July. It was any backfiring engine or backfiring second amendment right. Even now, L.A. was a vortex of trigger points.

Thus it was that Lenny's past led him to become a refugee of the L.A. Central Library, where it was very, very quiet.

Lenny sat in his memories well into the night, thinking about Whitt, trying to answer Simone's question of *why* did he join the Army. Finally he moved to his bed. As dawn peached the sky, his only conclusion was *fucking stupidity*.

On the day of the Kentucky Derby, Lenny and Simone met up in Periodicals. Simone got there first and was reading *Architectural Digest* with a certain amount of envy for a Venetian plastered wall in that green-blue crossover shade of teal. She was wearing a fascinator, feathers bobbing.

"Some poor birdy die on your head on the way over?" Lenny said, coming up beside her. But Simone noticed that he had on a pair of khakis she hadn't seen before and his dark hair was glossy-clean. They made their way to a quiet corner in History and huddled into the transistor Lenny had brought. They decided to stay inside to best hear the tinny radio. Simone produced two not-really-silver, but maybe silver-plated, cups she'd purchased at Goodwill. She filled the cups with iced mint juleps from her plaid thermos, adding a sprig of fresh mint, muddled by her pocket. The radio was just a whisper and they had to lean in close. Lenny could smell the papery books around them, the sharp bourbon, the warmth coming off their bodies. Overall it was a little peaty, but Lenny thought it as fine a May day as he had had in years. Spend a Buck won. *What kind of name is that?*

It wasn't long after the Derby that Simone got Lenny started in on his thousand origami cranes. He didn't do a true *senbazuru* because he didn't string the cranes together. He made them out of paperbacks from the Free to a Good Home bin, mostly tattered bodice-rippers or Jack-the-Rippers with vivid covers. Quietly as he could, he pulled random pages from the books. Then he used snapped crayons pilfered from the bucket in the Children's Department to draw battle scenes over the pages. Lines of olive drab men knee-deep in the shit of war. Explosions of red, yellow, orange so thick, you could run a nail through. Hueys, blades blurring the sky. His buddies. Whole, in pieces. Dead.

He never told anyone that he was the one who had killed Whitt, stupidly shooting his gun with his eyes closed. *I closed my eyes!* He felt stupider than his father, who froze for a bullet in Korea.

Sometimes he just wrote words in rainbow letters on his cranes. *I miss you.* Very simple messages, but really, not so simple. *I'm sorry.* One-by-one he folded the beautiful little cranes, long necks, sharp wings. He left them around the library in groups of two or three, like the *Watchtower* pamphlets. But he put them in high places, behind art installations, inside books, always a little bit hidden. He knew he was acting as loony as the other regulars, but the Japanese legend promises that anyone who folds a thousand origami cranes will be granted a wish by the gods. He didn't believe it, he didn't believe in his God or anybody's god. But why not? Also, sometimes he saw people find the cranes. Usually they just put them in their pocket or left them as they were. People liked the cranes. Once he saw a man unfold a bird; maybe he wanted to learn the creases. When he saw the drawing or words inside, who knows which it was, his face softened as if it were a note from his own mother placed inside his brown bag school lunch, right next to the red apple. Lenny thought, *That can't be a bad thing*, kept on with his project.

On the day that Lenny found Simone in Biography, he had a proposition. Simone felt his energy.

"You switch to double expressos this morning?" she asked, not looking up.

"You drawing pictures of strangers without their permission again?" Lenny could see she was working on the face of an old woman who sat reading nearby.

Simone accepted his deflection. "Yeah, look at her face! It's like a freakin' accordion."

"You, too, will sit in that chair," Lenny warned. Then he gathered his nerve. "What do you say we get out of here today." They had never left the library grounds together.

Simone looked up. "Like go somewhere. Together?"

Lenny felt as if he were Casey at the bat. Strikeout imminent. "Beach?" He kind of chocked the word out. "It's a nice day, not too hot," he added.

"It's always a nice day."

Strike three.

It wasn't really. What Lenny didn't know was that Simone didn't overly care to get that close to a big body of water. "Hey," said Simone, "did you know that in, like, 1928 the St. Francis Dam out past Santa Clarita broke—two-and-a-half minutes before midnight."

Suddenly Lenny was picturing moonlight over collapsing concrete. She had more to say. "A 140-foot flood wave took out the caretaker's family. Wham! Like that. Then it flowed down the canyon, two miles wide, all the way to Ventura! And 400-something people died. Worst U.S. disaster since the San Francisco earthquake." That was the kind of story that stuck with Simone. "Bodies washed into the ocean," she added.

"Well, I wasn't thinking Ventura."

Before Lenny could proffer an alternative beach, Simone admitted, "I'm afraid of water." Lenny's eyebrows peaked, his eyes expanded.

"You look like a meerkat," Simone said.

Lenny ignored her description of his face. "Famed water-colorist Simone Bouchard is afraid of *water*!?"

"Yeah. So, like, newspaper articles that say things like *The child drowned in two inches of water,* or *he was listening to a Giant's game in the bathtub when his wife pushed the radio into the tub* really snag my mind."

Lenny kind of smiled.

"My fears are not unfounded," Simone said.

"Oh, do tell," said Lenny, settling back into his chair. "Misery loves company."

Simone sighed, then told her story. "When I was about five, we were at my Aunt Nina's house. We all still lived in Pasadena then." This was when Simone Bouchard was still Staci Butcher. Staci could easily recall the bare legs of the adults, the women in summer dresses. Her mother in a daisy print, Staci loved the yellow dots in the center of the petals. The adults visited under the lattice shade of the deck holding drinks that bubbled around sunken raspberries, but she couldn't have that drink. She had a plastic glass of lime Kool-Aid, and Staci liked that color too. The only other kid at the party was Staci's teenage cousin, and he wouldn't come out of his room.

"I wasn't allowed alone in the pool; I didn't know how to swim. My dad promised to go in with me, but no one was paying any attention to me."

Her dad. Lenny took note.

Simone continued, "I was walking around the edges of the pool. There was a flamingo innertube and I reached for it, and I fell in." Simple enough words, but Simone relived the memory—the flamingo following the whims of the roving pool filter, the plastic smooth and bobbly. Her little hand stretched, she put pressure on the ring, but it escaped her and then she fell into the deep end. But, oh, what a world! She did not know it existed. Staci ran her hand down the green glass tile, through water that seemed made of sun. The air bubbles of her escaping life were pretty. It was so quiet. Staci thought she could drop to the bottom of the pool and walk to the other side. She knew to hold her breath, but for how long? Just as fear truly set in, her father dove into the pool, suntanned and blurry-limbed, and his familiar arm curved around her. He pulled Staci through a swish of sparkles. Then he had to go back in to find her pink glasses, the plastic frames floating in the water like a sad cartoon of disaster.

It was hard to breathe between the coughs, but when Staci finally got her lungs full, she understood that water only pretends to be your friend. She almost stayed forever in the quiet of a bubble. Her daddy put her glasses back on her wet nose.

"I could have died!" Simone told Lenny. "My dad dove in and saved me, my mom kept saying it was a miracle because no one was looking my way. My dad said he just *felt me missing.* Anyway, I'm just not comfortable at the beach. Have you ever seen photos of Valdez, up in Alaska, after the tidal wave? The houses are open like doll houses and you can see, like, the curling wallpaper and teacups and stuff. Water did that."

"What a wily bitch," Lenny said.

"Yep."

"Okay, so I have another idea," Lenny proffered. "Someplace I've been wanting to go, but honestly, I haven't got up the courage to go yet. Will you come with me? No water involved."

Simone understood Lenny was meeting her fear with one of his. It felt almost a privilege to say, "Sure, let's go!"

Simone got around, Lenny knew that. But for Lenny, his days were mostly spent on his front porch with ventures to the corner store, or to the library. Simone, Ruby and Garnet, Mrs. Ressel, those were really the only people he spoke to. So for

Simone, leaving the library and getting on a blue DASH bus was normal. For Lenny, it was almost Everest.

They headed down Sepulveda Boulevard. As the bus pulled up to their stop, Lenny looked out over the emerald and found himself mentally singing, *Put silver wings on my son's chest*, and he wondered if Vietnam would someday boil down to that stupid green beret song. Well, troubadours and jesters usually have the last word on history.

He thought he was ready for it, but when Lenny walked through the gates of the Los Angeles National Cemetery, he cried and he didn't care. Simone held his hand. He had hoped to settle some of his grief in the cemetery. He was glad the day wore a shroud of clouds, rather than skies of I'm-so-happy blue. As they walked through the rows of stone-cold death, Lenny believed he saw the whispery ghost of every soldier's soul. Resting, heads against their headstones. Sitting on their markers, cleaning their Springfield muskets, their Colts. M1s. The spirits of battles past recognized a brother-in-arms, nodded to him.

What Lenny didn't see, because his heart was tightly inward-wound, was that Simone had retreated too. She was not immune to the cold headstones and the names of young men who died because old men had told them to, moving troops as if they were no more than tiny, brightly colored blocks of wood from a board game of Risk. She left Lenny and armed herself with her ever-ready sketch book and a mechanical pencil with lead the just-right color of bullets.

Lenny watched children with their parents and wished he could talk to the kids about the reality the cemetery was silently broadcasting. But what is death to a child? A debt not yet believed your own. He watched young boys experience the cemetery like Buddhists tumbling through the here and now. Boys will ever love an endless lawn. The palm trees and cedar,

155

the artist-pallet roses—sweet-smelling subliminal affirmations of life—all conspired against Lenny's silent efforts. Add to that the in-your-face grandeur of the monuments and old iron cannons. Men turned statue! The whole thing backfired on Lenny's desire to save these potential future soldiers. Those boys might as well have been singing the *Battle Hymn of the Republic* by the time they left.

Lenny found Simone sitting on a bench, sketchbook in hand. He didn't ask to see her drawings; he was afraid of them. He sat down.

"You doing okay?" Simone asked.

"I'm thinking about my buddy Whitt," Lenny admitted. "We went on R and R together. We had a choice between Bangkok and Sydney. Whitt wanted Sydney." What Lenny didn't tell Simone was Whitt's reason—"*Lenny, you know we'll end up at Khoa San Road and Patpong. You know it. One offer, I don't care what of, I'll be lost. I can't handle it. I'll become one of those little goldfish that the prostitutes shoot out of their pussies into a fishbowl!*" Bob had told them about the goldfish. Lenny had seen worse ways to die, but Whitt was serious. Whitt needed rest more than recreation. Lenny agreed on Sydney.

"We got a car and went up into the Blue Mountains to Collingwood," Lenny continued. "It's a ski resort." How could he explain to Simone that leaving the jungle was like cleaning an infection, the mountain snow a bar of soap? "We rented a room from a family. Nice people—Mrs. Renee—she told us to call her that— made hot chocolate with real milk and bittersweet chips. We ate dinner with them. They had two teenage girls, really just like a few years younger than we were."

"Please tell me you left those girls alone," said Simone.

"Yeah, here's the thing. We pretended they were our sisters, that this was our home. We talked about it at night." Lenny was an orphan, so wanting a family, that was an easy fantasy for him. But it wasn't that. It was the war. The company of men. The Mekong and the River Styx. "Whitt kept offering to do chores. He said it was the best six days of his life."

That night a southern-style humidity rolled over Los Angeles. The ocean exhaled an overwhelming smell of clams and seaweed bubbling in salty water. Lenny pushed through the heat to go to the corner store for ice. The neon sign over the door, *Clyde's*, buzzed like flies as he entered, the heat only slightly relieved by the congested air conditioner. "It's a hot one," said the counter girl, holding a sweating Coke to her narrow chest.

Lenny opened the bag of ice and put a cube down his top. It ran down his torso like a cold heart. "City's on fire, all right," said Lenny leaving the small change in the plastic take-a-penny-leave-a-penny bowl. He headed for home, took an extra antidepressant. The changing pressure gave Lenny a migraine. He knew he could be headed for G.I. déjà vu.

It never rains in L.A., and when it does, it feels like a movie set for a musical. But this was a toss-and-turn night. There was a good deal of fisticuffs between the sky and the ocean, a buildup of bruised clouds. In the morning, the deluge struck. Half the rain evaporated before it hit the ground. But the other half was a slap in the face. When the library opened, the homeless ran in like they were escaping the whacking hands of an irate grandmother. Simone shook out her umbrella and headed toward a reading room.

Librarians know that the homeless tend to wear three layers of clothes, no matter the weather. While Simone made her way, she watched people taking off their first two layers, fingers considering the base layer, but knowing that would break the rules. They laid their clothes out under air-conditioning vents, over chairs. Place smelled like a big wet dog. Saint Bernard. Stoic librarians walked through the building saying

157

things like, *Keep it on the tile, folks. Not on the wood chairs, Esther. Paul, I don't even want to see you going for those pants!* Simone looked for Lenny but never found him that day.

Retreat: *To take all the treat away.*

The night of the storm, Lenny drank near half a bottle of Jack and fell asleep. He felt it was the safest thing to do. During the gale, the ghosts of soldiers-dead in the Los Angeles National Cemetery bloated into something like clear water balloons, wobbling within the collecting water. In the early morning, the small flood receded and the men were left covered in clumpy mud, turned to rough-hewn golems. Luckily for the living, no one saw the sludge-boys ooze their way back to the headstone carved singly for them.

That was Lenny's dream.

He thought he was dead, one of the soldiers hunting his stone. It made him almost laugh to think he had survived the meat grinder, Rottweiler-butcher-dog of Vietnam, only to be killed in a Los Angeles storm. *Los Angeles! Unfair!* But he wasn't dead. There was a bowl of bright oranges next to his bed; Ruby or Garnet must have left them. They had a habit of leaving little things for him. The half-empty bottle of Jack was still there. He wanted there to be a message in the bottle; he wanted to climb in, turn himself into a clipper ship, sail the whiskey seas forever.

He ate an orange.

Left out on the porch, the hoodlum wind had found Lenny's unfinished carving. There was his articulate haiku table, broken into syllables. *Oh well.*

A few days later, Simone found Lenny in the Children's room. "What are you doing here? I've been looking everywhere. You look like a creeper in here."

It was true; the moms had been giving him the stink eye and steering their kiddos away from where he was sitting. Lenny was reading *The Giving Tree,* that tear-jerker about a boy who takes advantage of an apple tree until the apple tree has nothing left but its stump for the kid-turned-old-man to rest on. "Ugh," said Simone, "gag me with a spoon. The apple tree should have smacked the kid in the face with a branch and told him to get a job."

"Gag me with a spoon?! Good thing you don't aspire to writing."

"I didn't make it up. Let's go. I got baloney and mayo. Do you know how hard it is to get baloney in L.A.?"

"They sell it at my corner store."

"Yeah, well, I'm not going to East L.A. My neighborhood is marginal enough." Lenny didn't actually know where Simone lived, but he knew she got "the family discount"—as in ridiculously low—because her Pasadena aunt owned the small apartment complex "of dubious reputation."

They went out to the fountains and Simone laid out her plaid blanket. It could probably use a washing. Lenny thought the sandwich was delicious, childhood incarnate, but he said, "What, no mircogreens?"

Simone elbowed him. Perhaps because Lenny had shared the cemetery with Simone, he felt able to ask her more about her phobia. "Was it just the swimming pool event?"

Simone knew exactly what he was asking. "Yeah, really just that one thing. But here's what I figured out, Lenny." She paused. Licked her always slightly chapped lips. Twirled her fingers through her bright hair with the paintbrush-black tips. "I didn't see my dad much after that. If I hold on to my fear of water, I hold on to my strongest, best memory of my dad. If I forget that fear, I'm afraid I might also forget the rescue. That proof of love."

"Whoa," said Lenny. "I've been to years of counseling and I don't know if I've ever figured out anything as good as that."

"Thanks!" Simone tossed her head. Picked up her sandwich. "Plus I followed glue-sniffing Kurt out on thin ice at Sawmill Pond and we broke through and I went under the ice. So there's that."

"Under ice!" said Lenny. "Scary."

"Yep. We were sixteen. I of all people should have known not to walk on an ice-covered pond unless there's a sign—*Ice skates to rent*—and a hot chocolate stand. But we were high on Maui Wowie, invincible, and Kurt's dogs where already on the island, so obviously the ice was thick, yes?"

Lenny laughed. Simone shrugged it off, although it was an awful memory. A memory from when she was still Staci.

When Staci broke through the ice, she wished for her dad something hard. But her dad was gone, skipping stones across the water, sunk. The ice didn't crack, didn't give fair warning. It just fell from under them in a circle the rough size of their bodies.

They went under. Staci's wool pea coat was like the stones in Virginia Wolfe's pockets, heavy like that. Staci felt no wonder, the way she did when she was a child in the glass-tiled pool, although her eyes did register the sun through the gold-green water, the algae motes suspended in the filtered light. Old tree trunks from the logging days below her looked carved from jade. She saw that beauty, but fear was what she felt. She pushed for the surface and took her suicide coat off at the same time. Her hands skated on the wrong side of the ice, but her head bobbed clear, so did Kurt's. They pulled themselves out, bellies on the ice like seals, but then the ice just broke again. Simone felt a cold panic but Kurt said, "We just have break our way back." They did it side by side, and they weren't so far from shore. Within moments Staci knew they weren't really in danger of drowning, but she couldn't help it, she screamed each time the ice collapsed.

Truly, there is water, water everywhere. In winter, Staci ran bare fingers over the stalactite icicles that turned their house fairytale. She tried to paint that nothing shade of white on white on blue. When a long-dead sugar pine was felled by the sheer weight of caught snow, Staci understood that water has its shifty ways. And for all that her mother tried to be, Staci would always miss her blurry, silent, slow-motion-savior father. Vivi convinced herself that Staci didn't miss having her dad, or because Vivi was not certain of Staci's memories, then having *a* dad. Vivi was wrong.

But Simone didn't want to think about her dad. She pulled herself back to Lenny. "I have an idea. Come with me." She packed up and led Lenny away from the library grounds.

Imagine that. Two outings in less than a week!

Simone took Lenny to the Museum of Jurassic Technology on Venice Boulevard. The outside looked like a deli shop. "This place is really just a *cabinet of curiosities*; they don't even claim the stuff is authentic," Simone said.

Inside, it was the sideshow at the night carnival. Lenny could have almost traded out the L.A. Central Library for the dark, Victorian-red-velvet-feeling space. At least for a while. He saw two taxidermied mice laid out on toast! Decaying dice titled Bad Luck. *Story of my life*. But Simone wouldn't let him stumble his way through. She took him to the portraits of the Soviet Space Dogs. There were five of them, but it was Laika that Simone wanted Lenny to see.

"Laika was the first one," Simone said, pointing to the Siberian husky and terrier mix. Laika's doggie face and elegant neck were backed by a wash of colors that rivaled Lake Tahoe reflecting a pink-sky sunset. Lenny knew Simone loved that deep-water look. "Laika died of overheating while in orbit," she said, then was quiet for a moment. "She was just a stray they picked up off the streets of Moscow."

"Aren't we all, from time to time?" Lenny said.

Simone looked at him. He got it; of course he got it. What it feels like to have Fate take advantage of you. "Laika, Zvezdochka, Belka, Strelka, and Ugolyok." She named each portrait. Lenny took a finished crane out of his pocket and tucked it behind an exhibition on the way out.

They went for ice cream, just like friends, sat on wrought iron chairs, the kind with friendly hearts scrolled across the back.

Lenny was almost surprised to realize he had spent another year in Los Angeles. He had lived it mostly in books, and in a mausoleum for books. If he shook his head, a dandruff of letters would escape his uncivilized hair. He couldn't envision change. But change doesn't require our participation.

April 29, 1986. The fire started in the fiction shelves. Did Fahrenheit 451 spontaneously combust? Or did that little twit Harry Peek, who said he did it and then recanted, eventually getting $35,000 out of the city for wrongful arrest, light a single match and turn 400,000 books to soot and ruin?

Simone heard the fire alarm; everybody did. The assumption was: another false alarm. That old building liked to hear its own voice now and then just to know it was still alive. She took her time collecting herself, her art supplies. She never saw the fire, but when she crossed the fiction department, a tiny current of smoke, just a wisp that smelled of the color gray, traveled over her shoulder and said *Get Out! This place is goin' Alexandria!*

For seven-and-a-half hours that fire burned, the largest library fire in the history of the United States, then and since.

Simone stood outside with all the others and watched the firemen go in shifts into the huge concrete building, come back out black as coal miners. Ashes of books drifted over. Simone held out her hands, wondered what story, sonnet or smut, was crumbling in her hold. She rubbed the soot into the lines of her palms, took the tales with her. She felt as if Lenny's house was burning down; it was.

And what of the inside of the library? Only the firemen saw the immediate destruction, heard the shelves collapse, felled knights in heavy armor giving up the crusade. The deep echo sounds. Hordes of fire, pitchfork peasants storming the castle. The firefighters alone witnessed the loss of history. And only one, Owen, he was just a kid really, saw two tiny cranes take flight when a shelf fell, the farthest crane's tail alight like the Firebird. The front crane kept its course, and Owen reached up and caught the delicate paper. (It wasn't until Owen was nearly seventy that he happened to unfold the memento and find the single red-colored word: *Live*, which made him decide to go for the chemo.)

The library staff managed to save an astounding 700,000 books. To keep them from molding in firehose water, they were shrink-wrapped and frozen within forty-eight hours. They would stay in that quiet state for six years, little Snow Whites, until the Los Angeles Central Library finally reopened.

Simone spent almost a week after the fire prowling the outskirts of the police barriers around the perimeter of the library, looking for Lenny. They had never exchanged addresses—why would they when the library offered such spacious living rooms? Lenny didn't have a phone so she had never given him her number. And she had gone L.A. on him and given him her made-up artist's name, Simone Bouchard—so much more *Marilyn Monroe*–sounding than Staci Butcher—

like that mattered. No one was hurt in the fire; that much she knew.

Simone never found Lenny. What she found was her desire to find him.

All those charred and fading words, the little literary deaths. A gloom of smoke marked the pyre, but L.A. can't abide a dark cloud. A pacific air came in at night and swept the sky blue. *There. Move on, you mortal fools!*

Simone sat out on the tiny Juliette balcony attached to her apartment. Bougainvillea petals offered a softhearted fringe for her view, but Simone's focus was interior. Lenny was lost to her. His kindness. Cuckoo-for-Cocoa-Puffs Lenny and the cheese balls he likes to make, rolling slices of limp American between his palms. The balls came out a little dirt-scuffed and somehow endearing. *How can I find him?*

The day of the Los Angeles Central Library fire, Lenny was in bed with a late-season influenza, or food poisoning from the Bueno Burritos food truck. He didn't even know about the fire until three days later, when thanks either to the ministrations of Ruby ("Oh, son, you got the flu-bug bad! I'm a-goin' make you some chicken bone soup.") or perhaps just the passage of three days' time, Lenny revived. From his sick bed, he had heard Ruby and Garnet's voices through the retrofitted wall put up between their two apartments when the house was segmented. But then again, the sisters were both hard of hearing and tended to shout, so it might not have been completely the fault of cheap construction.

"I think he might actually pass, Garnet," prophesized Ruby. "He's dog sick and he won't go to the hospital. Says he'd rather die at home."

"Oooh, honey. Don't talk like that. Where there's life, there's hope," Garnet encouraged.

"Yeah, Mama always said that," remembered Ruby.

Then there was a pause in the conversation before Lenny heard Garnet conclude, "Whatta we wear to the funeral? We still got them hats with the felt violets?"

When Lenny finally made it back to the library, over a full week had past. The building told its own story. The windows on both sides of the Flower Street entrance had been blown out by the fire. The white cement walls were scorched, marred by two sooty exit columns, the dark markings narrow by the broken windows, fanning up and out. To Lenny, the marks looked like sinister wings—a nightmare-phoenix perched atop the main portico. *All hope abandon ye who enter here.*

Bits of ash still floated in the air, along with the singular pasty scent of wet books. Lenny felt gut-punched and he had to sit down because he was still weak, and it was something sad to think about all those lost words. Turns out, even something as strong as a library was frail. Even the gigantic, red neon *Jesus Saves* sign on the Biola University building that towered beside the library like a guardian angel couldn't save the beautiful words. Lenny took it personally. Well, so did the librarians, and a lot of other shuffle-footed people too.

And where was Simone? How was he going to find her? He didn't know her address. He didn't even know her real name. Lenny was tired of losing friends. *Goddamnit.* It's why he didn't want any, because here he was again, no goodbye. To Lenny, the Los Angeles Central Library looked a lot like another body bag.

After the fire, Lenny took stock, wondered, *Should I stay?* He acknowledged that he liked L.A. But it seemed so much was gone—the library and Simone. Even the kid at the corner store had given up the cashier life. Over the course of evenings (and a bottle of what should have been labeled as potato moonshine), he wondered if he should try to get a job; God knows he could use the money. Time to get a haircut and buy some clothes that don't come out of a bin. Maybe he felt ready for life louder than a library whisper.

Lenny took to hanging out on the Santa Monica Pier. Not by the Ferris wheel and the arcades, although he appreciated the kids' voices like kites in the air. He went Otis Redding and sat out on the far dock with the quiet fishermen and watched them bring in mackerel and pearly-white sea bass. He listened to the ocean, and to the seagulls, who would risk it all for a snippet, staring down a human, so sure were those birds of their place in this world.

He spent some time thinking about jumping off the dock.

Fishing was a sinew from Larry's Sarasota boyhood; no thought required. It was cooler on the dock and he felt safer, closer to the skills of his youth than those the Army taught him. Less involved with people. Finally, Lenny went and bought himself a used pole and spent the majority of his time fishing and picking out sea shanties on an old guitar while he waited for the line to bobble. He wasn't so good with the guitar, but the pole was his wingman.

If Lenny caught sea bass, Miriam at Bueno Burrito would buy it. Ruby and Garnet took the mackerel, drenched the fish in olive oil and garlic, and sopped the whole thing up with French bread. The house smelled like Sicily. The days ran together, chronicled more by the quality of light than by the squares on a calendar.

During this time, Lenny came to see that the ocean and a librarian are both authoritarians—they set clear boundaries. But he was beginning to believe that perhaps he no longer needed those stanchions. Over these quiet days, it came to him that Simone's real last name was Butcher. "What kind of a fucked-up name is that? Ugh," she had said. He knew if he called USC, they would never give him information. Finally Lenny got the idea to call around to the other libraries and try and find Mrs. Ressel. He felt certain that the librarians had been rehoused, had new collections to boss around. Sure enough, Mrs. Ressel was at Beverly Hills. *Hoity-toity. They probably don't have a paperback bin there.* He got her on the phone.

"Oh, Lenny! You doing okay? You keeping up with the reading?"

"Yep, I'm on *Born on the Fourth of July.*"

"Well, that might not be your best choice!" It wasn't. The main character accidentally kills his buddy.

"Listen, do you remember Simone?" Of course Mrs. Ressel remembered the young woman who always had colored pencils sticking out of her twisted-up hair like bright ideas were rainbowing out of her head. She knew her real name too, had checked her out many times. She knew Lenny and Simone were friends.

"I'm trying to find her," Lenny said. "I know her last name is Butcher, but I don't know her real first name. Could you look her up?"

"Lenny, you know it's illegal to give out personal information."

"Yeah, but you're a rebel at heart, Mrs. R."

Lenny got the goods: Staci Butcher, Juliette Arms on West 39th, No. 18.

"She'll be happy to hear from you, Lenny."

She'll be happy. Imagine if that could be true.

He and Simone were friends, Lenny was sure of it, even though he was almost old enough to be her father. He thought back on the day they had huddled in the library and listened to the Kentucky Derby on a tinny radio. The way her face assembled each time they met. He was being silly. But a part of him was afraid that she would think he was a dirty-bum stalker, showing up at her door. Could be she just pitied him. Lenny knew that Simone had been a sojourner at the library while he was a full-time tenant. Since Vietnam, really even before, Lenny was used to people relegating him to the untouchable caste, turning away. Sooner or later.

Well, time to find out.

Lenny found Simone's place—The Juliette Arms. The two-story building's whole demeanor said faded belle, what with the balconies and vines. There were blackout curtains two-to-one over print or lace, and half of the vines were dead, looking as if the veins of the building had gone varicose. But it had brick bones. And a flock of red-masked hobo parakeets were perched in a mimosa tree, chatting like it was tea time.

Lenny knocked on No. 18. The door opened. Then things happened fast.

It is said love begins as lust, an E-ticket ride of inhaled pheromones plunging through two bodies. Lenny's first thought was, *Who is this beautiful hippie chick!?*

Simone pushed past the woman in the long patchwork skirt and the brunette braid-of-plenty. "Lenny!!" Simone yelled, and hugged him like he didn't stink, as if there wasn't a pretty good chance he would stink. But that was just self-doubt trying to come out of his pores. The truth was, Lenny was clean as a new razor, sharp in his new pants and navy sweater. Nutmeg and cedar in his aftershave instead of eucalyptus leaves in his pocket.

"This is my mom, Vivi," she said, stepping back to include her mother.

Lenny felt like a carnival prize standing there—hard to judge if he was worth the effort. But Vivi smiled. She'd heard all about Lenny, the Vietnam vet with PTSD and a sense of the absurd. "I hear you cheat at Scrabble," Vivi said.

Lenny knew it wasn't right to think it, but for a glimmer of a moment, he imagined that making love to Vivi would be like making love to a sunset. Or a mai tai. Just good like that.

"My mom's moving down from Tahoe!" Simone said, bringing him into the living room, and Vivi handed him a glass of freshly squeezed California orange juice at the same time.

"Imagine being able to push oranges out of nothing more than wood branches," said Vivi. "What a thing, nature."

Lenny couldn't agree more.

It was at a family dinner a few weeks later (and not the first one—Vivi loved to cook) that Lenny met Simone's Aunt Nina. Over lavender Earl Grey tea, Nina told Lenny the Juliette Arms was in solid need of a super. The wage wasn't that much, but a furnished apartment free of rent came with the job! Any work that the super couldn't do himself could be contracted out. Did Lenny know anyone who might be interested in the position?

All three women looked at Lenny with big eyes.

Lenny boxed up his clothes, his records and books, told Ruby and Garnet they could keep whatever they wanted of the furniture and household goods he left behind, and then he would schedule Goodwill to take the rest. He would invite them over for dinner as soon as he was set up.

The sisters found going through Lenny's stuff more fun than jigsaw puzzles, but still the same—assembling something understandable out of separate pieces.

"Look, here's his Purple Heart," said Ruby, finding the medal discarded in the back of the sock drawer with a few holey mismatched and a crushed box of "Oriental" cigarettes.

"Well, I'll be damned," said Garnet.

But then war is damned.
"Didn't know he had the Purple."
Ruby put on her reading glasses and looked closely at the medal; Lenny had drawn a Frito Bandito mustache on Washington's profile with a Sharpie.

The following spring, when the cherry blossoms made all their frivolous promises of youth, Staci (for Simone had reclaimed her birth name), Vivi, and Lenny took a trip to Washington D.C. To Lenny, who did not yet know he was a little bit near-sighted, the many petals looked like cotton candy, a lovely blur of pink. They went to see the long, soot-black Wall. Lenny seared his fingers over the names of his dead, talked for a long time to the stoned-faced Whitt. Then he headed over to the Korean Memorial to salute his father, Reggie. Cried again. A cheeky wind blew through the cherry blossoms, and the petals danced *Swan Lake*.

Farther down the Wall, Staci did a charcoal rubbing on rice paper over the name *James T. Butcher*. Vivi left a fading photo of the new parents holding their baby girl—Staci in a pink hoodie. Bunny ears. Staci never really got to know her father, until Lenny. Lenny, who made Vivi understand that Staci wanted to hear about her dad. Lenny, who taught Staci something about the men who fought and died, or fought and lived in *Kháng chiến chống Mỹ*—the Resistance War Against America.

Seven years later, the Los Angeles Central Library reopened, and Mrs. Ressel returned to her post. Over the course of the next few years, there came to be *the legend of the cranes*. People, mostly children, would sometimes find one of Lenny's unfinished *senbazuru* caged within the library. The children were not surprised in the least to find such a wonderous thing, and they would look for them as they would a four-leaf clover.

Mrs. Ressel knew who the artist was; of course she did. From time to time, she hunted the cranes herself, finding seven in all. These are now housed in a small display case, two cranes folded tight and perfect in their lines. One tells the story of the fire, the edges charred and scalloped, the face missing from the elegant neck. Four of the cranes are opened up, so that the war story is revealed in all its elemental, crayoned horror. The battle within.

Picture the friends now. Table set up by the mimosa tree on the lawn of the Juliette Arms. Garnet and Ruby in their felt hats, violets a-wobble. Simone in her Sex Pistols tee—*God Save the Queen*. Vivi in a white caftan moving over her body like a cloud in the sky. Lenny into his cups. Simone is passing out cereal bowls of lemon ice, the first and only sour thing to touch the friends on this July day in the City of Angels.

Greater Roadrunner

The Mojave Desert is the smallest and the driest of the four North American Deserts. It is a place for the marvelous and the oddball. There is the Wee Thump Forest of ancient Joshua trees, limbs outstretched, guiding the traveler Onward. Brown bats with their transparent wings, and the tiny desert night lizard whose babies look like toothpicks. The ghost flower, and bees that sleep—sometimes side by side—inside the petals of the orange globe mallow cactus bloom. There is jasper, chalcedony, and agate. Geodes that hold crystal universes inside plain brown packaging—an adapt metaphor for any desert.

The name Las Vegas is Spanish for The Meadows. There aren't any left. Las Vegas is a mirage—there's no water there. It's the elusive pot of gold at the end of a neon rainbow. The city grew out of the workforce that built Boulder Dam. Vegas was the dam's first customer.

One hundred and fifty miles northwest of Las Vegas, the desert hits its low point. Death Valley looks the lonely place. There's a reason the word desert is synonymous with abandonment. Most who walk through Death Valley take the name as fair warning. Who would live in the wooly dust, drink from that heavy water? Dare to call the red hematite and green chlorite streaks worth the trek through every shade of brown? Cough to find lungs flurried with chalk-white borax crystals. But some call it beauty. Some prefer to be alone. The Mojave may be boney, but there's a billion stars ablinkin'. A silk ribbon wind. When the rains come the flowers follow, tissue paper petals in baby doll colors. There are road runners, that joke of a bird, and stones that sail—don't think it isn't so. The ocean went away and left the desert. The desert doesn't care. Better to blow in the wind than hoist a sea.

THE SAINTS OF DEATH VALLEY

FRANCINE AND GRACE
California

There was a little-noticed annex of the Carmelite Chapel and Monastery of St. Giles of San Francisco located on Russian Hill. A lavender house—not an unusual shade for San Francisco—with a rather large garden hedged by bridal-bouquet hydrangeas and shaded by enormous Chinese yulan magnolia trees. It was there that five nuns cloistered in comfort and toil, led by Sister Francine. The Second Vatican Council ended the mandatory wearing of habits, so most days, the sisters were a casual bunch. They tended an apiary in their backyard, so prolific the whole house sounded like a radio between frequencies. The nun's small-batch bee products—soaps, candles, and honey pots—carried a label with Jesus's face haloed by bees—which, let's face it, is a kind of crown of thorns.

The favorite night of the week at the annex was *Dynasty* Night, in which the sisters would watch TV and drink tumblers of Chivas. So it was with some irritation that on a March evening in 1985, Francine left the front room because she could swear she heard a baby crying. On the mahogany turnstile, that small delivery space between the outside world and the cloister, was indeed a baby. Talk about a delivery.

The child was wrapped in soft white and there was a rose velvet bag holding what would turn out to be holy cards beside the bunting. Francine brought the baby into the house, and to the sisters, the child was a tiny miracle.

Francine went out into the garden to consider the situation. No need to turn on the string lights; the moon obliged. The magnolias were in bloom, full and open, and Francine's little inside joke was to think of them as Mary on the half shell; they looked like blessings. Francine tried to let the garden calm her, redid her little ponytail, running her hands through her short blond hair just to subconsciously massage her thoughts. But there was a pandemonium of the chatty cherry-headed wild parrots of Telegraph Hill perched in the magnolias; Francine could hardly think. She resolved there was nothing she could do; she would call the Diocese in the morning.

Inside the house, after a bit more Chivas and some pretty bad name calling, the sisters had decided to call the baby girl Grace Catherine. Of course, Grace should have been turned over to the authorities, but Francine let one day turn to two, turn to bubbles and bottles, and oh, the Carmelites just loved that baby. She had red hair! And her cheeks turned to cherries when she cried. Her ears stuck out just an adorable little bit. Freckles were her destiny; it was written all over her brown-eyed face. They couldn't let her go. Even Francine, or perhaps especially Francine, couldn't let her go.

Grace was, well, a graceful child. She lacked for nothing because she knew only of her quiet life. She had Bible lessons on a felt board, Noah's Ark, and a pillar of salt. Salt! She had chores, and there were errands to run, parks to play in. She had a school desk; she could count to 100. She had three dolls, but what she liked most was her rose velvet bag of holy cards. She especially loved the cards with the gold accents edging the clouds, highlighting the wounds. Grace did not have words or concepts to understand the cards, but she could perceive that there was grace in suffering. She thought of them as friends.

The sisters managed to keep Grace Catherine for five years.

When Father Ward made a surprise visit to sample some of their autumn honey beer, the nuns were busted. He shouted that they would be excommunicated and defrocked, which made them feel something like plucked chickens. Father Ward took Grace home with him until he could figure out what to do with her. The annex was not technically his responsibility, but he was the one who collected the bee products and had the most interaction with the house. Therefore, the one who *should* have seen Grace.

The only thing Grace had left of her Carmelites was her rose velvet bag filled with holy cards, pushed into her hand by Francine when Grace kissed all the nuns goodbye. She thought she was going to the dentist (she had been before) and had no sense of foreboding following Father Ward into his little Honda, although he didn't smell quite right.

Soon-to-be-ex-Sister Francine was nothing if not determined. The next day Francine paid Father Ward a visit. Grace was not present in the room. "Roger," Francine began, rudely using his first name, "how do you think it's going to go when I give an exclusive to the *Chronicle* about Grace—what took the Church five years to find the *poor* child? Just *who* is the mother? Better yet, who's the father? And I might suggest they do a little investigating into your use of the honey funds. . ." She went full *Dynasty* on him.

Roger gave a world-weary sigh. *Women!* Monks were so much easier. "Francine, what is it you want?"

"I want Grace. I want her now."

Roger sighed again, but got up out of his seat. Francine knew she had him. It was the easiest way out for him.

"And child support for two years so I can go back to school and get a nursing certificate."

Roger knew the Church was getting off easy. And it was no doubt a good choice for the child. Better than foster care. *Better than a scandal.*

When Grace joined them, she ran to Francine. Francine with her short dandelion hair and dark eyebrows that could talk for themselves. Grace knew those hazel eyes, that face, those arms that enclosed her, and the smell of lavender honey creamed into her skin.

A For Sale sign violated the front lawn of the lavender house. It sold to a gay couple who planned to turn the ground floor into a yoga studio and juice bar called The Downward Dog. The apiary had already been moved, but you better believe there were stings involved, and that honey never tasted as good again, never tasted of Chinese magnolias.

GEORGE AND PAULA
Death Valley

George and Paula Carroll were not natives to Death Valley, and it could be said they had no business being there. George grew up in the Salinas Valley on a walnut farm. It was a hand-carved childhood. Church on Sunday, white shirt and a black tie. A stern belief in God. But George certainly didn't listen when his father tried to tell his son that life need be no more than family, land to tend, and a clear view ahead. George heard that in the glitter gulch of Las Vegas, girls danced on tables in the casinos—in bikinis and cowboy boots! For George, it was the University of Nevada, Las Vegas, or Bust.

It didn't take all that long for George to come to agree with his dad. He ended his first semester on academic probation, generally hungover and broke, having spent his money one dollar at a time pushing bills against the skin of women who held themselves a millimeter and a hundred miles away.

George cashed in his chips and went back to the pay dirt of his soul. He earned a degree in Urban Horticulture and Water Conservation, Class of 1986, and fell in love with palm trees—those garden-variety showgirls. He spent his days in the contrived groves and gardens of a city that shouldn't even exist.

George's one-day-to-be-wife Paula was rocked in a different cradle.

Paula grew up in Salt Lake City under the gaze of the all-seeing granite eye of God carved into the architecture of the Mormon Temple. When she was little, Paula thought one of God's forms was cyclops. Symbolism is often lost on children. At the loftiest point of the temple, the gold-leafed angel Moroni blows his trumpet, Paula came to understand, for all the white people. When Paula learned that her best friend June couldn't get into the highest level of heaven no matter how many times she knelt to pray, clean white socks gleaming against her skinny dark legs, Paula felt the beginnings of the slow burn of repression. A kind of indigestion of the soul. On top of that, in 1978, she understood the apostle LeGrand Richards to say the promise of white skin in death through righteousness in life applied only to Native Americans, and not to Black people, not to June. Outrageous!

At only twelve years old, Paula told her mother that since June couldn't be with her in heaven, she didn't want to be a Mormon. Paula's mother, who was making banana bread at the time, beat her head with the wooden spoon, batter flying as if it were the spittle of God. She did not wish to discuss theology with her daughter.

As soon as Paula graduated high school, her mission was escape. It took a year of coffee shop tips before she could leave the goodbye note with excellent penmanship on the kitchen table. In 1986, Paula made her exodus from Salt Lake City to Las Vegas. *City of Saints* to *Sin City*. She wanted a boomtown that practically renounced religion. Plus the bus fare was cheap.

Paula took in the showgirls with their feather headpieces and slabby makeup. Every billboard either an enticement to excess, or a clean-up-the-mess attorney. The paper bag 6:00 a.m. drunks and the night marauders. Liberace. The truth is Salt Lake (or any city) really is no more moral than Las Vegas—Vegas just likes to talk. *Hey, girl, guess what I did last night?!* Paula might have been the only person ever to find Las Vegas uniquely honest. It's a town that sells its indulgences right on the street corners, sometimes on a sandwich board.

Paula trained as an EMT and that's how she met her husband. George fell out of a palm tree, broke his wrist, and suffered a concussion. He thought Paula was a nurse; of course he did. He'd never even heard of an emergency medical technician, and all doctors were imagined as men, the way all dogs were male and all cats were female when he was seven. Plus, he was in considerable pain, and not just in his wrist. It was a long fall, and the concussion caused his skittered thinking. The way the dark-haired nurse held his good hand on the ride to Sunrise Hospital seemed personal. He began to think she was leaning over him, exposing the edge of her white lace bra, just visible in her V-neck uniform, purposely. Best to pass out now, because there was a part of him that was fully aware that his thoughts were most likely inappropriate. He closed his eyes. But Paula needed him to stay awake. She placed her palm on his chest and his heart responded.

When George left the hospital, his arm in a cast, he was right-minded, albeit a little high on painkillers. He never expected to see the ambulance nurse again. But there she was! By the emergency room exit, exhaling from a cigarette; God, she looked good in smoke! He liked her little body, her short dark hair, curls akimbo. He went over to thank her. But mostly to get her number.

Paula looked him up and down. He was handsome in a *Hi-Yo, Silver!* outdoorsy way; he would never look comfortable on a couch. She had noticed the lines of him while he was laid out on the gurney, his water-blue eyes, sun-shot brown hair. Wide shoulders.

"What were you doing up in a palm tree?" she asked. Because really, she had to assume he was crazy.

"It's my job. I'm a freelance arborist. I take care of about half the palms in Vegas."

Paula held out her hand, wrist up. "What do you think of mine ... ?"

Paula and George were married in the Chapel of the Flowers on the Las Vegas Strip. Paula wore a vintage mini dress made entirely of crocheted she-loves-me daisies, and glossy patent leather Mary Janes. Creamy stockings. George wore a rented suit of midnight blue stamped with gold fleur-de-lis. They went to see the 1940s crooner Sonny King at the Bootlegger, and ate salt-crusted oysters that looked like miniature tide pools, drank champagne. The newlyweds were just so beautiful that night.

George had reserved a room at the Mirage and there was no need for candles; the strobe of the Strip pulsed right through the windows—the Nevada aurora borealis. Paula went into the bathroom and emerged only in her Mary Janes with their prim two-inch stacked heels. She was not a stiletto type of girl. Her hair was a backlit dark halo of curls. George thought her breasts looked the fruit of the *Phoenix dactylifera*—sweet little fleshy Halawi palm dates. Lucky for him he kept his fantasy image to himself. But Paula *was* a phoenix; he was right about that. She did burn that bed to ash and rise up and do it again, all with her Mary Janes still on, those shoes reflecting the neon lights of the city as if they were expressing little passions of their own.

Not long after they got married, Paula decided she was tired of old people and addicts—the most common ambulance pickups. Really, they both just broke her heart. She needed something a little sweeter so she enrolled at the Dreaming of Pastry culinary school to learn about things with French names and cream. Opera cake and madeleines. She didn't graduate first in her class—*Everybody knows that c-word Megan is giving Chef Maurice buttercream hand jobs in the walk-in pantry*—but Paula did win *la competition pour petit fours* because no one could dare deny the glory of her marzipan.

As a graduation present, George and Paula piled into their used Country Squire and pointed the avocado-green wagon north, keeping the destination a surprise for the graduate.

Paula closed her eyes. She assumed that when she woke up, they still would be crossing the desolate wild. Her body felt the wagon roll to a stop, heard the tiny pings of the cooling engine. She opened her eyes to the surprise of an oasis. An oasis! For a moment she thought they were still in Las Vegas at one of the casino gardens, but there was no adjoining neon city. She looked up at a hotel—the Inn at Furnace Creek—cool stone, windows set in sage-colored frames. A red tile roof. The inn was at the top of a hill, and below it spilled the oasis.

They got out of the car and walked through the maze

of palm. "Deglet Noor," George said, "Mexican Fan, there's a pomegranate tree!" Paula didn't need names—she knew beauty was a feeling. But she didn't know the history:

The Tonopah and Tidewater Railroad was built through the Badwater Basin, laying tracks in 1907 through the lowest elevation in North America to deliver red-and-white boxes of borax to a grocery store near you. Then came the luxury hotel built on Timbisha Shoshone grounds to augment the train business with tourism. Always there will be those who attempt the alchemy of dust to gold. Try to turn the desert green. It wasn't particularly good for the Timbisha, their only compensation the ability to sell their baskets in the gift shop.

Travertine Springs poured endless, earth-warmed water first into the swimming pool at the inn, then through the oasis garden. Happy-go-lucky rills silvered over falls, careened the fat palm trunks, slid into green ponds. Then the stream slipped on out to the mundane chore of watering the golf course. Paths crisscrossed the oasis, up steps, over narrow granite bridges. Benches announced the best views, suggested no action at all. George and Paula turned their eyes to the serrated Panamint Range—yes they were purple, yes they were majestic—bordering the far horizon.

"So, this is a little piece of paradise," said Paula, exhaling the grit of Las Vegas, feeling like they hit the jackpot. They sat on a bench and Paula watched the way the desert sun singled out the gold in George's brown hair. She understood for the first time why some people choose the desert. A cactus wren flew by. If they had waited long enough, they would have seen desert cottontail, kit fox, the stealthy coyote come the night.

They couldn't afford to stay at the Inn at Furnace Creek; they had reservations at the far less ambitious Ranch. But they could afford lunch in the fancy restaurant overlooking the grounds. Dessert was New York cheesecake and it tasted like it had walked all the way from Lindy's on its own two feet. "Sweet Jesus," said George, putting down his fork. "You could do better than this."

"I think I will," said Paula, who got up from her seat and asked for the chef. She thought maybe because she was short and nonthreatening, or because she had a sort of sugar-glaze about her, she made it back into the kitchen. But that wasn't the reason why. It was simply that Paula's timing was good. The last pastry chef had recently left in a cloud of suspicion over a missing order of saffron—the stuff costs more per ounce than gold. Meanwhile, all the desserts were arriving twice a week and a day old from a bakery in Las Vegas.

While Paula disappeared into the kitchen, George wandered the oasis, mentally naming plants and looking for bugs and rot, turning over new leaves. When he made it back to the restaurant, he found his wife in a white apron licking a spoonful of pink fondant while the kitchen manager spelled out PAULA, HEAD PASTRY CHEF with his Bakelite labeling gun.

"We're moving," Paula said, and George turned his eyes from his lucky-charm wife to the manager.

"May I speak to the head of grounds?"

FRANCINE AND GRACE

Francine adopted Grace (*that* took a bit of paperwork), now that she was no longer a nun, which she knew she never should have been in the first place. She rented a craftsman bungalow in Berkeley and registered Grace at Sacred Heart Catholic School. As Grace got older, it became a sort of joke between mother and daughter for Grace to introduce her friends to "my mom, Sister Francine."

At Sacred Heart, Grace went to Mass five days a week before class started, plus of course on Sundays. By the time she was ten, Grace and her best friend, Sharon, walked to Sacred Heart together. On foggy autumn mornings, the girls pretended the cloudy shroud was the Holy Ghost. Winter was rain under a shared dour umbrella. In spring, the blooming ornamental plum trees reminded Grace of the plastic flowered swim caps sold at Newburry's Five & Dime. Summer was hydrangeas, put a rusty nail in the dirt, the blooms will turn from pink to blue like a sleight of hand.

Graced loved going to church, had an esteem for the taste of Communion. It didn't taste like the body of Christ, which she imagined to be salted by His sweat and the spray of Galilee. To Grace, it tasted like His clothes, a circle of cloth. She pictured nuns in white wimples weaving the cloth on a loom while singing *Dominique, nique, nique.* Grace held the host in the top of her mouth for as long as possible to feel it melt like the rice paper around Chinese candy. One Sunday, Grace touched it with her finger and Sharon made her walk home with her fingers in front of her until Grace washed her hands. Twice. Grace wondered, but did not ask, *Why can't I touch the body of Christ?*

Grace believed that Francine, always awake by dawn—old habits die hard—attended early mass on Sundays, allowing Grace to sleep in and go later with Sharon. But what Francine was doing was communing with pinwheels of French crullers and black coffee while reading the *San Francisco Chronicle* at Dunkin' Donuts. For Grace, the rules were clear—go to church or chance Hell. Francine didn't want her daughter to worry about her mother's flaming soul. But Francine was done, or at least on hiatus with the Catholic Church. So she lied. Dunked another doughnut and ate the fib sweet.

Grace adored her mother. Francine tucked her into bed with stories about Francine's father, who had owned a bar. He served *the good stuff* up front and kept a bootlegging business running out the back door, selling cheap moonshine to the hardcore drunks. Grace thought bootlegger was kin to swashbuckler, and she pictured her grandfather in buccaneer boots. Grace knew that her grandmother *died young* and that Francine spent her academic years at a Catholic boarding school, then lost her father to pneumonia just before Francine turned eighteen. Grace assumed it was boarding school that led Francine to the Carmelites. The truth was that Francine was grieving and untethered, and like many of her generation, she followed the Pied Piper of the '60s over the Golden Gate Bridge straight to the heart of the Haight. She traded her frankincense for patchouli, her *opiate of the masses* for opium. It was a mistake. The flowerchild life was too tough, too much for sheltered Francine.

The Carmelite Chapel and Monastery of St. Giles was located within tripping distance of Haight-Ashbury. During the Summer of Love, Francine, strung out and tie-dyed, reached back to the comfort of her childhood and took sanctuary with the Carmelites. In later years, if anyone asked Sister Francine how she came to the Carmelites, she said, "I just wanted to stop sleeping on sidewalks and dicks—although honestly the Carmelite beds are almost as hard." But that was with her inside voice, her private little joke. Her outside voice said, "I was called by God." The truth was, the 1960s almost killed her, and though she was grateful to stay within the shelter of the Church, she felt she had gone to two extremes, never living a *normal* life. Well, she had it now, and Grace didn't need to know *every little detail* of how she got there.

Grace loved to hear about Francine's past, but it made her worry too. It did not seem to Grace that she would ever have any stories of her own to tell her future children. She was too young to realize that being raised by a defrocked apiarist nun was a pretty remarkable childhood. She worried that her life would be uneventful. When she grew up, of course, Grace came to know that no life is uneventful. It was a wasted worry. The only question would be, would she want to tell it?

GEORGE AND PAULA

Perhaps there were never two people more fit to live in the quiet of Death Valley. George's father was right all along about the value of small places, and the couple found it easy to leave Las Vegas, where the brightest stars are on billboards. They were assigned a small company home to rent, one of the Boulder houses, named not for stone, but for history. The houses were originally used to shelter laborers for the titanic raising of Boulder Dam in the 1930s, and later transported over 100 miles to Death Valley. When Paula learned this, she pictured a ramshackle line of shanties shimmering up the highway—a ghost town on the move in the glooming. But things will always come and go in the desert. When the Tonopah and Tidewater Railroad failed in 1940, the tracks were sent to Egypt.

When the wind blew, George and Paula could open their windows and smell the freshly cut grass from the golf course. After a rain, the air smelled of limestone and ozone. They had all of the valley to explore, the little blue pupfish in the water cavern of Devil's Hole, the super blooms of spring. Joshua trees and twisted old bristlecone pines, sentinels in a slot canyon. Sex is a great filler of lazy hours, an endless game of Twister. When the babies came—Addie in 1990, then Remi in '92, Blue three years after that—life could have become quite complicated. But Paula had her pastry and George his palms; eventually George became the head of grounds. Practically as soon as each kid was old enough to take the training wheels off their bikes, they were left to be raised mostly by the desert. *Just be home by the time the sun sets or you might die out there and we won't even know where to look for ya bones.*

The first time George could recall the feeling of losing his mind was when he couldn't remember his son's name. Oh sure, he remembered the name *Blue*. But that was just a nickname, given because the newborn's eyes demanded it. But what was his little boy's real name? George went over to the Last Kind Word Saloon—the place where all old cowboys long to die— and ordered a shot of peaty Talisker's. George could feel, could almost feel, the campfire whiskey roll through his veins, heart pumping the liquor to his brain, little bursts of electricity lighting him up. "George Finley Carroll Junior," said George out loud, but quietly.

"I don't know why you drink that crap. Tastes like cigarettes," said his friend Ben from behind the bar, pouring a second. "Old Overholt not good enough for ya?!"

"You still driving that piece-of-shit truck of yours?" countered George, and the buddies were off to the races.

Paula and George had few disagreements, but baptism of their children was one of them.

Paula would have been happy to leave religion at the altar, and certainly George was aware of Paula's reasons. But George had a lingering vision of unbaptized children consigned to Dante's gray limbo, where souls wandered through a forest of crowded ghosts for trees. When he put it that way, Paula pushed her dark curls behind her ears and said, "A little water never hurt anyone."

Beyond that platitude, following no set religious code, presenting side dishes but never the main course seemed to George and Paula a fine way to raise their children to be independent thinkers. But it is difficult for children to sort and categorize adult concepts. Adults talk so fast. Hands fly and children don't always know if they should duck or expect a butter biscuit. Intent is hard to discern. What do you mean— *When the bough breaks, the cradle will fall*? Thus it should be no surprise that when their inquisitive middle child, Remi, first heard the Psalm *Yea, though I walk through the shadow of the valley of death*, she thought it was literally written about Death Valley, and that Psalms were palm trees. She wondered which palm in the oasis at Furnace Creek was number 23. Should she count from the bottom up or the top down?

Well, the Carroll children's religious upbringing remained a splintered thing. Paula didn't care too much what they believed, as long as it wasn't *that moron Joseph Smith*. George was not one to talk of God so much as to show his children the desert, the amethyst hills and whirling-dervish borax dust bowls. To George, nature was divine. Addie, their first born, was entranced by the drum beats of the Timbisha Shoshone. Remi by the roving Baptists, whose revival tents rose like mirages in the summer night. One hundred degrees at midnight and the preacher calling down the brimstone. Their little brother, Blue went for the Baptist tables of fried chicken and lemonade. *To a growing boy, God dare take no other form than food*, could have been Blue's creed.

It was Remi who was most interested in watching visiting Buddhist monks spend three days building a mandala out of colored sand at Artist Point and then let the wind dissemble it like a naughty toddler. She'd heard the reverberating booms of the singing sands at Eureka Dunes—the terrible language of the mountain gods. She went with her dad to the Date Palm Chapel because sometimes he liked to go to the outdoor service. The kids could go or sleep in. It was up to them. Paula didn't go.

George did notice Remi's interest and he bought her *The Illustrated Children's Bible & Book of Saints* and *Buddhism for Western Kids*. Remi read those books to tatters and smears of peanut butter. But she didn't know if the stories were fairy tales or real.

Theology to the Carroll family was a Thursday soup—put all the leftovers in, stir, and hope for the best. "God's in your sheets, just as much as he's in any cathedral. You don't need to leave home to find God," was Paula's theory. That statement made Remi bring a flashlight to bed. In the dark, she pitched a tent with her feet and shone the yellow flicker into the tabernacle of her blankets, expecting to find at least the Holy Ghost or a little lamb. But all she saw was her own self in her own pink jammies, brown braids dull as ever, her searchlight projecting a harvest moon on the screen of sheets. It worried her a little.

Blue didn't worry about much. He had scabs to pick and popguns to shoot. A bike to ride and miles and miles of dust to moil into the contrails of his youth. He and his buddies would follow the Amargosa River to where it disappeared into the desert, looking for gold but only ever finding rust. Blue was wild as a red-tailed hawk, wild as burros. It is good to be a cowboy.

Remi sometimes called her older sister Haughty Addie. Addie's talents would pied-piper her right out of Death Valley; she was certain of it. Addie considered the world a music box—wild water over rocks, the chatty lawnmower—and every movement had a measure. Addie could listen to radio static and find an underlayer of plainsong. Give the girl a stick, and she'll conduct it.

Remi, as many a middle child, was truly the most overlooked. "Nobody much notices what goes on in the middle," was one of her mother's expressions, "unless you're an éclair."

George and Paula didn't realize that Remi would have preferred instruction to choice.

Remi wanted to know the forces and the rules. Picture her now, two skinny desert-brown braids, teeth so straight, she must have done something right. Nevada-blue eyes. Skin on the verge of a breakout; heart too. Thirteen years old in 2005, waiting for Grace to show up with her velvet bag of holy cards shot with gold. In early September of that year, it was Paula who would first spot Grace on the side of the road, thinking the girl was either a mirage, or on the verge of a glimmer-out.

GRACE AND FRANCINE

Grace wanted to live up to her name. She wanted the nuns at school to love her. She was ecstatic to be chosen to carry the roses up to the statue of Mary in her blue plaster gown, place those blood-red, love-red flowers at Mary's feet. Standing in front of the class, waiting her turn to set down her bouquet, Grace surveyed the other students, expecting to see a kind of adulation bestowed on her. But there was that *stupid* Anne, in the back of the class with her straight-across bangs, pulling her nose up, making a piggy face. Making Grace giggle. Sister Agnes yanked those flowers right out of Grace's little fingers—*You think this is funny?!*—and gave them to another girl, a *deserving* girl.

Grace didn't cause Anne to fall down on a Girl Scouts trip to Roller King; she didn't even *will* Anne to fall. No one thought it was Grace's fault that she wasn't able to stop in time, that she skated right over the speedbump of Anne's skinny arm. Besides, it might have been the fall that caused the break. Grace didn't know if she should confess how satisfying

191

retribution felt, for Grace was certain that Anne's broken arm was punishment for laughing the roses out of Grace's hands. That was how God worked!

Her catechisms taught Grace that just because she could do something, it didn't mean she should. She had to choose correct action, and she wanted to. Her indiscretions were small and private. She worried about the black spots on her soul, the weight of that darkness.

There are lucent September days that catch the phoenix of a dying season. On such a seventh-grade morning, Grace purposely threw her red rubber ball over the school yard fence. Sister Agnes told her to *hurry up*. It felt exquisite to open the forbidden gate into the ditch-bramble beyond. On the pretense of retrieving the ball, she picked blackberries from a wild bush and ate them while spying into the boys' playground. She didn't get caught. The berries stained her fingers red, and tasted sweeter, more inspiring, than the grape juice blood of Christ.

Such were Grace's youthful transgressions.

There is a small, poorly tended, retired graveyard well behind Sacred Heart Church. A grove of eucalyptus sheds bark in strips of paper, and the leaves smell of the best kind of clean. Of course, Grace always knew the graveyard was there, but it was sometime in her freshman year of high school that she first stepped inside the scrolled and arched iron gate. It had rained that morning, and Grace picked up and broke some eucalyptus leaves, rubbed the exposed veins against the veins of her wrist. There was something in the quiet nature of the place that drew her to return to the woods, always alone. The graves were secondary to her; she read the mossy headstones, experiencing the cemetery as if she would never belong to such a place.

But then Grace found the stone of Caroline Farrell (1930–1944), Caroline just the same age as Grace. Of course, Grace knew that children died, but seeing it carved in green-black granite—it was so much more permanent than a newspaper story, tossed at the end of the day. Grace visited Caroline, brought urban wildflowers. In a way that Grace could not articulate, she almost envied this girl who died, surely, in innocence. Puberty was confusing Grace. She wondered, when was the exact day that it became not about how she swam at the Strawberry Canyon community pool, but how she looked coming out of the water?

One of the nuns saw Grace resting on Caroline's grave—not lying down!—just resting her back against the stone. Grace's mother was called in for a conference—*It was that poor girl Caroline Farrell, killed by some vagrant who left bite marks on her body! Unseemly, disrespectful.*

Francine didn't see it that way. Graveyards inspire contemplation. If only Grace hadn't actually been sitting *on* the grave. "Honey, you probably shouldn't go back there," was all her mom said.

How could Grace defend herself? How could she explain that she was fourteen years old and didn't know what to do with her straight red hair, her new breasts, her bloody underpants, that she still wanted to be a little girl, ride a rusty bike? How could she explain that sitting in the graveyard with Caroline and the warm stones and the menthol woods felt closer to God than the pews at Sacred Heart? That the holy water font was smudgy from all the fingers dipped into the basin, while the rain in the grove was cold and clear. How could she explain that she was trying to craft her future in the shade-dulled sun of a quiet place? She wondered how could she possibly both live up to her name and become an adult. The older she got, the closer she felt to becoming a citizen of sin. She didn't know the words to express her feelings.

And why, oh why, was Bart Cooper *so cute?*

Grace felt doomed by her body and her floppy heart. Well, we all are. It was just that Grace's upbringing made her feel liable for it. Francine had come to question if she should have put Grace in Catholic school at all. But Father Ward's childcare payments had extended beyond the two years that Francine had asked for, as long as Francine kept Grace in Catholic school. Well, it was too late now. God knows that girl insisted on dressing up as a nun every All Saints Day, although by high school it was a more slutty nun. She worried that Grace took her religion too literally, too much focus on the rules and not enough on the wonder.

"Listen, Grace," she told her daughter. "You gotta take the church with a grain of salt." Grace couldn't help it; she pictured the pillar of salt. "Unless you're in a convent, the place is run by men. They have control over you. Ugh!" By then, Francine had become a feminist, but Grace had just become more confused.

Bart Cooper did ask Grace out to a movie, in their junior year. He said they were going to see *The Last Samurai*, and Grace thought they were, but when they met up at the theater, Bart wanted to *just go walk around.* Oh, how exciting your own city streets if you are seventeen and the streetlights— *Stop, Slow, GO*—are your only chaperone. It was December and people were out shopping, music spilling from the shops. Grace felt as if they were breaking all the rules just to be part of that night. Bart reached for her hand. She took her mittens off. When they headed back to the theater, it started to rain. At the back of the building there were collapsed boxes and Grace sat on the cardboard. Bart made a sort of homeless shelter around them, then sat down too. Leg touching leg. Bart kissed her. Grace felt awkward, but it was hard to think over the thrumming of her body, and then his hand was on her breast.

It wasn't the full-sized portrait of Jesus with his flowing hair in the hallway of Sacred Heart that made Grace stop Bart's hand, break the kiss—although that image did come to her. It was more every schoolkid's innate knowledge of their place in the social caste. Bart was a jock, dirty blond hair with a wave like the California coastline, billboard smile. He was popular. Grace was in the Ecology Club. She was pretty too, she had those eyes, hair like burning wood, although she didn't yet believe it. There was a part of Grace who still saw herself as one of the kids that used to have to pull their retainers out for lunch. She couldn't buy that Bart wanted her for anything but her new boobs. She might have been right. But gosh, what a kiss! What a thing—a body.

Grace went home that night (*How was the movie? —Oh, pretty good. You know, Tom Cruise*) and pulled out her bag of holy cards. She barely remembered her first five years at the Carmelite Victorian annex. Mostly she remembered the bees and a feeling of safety. Sometimes she played the cards like tarot—laid them out to get a glimpse at her future. But that's really not a good idea when most of the saints are martyrs and died in some horrific way. Out of the rose velvet bag came Saint Eulalia of Barcelona. Eulalia's fate was to be placed in a barrel with shards of glass and rolled down a street that would be named *Saint Eulalia's Descent.* Grace sighed. Put her head down on her pillow and pretended it was the expanse of Bart's chest.

Grace believed that repentance was possible through ashes on her forehead, that water could be holy. But she was also brought up in Berkeley, where rebellion brewed in the coffeehouses and the college students were never interested in surfboarding or how many kids could be stuffed in a Bug. They wanted to change the world. There was always a war to fight.

Telegraph Avenue is the main street in Berkeley, running downhill from the university toward the San Francisco Bay. When Grace turned seventeen, she got a job at Carta Fiorentina, a stationery store on Telegraph that specialized in marbled Florentine paper made by hand in a back studio. The shop smelled of good paper and paint, and the gold accents on the finished work reminded Grace of her holy cards. While she was still in high school, the owners encouraged Grace to wear her school uniform with the Stewart Black plaid skirt when she worked; it fit the general theme.

On workdays, Grace took the bus and then walked down Telegraph. Grace watched the old hippies on day trips, the college students, lax or animated, filling the tables at outdoor cafés. She watched the students pass out flyers. The bells of the university campanile heralded the hour. But Grace didn't feel she belonged to the vibrant street. She belonged behind her silver cross. The Gulf War was on TV, the protest was four blocks away, but she only walked three.

A few years later, Grace got into UC Berkeley on a Carmelite scholarship. *(Who knew?!)* She at last became one of the college students she had so envied. She upgraded her fashion from tartan to Madonna (the singer, not the mother of God) in a bid at irony. After all, Madonna loved her some crosses.

But Berkeley made Grace feel awkward—its purposeful counterculture was a demanding idol. She would have fit in better at Holy Name. She studied history because she thought hers was dull. All that was left of the '60s was a lingering in the air brought over from the after-burn of the weed still smoking in the Haight. But there were plenty of new bandwagons. Osama Bin Laden saw the Twin Towers as Sodom and Gomorrah and President Bush as a pillar of saltpeter. The Janjaweed were scorching the earth of Darfur. Matthew Shepard was reaching a type of sainthood for the gay community. Grace made a holy card of him at Carta Fiorentina, Matthew depicted as a wheat-gold effigy broken on a split-rail fence. The card was beautiful, with fleur-de-lis of barbed wire, and a tiny bicyclist sporting gold-leaf wings in the upper corner representing the man who found Matthew—at first mistaking Matthew for a scarecrow. Grace used the card as a bookmark. It was just a project for her art class to her. She joined no cause. She covered her Catholic past in vintage Blond Ambition outfits, wrote her papers at Three Worlds Café, and expected nothing to happen.

On the last day of innocence, Grace was reading Camus. Christos Alexander sat down next to her and shredded any remaining stitch of plaid skirt right off the face of her thighs. Her hand shook as she put down her coffee cup. His stare was blue caffeine.

"Anybody sitting here?" he asked, scraping a hand through his Greek hair. The place was practically empty. He wore a White Stripes T-shirt, his jeans authentic hobo or left-over Nirvana-curated grunge. He vibed musician or artist, or welder. Something non-student and grown up.

Grace didn't say anything.

Christos, sitting down, shrugged toward Grace's open notebook. "What are you writing?" he asked, ignoring Camus—his focus on the personal.

Grace would rather die than tell this *man* that she had to write a paper comparing and contrasting Arron Burr and Andrew Jackson. She knew she was blushing, probably looked like a burning bush. "You from around here?" was her answer.

Grace was looking for the real world, and he was looking right at her.

Christos was older than Grace, and he had been in the Gulf War. He was intense; he had scars. He was direct and addicted and had a burned-out soul from accidentally killing a little kid and the kid's mother on the *Highway of Death* outside of Kuwait City. Or maybe he did it on purpose. Sometimes the story changed. Christos did not know that Grace was a virgin, didn't know that she was more interested in feeling the pressure of his trigger finger, those killing hands, on her skin than any other part of him.

Grace told her mother that Sharon was subletting a furnished apartment in San Francisco and that Grace was joining her, would be working at the Carta Fiorentina on Maiden Lane for the summer.

"I thought Sharon was in Los Gatos?" her mother asked, her eyebrows knitting together.

"Yeah, for school, this is just for summer. We'll have you over for dinner." Grace wondered where she had learned to lie so smoothly. "We have a bay window!"

Of course Francine believed her, even thought it was a good idea for Grace try something new. San Francisco was practically their backyard; she wasn't going far.

But Grace's move was only to Point Richmond, into Christos's studio, which smelled of old bong water. Christos showed Grace his illegally constructed driftwood sculptures of prurient themes out on the mudflats of Emeryville, between Berkeley and San Francisco. They were just drifter's shit. He wrote violent poems on her skin and they were shit too, but now Grace was softly high, and the words sounded like the pealing bells of the campanile. She made Christos tell her war stories and she imagined Nighthawks over the desert, infrared goggles, camels on the highway, spittin' mad. She confused the smell of his sweat for the scent of date palms by the Euphrates River. Grace thought Christos knew something real, while all she knew was the poetry of prayers.

It happened so fast. Christos took Grace to the Glory Hole and the Hit Club on the dirty side of Oakland. Grace got high and danced by herself. Other men moved into her sphere, and Christos watched from the bar. Grace lost her job at Carta Fiorentina because she didn't show up. Christos sold coke, and sheets of LSD that looked like Cracker Jack tattoos. Red-threaded pot. Whatever came his way. But a lot of it never hit the resale market, and they were broke. Dinner was Rice-a-Roni.

Their apartment bedroom window was shattered, the fog from the bay came inside, made itself right at home. Grace woke up under a ghost blanket. In the mornings she could smell the cold ocean air in the length of her red braid, could lick the salt off her arms like a cat. She was hungry. So she did. She looked out over a sci-fi skyline provided by the smoking stacks of the Standard Oil refinery, felt the shadow of World War II in the deserted burly Kaiser shipyards—yards that once produced three ships a day bound for troubled waters. Grace fell back to sleep to the long-distance loneliness of freight trains.

Christos had this idea. "The girls always smelled good, and they were, I don't know, plump"—he put his hands out as if he was touching flesh—"and they wore those belly-dancer clothes, silky. There was candy." He was reaching for images, trying to sell her something.

Grace had a good imagination. She saw rosemary-scented oil baths, Persian silk, fat green pistachios and rose-flavored Turkish Delight. For a moment Grace was the Little Match

Girl lighting her last match, looking in on the feast. Then he said, "Only one man a night. I'll set it all up . . ."

The cross Grace still wore around her neck, the one Christos liked to tease her about, might as well have glowed with the Holy Ghost. Grace girded herself with all of her past and all of her strength, all the power of the redheads, told Christos to *fuck off*. Oh, what a satisfying word!

One week later she was crashing with Sharon in the Los Gatos hills and starting a new waitress job at the Good Earth. She was eating nothing but whole grains and fruit. Jake Jamerson was the cook, and he was a hipster, but all shined up. *Nature boy*, and he could make a mean grilled cheese with Havarti. He only did drugs he could grow: organic pot in a pot. Jake said, *Move in, I have room!* It was easy to slip into his clean sheets, his earth eyes, and there Grace was, pregnant, and she may as well have flipped a coin to guess the father. While she was taking all those drugs with Christos, she forgot to take the one she really needed.

Grace dreamed she had a baby girl. Even though she was just born, the baby asked Grace to name her Twentieth Century. From the moment Grace found out she was pregnant, she knew Twentieth Century was in trouble. She didn't go to Francine for help, not to Sharon, or anyone. She didn't want help because she needed to make up her own mind. She believed people only ask for advice when they want to hear themselves talk. *Yap, yap, yap.* Also, if she asked her mother for help, then her mother would know.

Grace grew up with Valentine's Day cards, decent cuts of occasional steak, new dresses for Easter and the first day of school. Herbal Essences shampoo. She was not the kind of girl who doesn't know the father of her baby. But then again, she was.

*   *   *

Grace went alone to Big Sur, wandered the tide pools, little wombs of nebulous and darting life. She thought of all the drugs she had taken. Coke took her up, pot brought her down, LSD took her over the rainbow.

Grace imagined telling Jake she was pregnant. Somehow she pictured it happening in the kitchen at the Good Earth while he was pulling a sheet of granola cookies from the oven. His face would light up and he would ask her to marry him! They would marry, not in the Catholic Church, but in the Muir Redwoods just north of the Golden Gate Bridge. Very early in the morning and Grace would wear a veil of fog held in place by a single gardenia.

What a pipe dream. Straight out of a bong.

And how was it she was pregnant anyway? How could she be pregnant when the sex with Christos was so bad? Wouldn't conceiving a whole new life require the ingredient of plea-sure? Shouldn't it be the orgasm that *sparked* life? Well, Chris-tos and Two-Shakes Jake certainly had theirs. *Ugh.*

For twelve hours, Grace stayed by the ocean, the waves pixilating; she was inside the Magic Eye. It was the last Crack-er Jack LSD tattoo that would ever dissolve on her tongue. Grace lay down on the gold-standard sand. She tried not to picture Twentieth Century, destructive drug dripping through her thimble-brain, DNA contorting. Forever, she knew, she would feel the guilt of purposely drugging her un-born baby. But that was the point. To keep the baby unborn, Grace needed to wreck the fetus, otherwise, how could she let Twentieth Century go?

Grace pawned her high school graduation diamond earrings and showed up for her appointment at the Bay Area Wom-en's Clinic. In the waiting room the nurse gave her Valium to relax and she sat around pretending to read magazines with the other woman. She looked at them all. There was a blond girl with her blond boyfriend. She was crying and he was supportive. Grace wondered if crying made her feel less guilty. *For the love of God, if you want to keep your baby, get up and walk out.* On this day Grace felt an intolerance for indecision—she couldn't afford it. There was an older woman who looked like she lived in a shoe. *Had so many children, she didn't know what to do.* The tall Black woman, she looked strong enough to use the hanger.

Grace liked the Valium. They called her into a dim room with a single bed, a big overhead light, and those metal stirrups. She put her heels in the stirrups and the nurse pushed her legs apart. The nurse's fingers in thin membrane gloves came sliding, sliding into her. "You're about ten weeks," she said.

Grace wanted the nurse never to have said that to her. It made the baby so much more real. *Soft blankets and milk, little fingers and bassinets.* The doctor came in. *Onesies, powder, diaper pins.* He turned on the dilation and curettage engine with its efficient vacuum aspiration. *Bubbles and nursery rhymes.* He put a tube inside Grace, deeper than anything had ever been before. *Rocking chairs and lavender.* The slender tube scraped and scooped and it really didn't feel like much at all. Grace tried not to think about what it felt like to Twentieth Century.

Our Father who art in heaven, hallowed be thy name.
Hail Mary, full of grace.

And then it was done. Grace was transferred to the recovery room, where she sat again with the other women. Staff gave the women orange juice and cookies like nursery school. Everyone actually seemed to feel a little better now that it was over. Grace could see that the blond girl had transformed herself back into a cheerleader. The older lady didn't look so old.

But Grace was wrecked. She went home to her mother, Sister Francine. To the arms of an angel.

Well, let's face it. An angel who thinks Jesus walks on water, but has conflicts about institutional religion.

As Grace told her mother her story—romance novel, horror—it was hard to keep up with the genre. But in a way, Grace was reciting Francine's diary: Child who loves the pageantry and the rules when she is little, comes up against the sticky rapture of desire. Raised on Bible verses and Nancy Reagan's *Just Say No*, Grace held herself in innocence as long as she could. Francine had tried to save Grace *from the drugs and the dicks*, but now she believed all she had done was allow history to repeat itself. Francine just listened and ate her child's sins.

The hardest thing for Grace to tell was about Twentieth Century. Especially the day at Big Sur, taking LSD to make sure she would go through with the abortion. In the end, she couldn't tell the Big Sur part. It was just too awful. She shouldn't have done it; it somehow felt worse than the abortion itself. Some actions stay with us forever, and Grace knew this would be her albatross. Carcass around her neck.

"Here's what we are going to do," Francine at last said, telling Grace her plan.

Together they went to Britex, the fabric mecca in San Francisco. They sewed a jumper of woodland animals—fox and badger, and a pixie-hooded jacket. They bought ready-made rose socks and a rose angora blanket, soft as bunny ears. And a little stuffed bunny. All of this Grace and Francine settled into a fair-sized, thick cardboard stationery box from Carta Fiorentina, the paper covering as beautiful as any holy card.

On a cloudy night, the momentary mother and grandmother went to the way-back graveyard of Sacred Heart. Grace nodded to Caroline Farrell. *Farewell.* They used a garden trowel to dig a shallow—well, it must be said—grave, under the eucalyptus and the trumpet vines. Settled the box within. Then they scattered earth and paperbark, and rattles of eucalyptus pods back over the disturbed ground. No marker, but they would always know the spot. Walked away hand-in-hand.

"Do you feel like you want to go to confession?" Francine had grown to believe that forgiveness is granted through personal contrition, that one did not necessarily need the intermediary of a priest in a confessional box. In fact, confession now felt a little voyeuristic to Francine. A sort of *Days of Our Lives* for priests denied personal fleshy messes. But she thought her Catholic daughter might benefit from going.

"I looked it up. I'd have to go to a bishop." Big sin.

Of course, Francine knew a bishop—Roger's boss. Francine almost laughed. Roger would be livid with her, raising a daughter who had an abortion. Still, she could take on Saint Sanctimonious for her daughter's sake.

"But I don't want to go anyway," Grace said.

Francine was nobody's fool. She knew her daughter. "Is that because you don't believe you can be absolved?"

Bingo. "And because, given the same circumstances, I'd do it again." Hard admission. *Maybe not the Big Sur part.*

They walked through the angel-light of streetlamps, through the scents of summer after dark. Well, some things just need to sit awhile.

School would start in a few weeks, Grace's junior year at UC Berkeley. But she no longer wanted to major in history. She had one now. What she needed was a future. Francine, perhaps overcompensating for Grace's grief or guilt, bought her a fifteen-year-old Pontiac Grand Safari with exactly 722 miles left to live (surprisingly close to the purchase price) and suggested Grace *might want to go on a road trip for, maybe a month? You know, get away from it all? Come back and we'll figure it out. Things will be better then.*

Grace had this vision of the two of them scrubbing the house, themselves, their souls with Pine Sol. Hanging their souls out on the line like carpets and beating the dust out with a broom. Get some of those black spots out. They would be better then.

She went to look at the car. "Really, a Grand Safari!? I'm going to look like a creeper!" The car clearly had suffered all kinds of domestic abuse. But really Grace loved it. It was the greatest shade of red and it would hold all her stuff.

Francine had tried to get money out of Roger to send Grace to a retreat at Esalen in Big Sur, but given the fact that Francine could not tell Roger of Grace's transgressions (*She's* depressed, *Roger!!*), and given Esalen's New Age, Eastern philosophies, Roger wasn't going for it. Maybe Francine should have just come up with the money herself, because instead of the controlled grounds of Esalen, Grace bought herself a golden ticket to the party on the Black Rock Desert, as far away from the California coast as a landscape can possibly imagine.

Grace was going to Burning Man.

Grace left the warren of the Bay Area, headed east. It always surprised her how quickly the maze of the city unwound into barely developed, grassy hills. You have to call these hills *rolling*. In spring, the grass is the shade of parakeets, stippled with poppies and yellow-brick-roads of mustard flowers. Now the grass was August-dry, dairy cows crowded under the wide branches of stoic oaks. It evoked old California to Grace. She passed the Pinole oil refinery with its Necco candy–painted holding tanks. Soon came the delta and Sacramento, the city built on gold nuggets and roadside produce stands, and then over the Sierra Nevada Mountains. Those mountains mean business.

Grace wanted to make Reno by nightfall. Driving down the twisty Mount Rose Highway, the put-it-on-a-calendar beauty of California just gradually trailed off. Grace hadn't even really noticed until *poof*, it was gone. *Welcome to Nevada*.

August isn't Reno's best month. Here's the seven-day forecast: Hot and dry, and don't throw your friggin' cigarette butts out the window.

And the desert was just getting started.

Grace spent the night at the Peppermill, her first casino. The main casino was a blotch of color and sound, the clanging bells of the slot machines with their whirling faces, the pour of a jackpot, the slap of the cards in a dealer's hands. Cocktail waitresses dressed mostly in flesh. Buffets of shrimp, curled up in death, lemon-glossed. Grace loved it! She ate the shrimp.

The next day Grace continued into the heart of the desert. She never felt so alone. She had delayed going out to the playa until there were only three days left of the festival, because she suspected Burning Man might not be the best place for a Carmelite wanna-be fallen from grace. *What would Jesus do?* Well, she kept driving. So that was that.

Grace stopped in Elroy at the Native American mini-mart just to look for signs of joy in the effervesce of a fountain Coke. Back out in the parking lot, Grace saw a woman approaching on a fat-tire mountain bike, sweating something fierce. Grace walked over and handed the woman her Coke. "Thanks, oh my God, thanks!" She finished the thing.

"What happened to you?" Grace asked.

"My fucking car broke down."

The woman had a huge backpack on, her sunburnt biceps all spinached up like Popeye. She looked capable. "You need a ride to the Black Rock?" Grace offered. It was obvious where the woman was headed.

"Would ya?! I've been hitchhiking. Not easy with a bike."

"Where's your car?"

"Lodi! It's always fucking Lodi."

"Oh Lord," said Grace, opening the back door for the woman to toss her backpack in.

Fresh Cokes in hand, Grace and her new friend, Barbarella, headed out. Grace pointed the wagon toward the Black Rock Desert, mountains on both sides funneling them forward. There was no natural color but brown, so the Grand Safari sparked like a ruby slipper. The sun came through the windshield, little dust motes everywhere. They passed a far-off view of Pyramid Lake that could have been a delusion. A band of mustangs that would not look at them. It was a pencil sketch of land. When they finally got to Gerlach and then out onto the playa, Barbarella gave a low whistle. "Looks like there's a scorched earth policy here."

The playa is an alkali basin, dried up and cracked. The only inhabiting animals were humans, and they were transient, population 35,000 in Black Rock City. But in the sagebrush dunes surrounding the playa, the puny kit fox with its big ears, the kangaroo mouse, wondered *What new Armageddon is this?* and took cover. Maybe a jackalope loped by—who's to say what's real in the desert? It's true that when the playa floods, the dormant eggs of the fairy shrimp hatch and grow three inches in the ephemeral water. There is ever magic in this world.

Black Rock City is built in a semicircle, a mile and a half across. In the middle stands the Man—an artful effigy infused with combustibles and, like a monk's mandala, built to blow.

Scattered across the playa, fantastical art, most of it big, most of it hands-on, *right this way, step right up,* most of it built to blow your mind. Mutant vehicles scutter around—golf carts to parade floats all dressed up like Timothy Leary and Mardi Gras had a baby.

Grace and Barbarella set up camp; Barbarella had plenty to share. She earned her patches—*Adventurer, Eco Explorer, Take Action*. Barbarella pulled a bottle of tequila from her pack. They drank it straight from the glass neck and bit into limes that were born in Costa Rica. A little drunk, they saddled their bikes, Barbarella tossing the tequila into the incongruous pink wicker basket lodged between her handlebars. The liquid sloshed through the confines of the bottle in little golden waves.

The women headed out of the campgrounds and into the no-car zone, into the bizarre.

A girl on a beach cruiser bike glided past in a cherry crinoline half-slip and a 1950s pointy-cup bra. Barbarella almost followed her. A drag queen on stilts. Mad Max passing out Twinkies. A piano on wheels playing jazz. Was that a pirate ship? An octopus, a movie theater, a Victorian bar.

They passed a tent offering to reinstate your virginity and Grace thought of Christo. She had liked the ropy scar across his shoulder. But he was always twisting her arm. She thought of Two-Shakes Jake, and laughed. Well, what's to be done about it?

A fire-breathing fish swam by, singeing the desert air, giving it a taste of its own medicine. The Billion Bunny March started up. All those fuzzy ears. Grace and Barbarella watched the parade, most of the women topless and bouncing. "I feel like Empress Nympho," Barbarella declared, and started pointing and singing, "*Yes, no no no no no no no, yes, no no, yes, no no no no no no, YES!*"

As night fell, Black Rock City lit up with neon—the official element of the State of Nevada. Laser shows, music, minor fires started to burn. The women went to District and Slut Garden, Barbarella danced in a window box, she was just a silhouette, a marionette to the music that did not stop. Everyone wore glow sticks—hula-hooped round wrists, bandoliered over chests—so they wouldn't get run down by the mutant vehicles. Everyone was high. Was everyone high? To Grace, it was a cacophony, she couldn't find a balancing cadence, while Barbarella turned herself into a set of drumsticks. Barbarella joined everything. Grace stood back and watched. Wretched voyeur.

Near midnight Grace saw a dark girl, almost a shadow, but that was not uncommon. The only light coming from her was a sort of halo of hummingbirds, neon glints under their rapid wings. Grace tried to get closer, she wanted to see those whirly birds, but the shadow seemed to continually move off, the way a rainbow does.

In the morning, Grace had to disentangle her legs—*which ones are mine?* She and Barbarella had lost the way to their camp, ended up sleeping in a commune called the Hen House. Grace had all her clothes on. She considered this a win, given the tequila. Grace peered over the piles of sleeping women in various stages of attire. Caramel sunlight filtered through the canvas walls, and Grace did see the painterly beauty of draped limbs. One of the slumberous still had on her bunny ears—one ear up, one down. In that obtuse light, Grace momentarily mistook the pink polyester center in a white fur surround for an albino vagina. It only lasted a moment, but Grace knew she was never going to fully recuperate from that image. Easter may always be traumatic for her now, as if a man nailed to a cross wasn't bad enough.

Grace quietly went out into the dawn. There was a layer

of smoke in the air, the smell of ash and early morning pot and coffee. There was pulsing music already at District. Grace found her bike (*amazing!*) and threaded her way back to her car. She loaded all of Barbarella's belongings out of the car and into her backpack, laid a pair of lipstick red panties on top, like a beacon. She never learned Barbarella's real name.

The Man had not yet burned, Grace had yet to go to the temple where people left photos and poems, loss and regret. She didn't care. Burning Man was not for her. There had to be a place between the hard-and-narrow church pew and the borderless green-grass of hedonism. She wanted to rest in the middle space. Grace still had her holy cards with her; she wondered if she brandished them, would half the people on the Black Rock turn to salt, or minor saints?

What a bunch of jackalopes, what a grand safari. She couldn't really handle it. She headed south.

THE SAINTS OF DEATH VALLEY

Driving back from Death Valley Junction, Paula thought she saw a ruby aura around the shadow outline of a woman. It was hard to judge in the wavery heat—if the woman wasn't a mirage, certainly she was on her way to becoming a ghost. Paula caught up and pulled over next to a young woman standing beside a ruby Pontiac. The traveler's face looked as if it had just pulled a fresh batch of freckles out of the oven. She wore a bone-in pearl corset (something you don't see every day in the desert) and her shoulders were almost as red as her hair. Conflicting religious necklaces around her neck, black cargo pants tucked into alkali-dusted combat boots.

"Watta you doin', it's going to one-ten today," Paula asked, rolling down the window.

The young woman leaned hard into the escaping air-conditioning. "Depending upon the kindness of strangers," she responded, and her bottom lip split when she smiled, giving away her physical state. She'd been out there for some time. "My car died."

"Okay, Blanche, get in." Paula thought the girl looked like she could not be much more than twenty, shouldn't be traveling long distances alone; no one should, in the desert. "I'll get you to a service station."

They exchanged (real) first names and Grace handed Paula a holy card. She meant it as an act of thanks. It was a good one too—St. Catherine racked on her wheel, sparks of gold pinwheeling around her. Paula held the card like it was shit. Did she pick up an evangelist? Grace saw the look.

"Okay, I know it's ridiculous. These cards—" She had pulled the card from a velvet bag. "I intended to leave them at Burning Man, but I left, so now I have to give them away a card at a time."

Burning Man. *That explains the outfit.* It didn't.

Paula stepped on the gas, threw the card out the window. Catherine wheeled head over heels through the Nevada desert, landing at the feet of a kangaroo mouse, who jumped right over the card, and kept on going down the folded mountain pass to an ephemeral stream that would be gone with the hour.

Paula peered at what she now saw more or less as a lost child—at her loose braids, the ratty backpack she pulled from her stranded car.

"You have a plan?" It wasn't appropriate for her to ask, but it felt like a mother's prerogative. Even if she wasn't the mother.

"Las Vegas, I guess."

The young woman was so dusty, if not for her hair and sunburn, she had lost all her color. Something about her reminded Paula of herself; Paula had fled Salt Lake City as soon as she could. *Moroni and his Mary Kay lips.* She might have been imagining it, but the young woman had a sort of jump-off-a-cliff desperation to her. Las Vegas thrives on that edge—puts it on a marquee and sells it. Then keeps most of the money.

"Death Valley's kind of out of the way . . ." Paula pushed.

"I'm in need of an oasis. I heard you have one."

True enough. "So, where'd you say you're from?" Paula asked.

Grace surprised herself and said, "The Carmelites."

And she kept on talking. She told Paula that she was not sure if she should return to college, that she was in a bit of a crisis, how Burning Man was too intense for her—life was too intense for her—and that she felt she needed to retreat and regroup.

The more Paula heard, the more she knew George wouldn't mind, didn't think he would mind too much when she impulsively said, "Why don't you stay a few days at my house with me and my family." Paula looked Grace directly in the eyes to convey safety, although at five-foot-four-inches, threatening was not one of Paula's best attributes. She tucked her black curls behind her ears, exposing that small part of herself. "We have three kids," she added; what could be safer? If George was unhappy about it, well, it would only be for a day or two. The child just looked like she needed refuge.

"I have money, I can rent a motel room," Grace said, running her tongue over the minerals crystalizing on her teeth, "but I think I'd like to. To stay with you." She was used to the charity of others, believed in it. And Grace didn't particularly want to be alone.

They arrived at the Boulder house, went inside. "These are my girls, Addie and Remi," Paula said, the sisters looking up from the TV. The older girl, Addie, was a tall copy of her mother, with her black-cat hair. Remi had braids the color of the desert. "Blue is around here somewhere." Grace didn't know if she meant the third kid or the dog.

"Grace is going to stay with us for a couple days," Paula informed her daughters.

The girls said *hi* with their voices, but their eyes, taking in Grace's corset and cargo look said, *Are you crazy?*

Paula led Grace to the small enclosed porch George had added on to the side of the house. The wall of windows made the porch room unbearable during most days, but on a clear night it was Starship Command. Addie and Remi followed, silently.

Grace shrugged her backpack into the corner; it settled like a hobo.

"Addie, get the broom," Paula said. "Remi, get some clean sheets and the nice blanket." There was a pullout couch that, when open, would take up most of the space. Addie swept clean the chili-pepper-red tiles and threw away her mother's struggling herbs—parsley, sage, rosemary, and pot. (*Those little hypocrites!* Then later, *That's for your dad's headaches!*) She plugged in a huge fan that chopped at the heat. Addie wished her mother would put Grace in with Remi and give her this room. When Grace left, she was going to ask for it.

Remi helped Grace make the bed. Remi was piqued by Grace's bright hair, and the cross, the yin-yang symbol, and the dharma chakra wheel (*Was she a sailor?*) Grace had strung around her neck on silver chains. Remi had overheard Paula tell George over the phone that Grace was raised by Carmelites, which Remi could only picture as a low-calorie ice cream topping. Yes, the new girl was intriguing.

Later, Grace called Francine. Pictured her mother on the

other end of the line, her bumblebee hair. "Mom, you'll never guess where I am."

"Paris!"

"Ha ha. I'm in Death Valley. At an oasis. There's a golf course."

"Are you taking up golf?"

"Yes, I'm quite good. The Wheaties people are on their way."

"Oh nice, but you know, you're not going to look so great on that orange box—what with your red hair."

"Actually, I'm staying a couple of days with a family." Grace knew that would send Francine's freewheeling eyebrows a-flying.

A family. It is hard to let a child go.

"The Carrolls, they're really nice," Grace continued. "They have three kids. I want you to talk to Paula, the mom."

The mom. I'm the mom!

"I think I want to stay here for a while. I mean, I don't know if I can stay with the Carrolls—there's one bathroom—but in Death Valley."

Francine tried to picture her daughter below sea level. Living with *a family.* What were they, the two of them? She felt a butter knife of jealousy. Made it melt. "Baby, put Paula on. If you say it's a good place for you, I trust you." She still did trust her, despite Grace's actions over the summer. Mothers can be like that.

Paula got on the line. "I found her by the side of the road and brought her home like a puppy. I'm feeding her table sweets."

Francine's instinct was to like her. It takes a village. But even still, she would be driving out for a visit as soon as she could schedule the days off. *A family! Pfft.*

*   *   *

A few days gave way to months; no one talked of Grace moving out. Paula gave her a job in the kitchen making rosettes of many colors laid out on wax paper rows. When the sun receded from Grace's skin, the girl looked like waxy magnolia petals, she looked as if she belonged in a canopy bed. Paula had never seen a girl more in need of a large plate of desserts.

Grace helped Blue with his homework, no small task— *For goodness' sakes, Blue, i after e!* She took Addie to her dance lessons at the Amargosa Opera House. Jumped with Remi on the heat-stretched trampoline in the backyard—star jump, swivel hips, jumping jacks. *Now do it higher, Remi—fly!* She was good with the kids.

Francine did come out, more than once, and they had barbeques under skies so big, it was heartbreaking. Francine had never before truly seen the Milky Way. She thought it the bridge to Heaven. She could understand why Grace was lingering in the oasis, and it was easy to see that Paula and George were not the type of people to ask Grace to move on just because they only had one bathroom. Although George did say it was easier to go to the stalls at the Last Kind Word than it was to get a seat in his own house.

George and Paula didn't pay enough attention to realize that, when it came to doctrine, Remi would have preferred instruction to choice. Paula had grown up with no choice and offered her children the opposite. George need only bite into the flesh of a date to taste the body of Christ, and he was grateful. Grace was carrying around her black-shot soul, working on atonement, wondering if she might need a new religion to gain it. Remi was rummaging through the transcendental looking for a good fit.

Remi was thirteen years old and she wanted to understand the forces and the rules. Nature has no morals. It is raw and it is beautiful, and Remi knew—it is opportunistic. Anything that can kill you, will. From a killing-you-softly mosquito, to an eating-you-alive mountain lion. If the lions don't get you, the heat—that true apex predator—will. Nature doesn't care. Beauty is a by-product, not a goal. Remi understood the environment. It was philosophy that puzzled. *The Alfie Questions*, her mother called them. Paula sang *What's it all about, Alfie?* and Remi didn't even know what that meant. Remi wanted a burning bush. She wanted divinity (not the candy!) and definitive answers. A child isn't good with shading—just look at their artwork—if it's not in a box of sixty-four colors, it doesn't exist. Some kids only have eight.

Remi was young enough to like the idea of Ten Commandments; she'd first read about them in her *Children's Bible*. Ten seemed reasonable. She was also young enough to believe she could obey them. Remi took to hanging out with Grace and her velvet bag of holy cards. The illustrator of Remi's saints book had used watercolors—such a soft sell. Grace's cards made the saints come alive—drops of vermilion blood from open wounds, girded for battle, standing for God. The lessons were black-and-white.

Remi became an acolyte.

Remi instigated discussions on teenage theology, starting with Remi's curiosity of Grace's necklaces and moving to the important things like is there a Heaven, to the really important things like who has the best outfit. "Witches, when you get right down to it," concluded Remi, and on that one and Grace couldn't disagree.

Eventually Grace asked Paula if it would be okay if she moved in with Remi and gave Addie the patio room. "Remi's with me like half the time anyway, and I think I'd make some real points with Addie." Everyone knew Addie coveted the red tile room. Paula was fine with it.

"Would you like the top bunk?" Grace asked Remi, indicating the bed that Addie had stripped so thoroughly. The mattress looked prison-issue with its red ticking and sagging center.

Remi put her hand on the ladder, her pure blue eyes wide—it may as well have been the stairway to heaven, eternally denied by her older sister. And now it was *hers*?!

On a day off from the kitchen, Grace took a ride into Las Vegas with George. He needed supplies, she needed a car—the Grand Safari never recovered. On the drive, she learned all about soil with high salt content and pH scales. "I'm trying to grow this stuff with a pH of 10.5. The alkaline! And don't get me started on what happens in 125 degrees. I once saw a burning bush—I'm talking spontaneous combustion, not Moses. But Holy Moses!"

They had no reason to go to the Strip. They drove the periphery and Grace saw the old ranchero-style homes with flat, gravel roofs, front yards of prickly pear and saguaro. Scarecrow cactus guarding nothing but yards of rock. George helped her buy a beater at Atomic Auto, and the old Toyota truck seemed disappointed when Grace drove it farther into the desert instead of toward the ocean—the truck resisted every climb like a mule. But mule was that truck's destiny, because Grace had decided to become her own version of a Carmelite—and it involved building a chapel.

Death Valley is part of a 300-million-acre national park. The park rangers who work there are parched. The people who live there are fringed; it's just the way it is. So when the young woman with hair the color of polished carnelian started carefully stacking rocks to create a small room sidled up against a seldom-visited gorge by Zabriskie Point, no one cared. Or most possibly no one of authority even saw. The occasional intrepid tourist stumbled on the narrow trail, looked up, and noticed the splotches of orange lichen on a gray limestone rock wall clinging to the mountain like a poorly built Pueblo cliff dwelling. Of course that tourist would follow that trail—was it a . . . *discovery*? Imagine their surprise upon finding a bone-white plastic lazy Susan fit into the stones, perfectly free to be set in motion. Just asking for it. Really it was irresistible not to twirl that turnstile. Mostly the plastic would do nothing but release a layer of orangey dust into the air. But if a person felt the urge to put something on the lazy Susan, anything at all—a small stone with a quartzite vein the nowhere color of ice, a cactus bloom sticky and wilting, a Lincoln penny—then a holy card would replace that offering, gold and all the royal colors glinting in the unforgiving sun. While this exchange was taking place, the self-proclaimed prioress of the desert, and often her aspirant too, could be heard giggling from behind the stone wall, but never, oh no never, ever seen.

Oh, what a fine story, what a fine souvenir! A great exchange. But most times no one was at the enclave, neither tourist nor nunette. Just the whirly wind on the plastic merry-go-round. At the Unofficial Our Lady of Cake Carmelite Chapel-lite.

In the Furnace Creek kitchen, Grace moved up from rosettes to cheesecake. She perfected an Apple Charlotte that made the menu. In her off hours she drove around the desert in her old mule truck looking for unusual but movable rocks. The young men who worked under George at the golf course took an interest in the pretty young woman with the lead foot. The one with hair to her shoulders the color of the tail of a comet. Remi was watching from the truck when Jared, in his Dockers and polo shirt, his muscles and his name tag, asked Grace if she wanted to go for a golf cart ride with him on the greens after dark. Made it sound all *Midnight at the Oasis*, which it technically was. He shook his set of keys like a chatelaine, proof of his authority.

"What'd Jared want?" Remi asked when Grace got back in the car.

"To romance me under the stars."

"What'd ya say?!"

"I said my boyfriend was in the Marines."

"Good. You see that mole on his face?"

"Yep."

"Looks like he fell asleep on a Rolo."

Grace snorted. "Oh, you're a rough one, Remi. I feel sorry for the boys who go after you!" What Grace did not say to Remi was that she wasn't overly confident about sex at all. It hadn't gone particularly well to date. She didn't lace her corsets so tight to push up her boobs; she was binding her heart.

Twice a week Grace drove Addie to her ballet lessons. Oh, in Death Valley a child could expect to learn to shoot a gun, track a bighorn sheep, even jump on a backyard trampoline that is succumbing to heat exhaustion. But ballet lessons? Thanks to a flat tire, a child could.

In 1923, Pacific Coast Borax built a complex including a recreation hall. Corkhill Hall has seen church services, funerals, union leaders shaking sabers made of steely words, and yes, dances. But never had that hall seen the likes of dancer Marta Becket.

In 1967, Marta's car got a flat tire, and in the time it took for the tire to be changed at the Death Valley Junction service station, Marta changed her life. She had been part of the corps de ballet at Radio City Music Hall, had played Carnegie. But she bought Corkhill Hall and traded New York to dance to an audience of *none*. So she painted the walls of the hall with a sixteenth- century court with royalty, bullfighters, prostitutes—her tromp l'oeil audience on the walls of her now-named Amargosa Opera House. Eventually the living audiences came, if only to see the oddity.

Then the young kids who wanted to stand on their toes came to Marta and asked to learn to twirl and twirl and twirl and *jump*! Addie, with her dark-dark hair, was one of these kids, perhaps the best, because she understood the secret language of music, could dip into that silver stream and come out all a-sparkle.

Remi usually came along for the ride. She and Grace watched from the farthest back seats, right below the court jester. "God, what a hoofer," was Remi's take, closing her jewel-blue eyes. Remi was not interested in dance—the Hokey Pokey was still her best number. What Remi was interested in was those cards in Grace's rose velvet bag. Remi had bigger dreams than Addie. Remi didn't want her name on a marquee; she wanted her likeness, gold and violet-blue, on a holy card. She had decided she wanted to be a saint.

Saint Remi of the Desert.

Paula had her head in the oven. George was somewhere under a tree. Grace fed Remi the cornflakes of religion; took her to the Date Palm Chapel on Sundays, out to the Bedouin-tent revivals of the holy rolling Baptists, where Remi raised her palms up, open them to *Je-sus*, and Grace put gingerbread men with raisin eyes in the collection baskets. They went to the powwows at Indian Village, 197 feet below sea level. The Timbisha called Death Valley *Tumpisa*—meaning *rock paint*—a place that used to belong only to the Red Rock Face Paint peoples.

Up at the Our Lady of Cake, Grace would hoist a ladder so they could climb over the wall; the second ladder already in place on the other side so they could climb down, pulling the first ladder after them. They kept a small weatherproof box with the holy cards, their books and a few treasures and talismans that had been delivered on the lazy Susan. In the quiet of the cooler days, they carved petroglyphs into the sandstone walls, the outline of their hands, stars, and coyote-in-the-moon. It was their version of the paintings at the Opera House.

Years later a tourist named Simon Ha would find the drawings, looking through a chink where the lazy Susan used to be. Simon thought the drawings were authentically old. And when he found out otherwise from an anthropology grad student out of the University of Nevada at Las Vegas, Simon stayed behind and carved *fuck you* over the drawings because he was disappointed and embarrassed when the grad student pointed out the drawing of the truck—"Looks like a Toyota." But Death Valley is a dry place and sooner or later those scratches, that graffiti, *would be* petroglyphs and Simon had deprived the drawings of one possible destiny. But neither Remi nor Grace would ever know this part of the story.

Behind the walls, in the shade of the chapel-lite, Grace read a paperback copy of *Comparative Religions* that she'd bought back at Moe's on Telegraph in Berkeley, where new and used books are shelved side by side. Used struck her as infused with an earlier reader's sparking energy. Grace had bought her yin-yang and her dharma chakra wheel necklaces at one of the ubiquitous Nepalese stores—prayer flags fringing the windows. Grace bought some of those too. Now she strung the colored flags across the back of the desert chapel.

"Pretty," said Remi, pushing her peanut butter braids back, "like the Mexican paper banners." Remi was thinking of

221

the *papel picado* fiesta banners she had seen in Mexican restaurants in Las Vegas.

"These tell a story if you know how to read them," Grace said, thinking of the stained-glass windows at Sacred Heart, the stations of the cross. Grace touched the center of the flag. "*Lung Ta*—Wind Horse—for speed and transformation of bad fortune to good."

Remi pictured a barely visible horse, a galloping soap bubble warrior-of-Buddha horse.

Grace ran her fingers over the writing around *Lung Ta,* "These are mantras, four hundred of 'em, like prayers. The Tibetans believe the mantras will be blown by the slightest wind to spread compassion. They are not individual prayers but for the benefit of all." Grace loved the image of prayers coming to her on the wind, blowing by, tangling her hair.

"I think the Mexican flags kind of do the same thing," said Remi. She wasn't wrong.

Grace was working on what she came to think of as her *empty space*, or her *godless space*. (Paula would just call it the *Alfie* questions.) Grace read to Remi about Buddhism—"The world, it's not real. It's a cosmic dance."

Remi pictured the Hokey Pokey.

"You can never give enough loving-kindness, or compassion. If you have joy in other people's joy—how can you not be joyful!?"

Remi wondered if she could live up to that; Grace already did.

"Emptiness is emptiness. Sky is blue, grass is green. See reality as it is, without projections. Words are not the ultimate truth. Experiences are reality."

The teenager on the brink, and the young woman on a break, thought about these concepts. Possibly they resonated because Death Valley is itself such an elemental place. Bare bones. There is no sugar coating reality in the Badwater.

"You are responsible for your own salvation," Grace continued reading. "The goal is to end suffering. Suffering comes from desire. Decrease your desires and decrease your suffering." Grace continued to read aloud, but inside her head, words were popping: *You are responsible for your own salvation. What, no need for a bishop!?*

Grace thought of Jesus, she thought of Buddha. One born from a virgin, one born from his mother's side. She discussed this, as she did so many things on so many night calls with Francine, who said, "Really, what's wrong with a holy person coming straight out of a vagina? Straight out! Men are idiots!"

"I like both these prophets; can I like both these prophets?" she asked her mother.

"*The more I seek, the less I know*," said Francine, quoting the Red Hot Chili Peppers, who weren't the first to say it.

"I'm ping-ponging from god to god!" Grace said.

"Grace, stop worrying about the peripherals. Look for the shared morals in the religions. Those are the truths."

Grace thought that was a good idea. She was seeking forgiveness. She wasn't moving away from the Catholic Church. She was expanding.

Grace and Remi distilled the rules that resonated with them:
Remi's were: No killing, no stealing, no lying.
Grace added: No sex outside of morality. Remi blushed.
Remi added: Don't be jealous of other people's stuff.
Grace concluded: Be nice.
Easy, easy rules. They repeated them like a rosary until they looked like this: Nokillingnostealingnoyingnosexoutsideofmoralitydon'tbejealousofotherpeople'sstuffbenice.

Then Grace shortened it to Supercalifragilisticexpialido-cious. They knew what it meant.

But here's the thing: A picture is worth a thousand words. And Remi was deprived of color. Color in Death Valley is a migrating bird wondering where it took the wrong turn. In the desert, violet is its brightest on the face of an Anna's hummingbird, scarlet its deepest on the silly crest and puffed belly of the vermillion flycatcher. The truest white is a great egret, looking like a dorky angel. Color is hard to come by. So despite the lessons in comparative religion, Remi remained most interested in Grace's rose velvet bag of holy cards, shot with end-of-the-rainbow gold.

Behind the stone wall, Grace sometimes asked Remi what she wanted to be when she grew up. Finally, one day Remi answered truthfully: "I want to be a saint," she said.

"A saint?! Well, you're a whirling dervish on the trampoline." Grace assumed she was teasing.

"Don't say that. I'm serious. I want to be on a holy card." There. She said it.

Grace still thought it was a joke. "Might be easier to make it on the cover of the Rolling Stone magazine. Take up guitar. Desert grunge."

Remi gave her the blue evil eye. Two of them.

"Well," said Grace, now understanding that Remi wasn't kidding. A little afraid for her. "Saints *cannot* be timid," she postured.

"No," agreed Remi, flinging a peanut-butter-colored braid off her shoulder.

"And there is usually an ordeal, although one might think living in Death Valley is ordeal enough."

"Living with *you* ought to be ordeal enough."

"What kind of saint do you want to be?" Grace pulled out the cards, fanned them like a fortune teller, or a card shark.

This set Remi thinking. Certainly not Prince Igor Constantinovich of Russia. He was so handsome with the gold of his war medals and his smart uniform, but Grace knew her saints and she told Remi he was murdered by Bolsheviks in the Urals, his body now under a parking lot in Beijing. Igor was exchanged on the lazy Susan for a scruffy blue button.

Of course, Remi liked Saint Francis, looking like Cinderella with doves on his shoulders and bunnies by his sandaled, earthy toes.

Grace touched the Joan of Arc card. Barbarella came to mind. Grace wondered if there was a saint for lesbians—everyone deserves a saint! Right then Grace pinned her hopes on Joan of Arc, whom growing up, Grace believed was *burned like a steak*.

"Saint Thérèse," Remi finally said. "I want to be like her."

"Thérèse of Lisieux, the Little Flower of Jesus. You want to be the patron saint of florists?"

"No, stupid. I want to follow her Little Way. You don't need heroic acts. Small acts done with love."

"Yeah, I don't know about that. She got lucky. Usually it takes a painful death to make it on a holy card. Like really painful." Grace handed Remi the Saint Philomena card. "See the two anchors (gold) and the three arrows (gold)? She vowed to be a virgin, and when she refused to marry Emperor Diocletian, he had her scourged, drowned with anchors, shot with arrows, and finally decapitated."

Remi rolled her eyes, disgusted. "I knew you would make fun of me! I knew I shouldn't have told you. Don't you dare tell anyone else."

"I'm going to tell people that you want to be a saint?!

Good God. I tell your mother that and she'll wash your mouth out with borax."

The conversation was left, Grace hoped in immurement, behind the stone wall. But it wasn't. In a flash fire of self-awareness, Grace realized that she, too, wanted to be saint. Her early influence with the Carmelite nuns—she still associated the hum of the bees with the low murmur of God's voice. Catholic school with its straight-lined plaid skirts and sweet submission. What better goal in life than perfection? A child can believe in it. Probability gets confused with God. It's pretty to think there's a Hell. Before puberty, sainthood seemed attainable.

But the moment Grace followed Christos out of Three Worlds Café, she reached for the cat-o'-nine-tails. There was a part of her that was attracted to his dark, rain-cloud soul. Perhaps she thought her white body would be a poultice. But he covered her in bruises and she tried to call them poems. And then happy Havarti Jake. *Let's get high. Let me fuck you* this *way*. All of it leading to Twentieth Century, the idea of her now shrouded in rose angora beneath shredding eucalyptus trees. Oh sure, there were saints who started as notorious sinners—Saint Pelagia, Saint Mary of Egypt. Certainly Mary Magdalene. But Grace could think of no holy card for a woman who had an abortion. Grace discussed this heart-and-soul question with no one.

But still . . . *You are responsible for your own salvation.*

Grace realized she had been playing patty cake with Remi, and baker's man with Paula. Remi's innocent declaration let her hear how ridiculous the goal was. Grace realized she *didn't* really want to be a saint anymore. And if she wasn't, it should not automatically qualify her as a citizen of sin. Could she grant herself this indulgence and allow herself to be loved by God? Did she have to sacrifice one for the other? She had spent two years in her celibate desert, discussing God with a child!

Theology could be fireflies blinkering glimpses of the Divine. Not a burning bush. She had to give this some thought.

A few months later, Grace went again with George into Las Vegas—*You forgot the list, George!*—Paula catching them just in time. Paula and Grace shared a look. The family all knew George was getting a bit forgetful. They didn't talk about it; they just compensated.

Grace was quiet on the ride, and George gave up on trying to start conversations and turned on an old Hank Williams CD. Seemed like the right kind of music for a person who just wanted to look out the window.

While George hunted the great wide aisles of Home Depot and waited for his lumber order, Grace took his truck over to the seedy Arts District, which was trying to convince tourists that *graffiti* is Italian for mural. She went to Buffalo Exchange, where the smell of old lives defeated the citrus diffuser by the cash register. Grace fingered outfits that Francine would love, pieces resurrected from the Haight with suede fringe and paisley, but it was still the '80s that lit Grace up. Madonna remained her fashion saint. Fingerless lace gloves and crinoline. A bustier—the whale bone may have been plastic, but there's a garment that lives up to its name. She didn't get to wear these outfits much since she left Berkeley, and she was beginning to feel that she had to find a place where her clothes could walk around in public and not get shot like a deer out of season.

At the checkout counter, there was a row of Mexican religious candles, the kind in cylinders of glass, holiness evinced in portraits of deep colors and glitter. Oh, how that glitter would star a dark room! Beautiful. Grace bought Remi an Our Lady of Guadalupe with her full-body halo.

With a little more time to kill, Grace ordered nachos at the nearby Casa Don Juan. (Yep, *papel picados*, party on a string.) "You want a margarita with that?" asked the waitress in a full skirt of many layers and nurse's shoes. Grace hesitated; the waitress caught the melancholy slump in Grace's shoulders. "Let me tell you something," the waitress laughed. "Margarita make everything better!"

Who was Grace to argue with a philosopher such as this?

George and Grace headed home. Hank Williams, who had died at the tragic age of twenty-nine, sang about *setting the woods on fire*; he sang about being young. George and Paula were not oblivious to those in their care; they just believed in letting kids fall off their bikes. But Grace was starting to look as if she needed a push. They had come to love Grace; who wouldn't? George pictured the time she walked by Blue and his buddy Carson fighting over equal shares of a sugary drink they had bought out of the vending machine at the golf course. "Only virgins and posers drink that crap," she had said as she walked through the room without even a pause, transforming the drink into the toxic sludge it already was. She had that easy way with the kids, a sort of slutty-dressed Mary Poppins, red bra strap ever at the ready. Paula and George would love to keep her. But they were well aware that she was an adult sleeping in a bunk bed in a room that smelled like teen spirit.

OUR LADY OF GUADALUPE

A year went by. Remi turned fifteen. She quit going out to the Carmelite chapel. She felt like a science experiment. She started her period—a lava flow, an eruption of Mount Saint Remi. Her body was turning on her. Remi wanted to shellac someone, anyone, on a constant basis, every conversation was karate. She wanted to kick. She wanted to kiss that stupid boy, Bryan. Bryan! The girl didn't know what she wanted.

So she jumped on her trampoline. Especially at night, because airborne, she felt twelve. Remi was unaware, but she was beautiful on the tramp. Graceful, and on nights when the moon was a nick of silver, she was nothing more than a shadow, brown braids like reins come loose. She never missed her move, always made an Olympic landing. The only color in the night, the Milky Way a-shiver above her.

When winter came, the first rain drops fell and turned to little puffs of dust on the hard, parched ground. It looked like suicide. But eventually the water soaked the earth, and come late March, flower tapestries were thrown across the shoulders and valleys of the desert, exhaling a light of many colors. Paula went back to her roots, to petit fours, exquisite squares of cake—lemon, raspberry, rosettes and violets frosting the top. Little bites of spring. George found moss growing on a stony ledge. Moss! The ribbons of Addie's ballet pointes crisscrossed her maypole legs. Blue *borrowed* Addie's tarot cards and put them in his bike spokes—the Magician and the Fool—she couldn't miss just two—and roared off on the quest-of-the-day. Francine came up for a week's visit, and as always happened when Francine was there, Grace had eyes for no one but her mother.

Remi jumped.

Later that summer came a hot night, too hot to be a longer word than that. Remi couldn't sleep. She got up and lit the Our Lady of Guadalupe candle. It was augmented now by one of Paula's Thanksgiving tapers because the original candle had long ago puddled low in the glass cylinder. The thin candle rose a few inches higher than the holder, and Remi liked the look, a little hello-halo of flame. She lay in bed and watched the flicker.

Grace wasn't in her top bunk—she was out at the Baptist revival, *shakin' it for Je-sus*. Remi hadn't wanted to go. Too much work. She had declared herself a naturalist like her father. The fact that grape soda lupine grows three feet tall and smells like its name was proof enough of the divine for Remi. Grape soda! In the desert! It takes a God to come up with that. It sounded good, but basically it was just an excuse for being lazy.

Remi thought she heard a buzzing sound, far off, like bees on the move. Probably the hum of the Baptists. Finally, she gave up on sleep and headed outside. The waning crescent moon seemed a sliver of ice, and 95 degrees felt cool. She went to the refuge of her trampoline. Upward bound. She could jump with her eyes closed, so sure were her bare feet. So she did.

Paula woke up too. She heard the high-pitched, tinny sound, opened her eyes. "You up, George?" She thought he was shaving with his electric razor. *In the middle of the night!?* He really was getting worse. The bathroom was dark. Everything was dark. The sound was coming from outside.

George wasn't in the bed. *Shit!*

The two of them, old lovers, they didn't much talk about George's freewheeling memory. What did it matter if he sometimes couldn't remember the Latin names for the stupid palm trees? Why did that frustrate him so? She didn't care if he came home with beer instead of butter. Who doesn't like beer?! And if it was butter instead of beer, well, she'd bake some sheepherder's bread in the Dutch oven. What is marriage but prolonged tolerance? And it wasn't that bad. She didn't think his memory was that bad.

Paula put her sneakers on and went out the front door. Shifted her ears from side to side. Where was that sound coming from? She had to pick it out in between the strands of gospel music.

Reverend Bernard was bringing down the house. The revival was set up in the Mission Gardens. The high arch of the whitewashed adobe entrance shone as if it were the Pearly Gates. Magenta bougainvillea trailed over. Palm trees swayed, and *Thank you, Jesus, for the breeze!* Three women, whom the Reverend hired as much for the girth of their thighs as for their voices, were leading the gospels, "Alabaster Box" and "You Got a Friend in Jesus." Bernard's wife was laying out the cold fried chicken on long tables, lemonade in glass pictures sweating in the night. The stars of the Milky Way looked as if the souls of all those who went before us were peeking out from heaven. Everyone was moved to raise their hands in praise. Everyone was singing, Grace too. Top of their lungs.

It was beautiful. Really it was.

Paula made the oasis. It wasn't hard to find George. He was the one with the chainsaw.

Inside the Boulder House, Our Lady of Guadalupe's little flame had been pushed by the small backwind of Remi's body as she exited the room. And the little flame had taken the opportunity to grab hold of the curtains that had been just beyond its reach. Everything in this world has a mindless bent toward movement. Up, down, over, under. The flame was just a tickle on the linen, but a loose thread threw the fire a lifeline. It wasn't quick. A thin column of smoke rose toward the ceiling and then mushroomed out. It had the color and consistency of dove-gray silk, bolts of silk rolling off the spool.

A shadow color. Full of all the things it ate. It took a long time with the savory oak of the bunkbed. The house itself was solid and would stand like a Sequoia after a lightning strike. But all the things we buy now—synthetics, things with pretty-sounding names—*vinyl* and *plastic* and *acetate*—burn like a son of a bitch. And flour. Would you believe it? Paula had made biscuits for dinner. Blue did the dishes. What a disaster. Flour in eddies, flour dusting the air. Dozens of other little things around the house, flavoring the smoke, building density. Toxicity. Not all the Boulder Houses were equipped with fire alarms. Of course they should have been—ask the head of grounds—didn't he take care of that sort of thing?

Reverend Bernard had provided a piano—that was a son of a gun to set up. If the stars themselves could sing, surely they would sound like the tambourines. What a lovely jingle the little zills made. People were stomping. *Glory, glory, glory!* Grace said. *Glory!* Could be the Lord was enjoying the concert.

George was boiling with frustration, bursting with it. The names just wouldn't come to him. Skidded right by, on the periphery of memory.

Washingtonia filifera. Phoenix dactylifera.

He could not manifest those words. He gave up on the hard ones and tried to find just the names for the wildflowers—the Mojave wildrose, Panamint daisies, mariposa lilies. Child's play, just flower names.

Rosa acicularis. Calochortus. Enceliopsis covillei.

Nothing. He tried the jackalope, that desert jokester. Laughing at him now.

Lepus antilocapra

Empty. All the names were gone, mandalas blown in the wind. Sands in an hourglass.

Looking back, Remi knows she smelled the smoke before she heard the sirens. There came a tipping point, when the damp grass, the curated smell of the golf course was overcome by an out-of-place smokehouse scent. It smelled something like the whiskey her dad liked to drink. But it was the sirens that opened her eyes. Her body turned to ice, but still she jumped, an automaton of a girl. She didn't know what to do.

It's the smoke that's the killer, if it can't find its vent. The fireplace chimney was closed. Only threads could escape. The windows were shut. Every room had a fan that would push, push, push the smoke around until the plastic blades melted into Dali-esq sculptures. Every bedroom door was open to help the flow of the fans. The smoke followed the rivers of air.

Blue had a summer cold; he was off on the wings of the green dragon Nyquil, that absinth tincture of childhood. He'd kept sneezing in the kitchen when Paula was baking. "Take some cold medicine at bedtime," his mother had said. He was old enough to do it for himself, and young enough to double-dose on purpose. For the fun of it.

Addie, perhaps she had the best chance, in the glass room. But there is nothing that an seventeen-year-old girl likes better than aerosols and polishes—she was forever forgetting to put the lid on the nail polish remover. Clothes in piles. Books, whose only natural enemies are school boards and bonfires. Addie dreamed she was dancing pirouettes across the floor—again and again and again!—until she was out of breath.

Out at the oasis garden, the lighting was exquisite. Luminary stars, and so well-placed fairy lights on the crisscross paths. In this artist's glow, George had turned Laszlo Toth, that crazy Hungarian who delivered twelve awful hammer blows to Michelangelo's *Pietà*. For isn't the oasis at Furnace Creek—with its magnificent grove of tawny-barked palms, fruit that could keep a wanderer alive in the Badwater—a masterpiece?

George's Husqvarna chainsaw chewed into the palm stems like a fevered beaver. By the time Paula got there, four were down, crown of fronds a-topple like vaudeville showgirls that had slipped on the banana peel. Paula was aghast. She yelled for George to stop, but he was starting on a fifth tree, and she feared that if she touched him, the rabid Hasqvarna would sink its teeth into her.

The sirens started. What a wail, that heart song of disaster. But the fire crew was confused. First, they got several calls that a crazy man was cutting down the 100-foot palms in the oasis, and they headed that way. They had axes of their own. But then there were conflicting calls about a fire, and they could see dark smoke. Over at the Boulder houses. They diverted to the fire.

When the sirens started, the revival folk stopped singing. Now they could smell the smoke, see the ghost of it coming from the north. With their voices stilled, the sounds of a chainsaw grew. They heard a tree fall, a sound only lumberjacks and big game hunters seek, the *womp* of it. Grace took off. She had only to traverse the front of the Furnace Creek Inn to reach the oasis.

Remi could see from her trampoline's angle, the firemen who broke through the glass of Addie's patio room, shattered the whorls and labyrinths of smoke. The smoke poured out, a fire-breathing scourge on the loose. The men in padded coats and the black boots that Remi had put coins in at the annual fundraiser pulled Addie through the window and put the coughing girl in the ambulance. Blue right behind, carried in yellow arms, but head up. Alive!

But not Remi's parents. They didn't come out. *Dad wouldn't wake up if the house was on fire.* That's what her mother always said, her husband's snoring the metronome of her nights. Paula smoked so much, she would have thought the smell was just her own menopausal sweat on a hot, hot night.

Still Remi jumped, braids akimbo. No one saw her, so entrancing was the fire, and no lights shone her way. She watched the comings and goings, the water arcs, all the neighbors. The atomic bomb worth of smoke. When it was conclusive to Remi that no one else was coming out of that house and into a speeding ambulance, she steadied herself and began a series of jumps intended to launch her as high as possible. When she reached that summit, as high as she had ever been, she realigned her body, took it out of center, and flat-lined into a horizontal slab of meat. For the first time in her life as a jumper, she landed on the metal frame. Her shoulder, her new breast, her just-below-the-surface ribs. Hip and thigh, her ankle caught and twisting. Her face. What a satisfying pain.

Grace rounded the grove in time for the beginnings of the wreck of the sixth tree. The shock and the percussion. In the pale light, the palm fronds on the tree George was attacking were shaking as if they had their hands up in surrender. The mind is a swift calculator, and Grace pushed her legs past burn because it looked to her like Paula, trying to climb over the helter-skelter of the felled trees, was about to get felled herself. Shouting was useless because the sound of the Hasqvarna was a visceral, straight-to-the bones loudmouth. She tried anyway. Might as well spit into the wind.

There are those who believe nature has a consciousness.

That an avalanche is the mountain shrugging it shoulders, scratching an itch. House plants prefer Beethoven. Tree roots send out nutrients and information to others in their grove. George believed this, although he would never try to put it into words. Words are just a mud puddle.

One truth is that just as the sixth *Phoenix dactylifera* was *land ho*, George changed directions. One could not say if he purposely stepped into the tree's falling trajectory, or if already fallen fronds gathered together to magic-carpet him away from his Hasqvarna. Or maybe he just slipped. It is disputable. But what is indisputable was that George was crushed, and those same earthed fronds curved up and around him, as if to hide what they done did.

Paula was not so cradled by the fronds; she was caught on the edges of the falling crown, slashed and pummeled. Colleterial damage to her husband's long-ago concussion combined with his unfortunate genes.

Everyone was headed toward the house on fire, but Grace was with Paula and George. Without the savage voice of the Hasqvarna, the oasis grove reset. The rill burbled. A wind jostled the frond crowns of the survivors, and they had plenty to say with their papery voice. Grace prayed aloud, *Our Father who art in heaven*. George was beyond her strength to pull from the wreckage, but Paula, she extracted like a precious, sweet little fleshy Halawi palm date, so worthy of all the praise.

Remi woke up at Sunrise Hospital in Las Vegas. Morphine stilled her riptides of pain, the ocean of bruises that mottled her skin. Washes of greens, purpled edges, yellow eddies. Her nose and three ribs were broken. Her ankle badly sprained. She had a concussion, a punctured a lung. She went back under and dreamed of her mother:

"*I want you to bring a priest to me. I want you to bring me a Marlboro. You've got your orders now,*" her mother said from her own hospital bed. So Remi knew her mother was dying. And she knew her mother still wanted to get into the celestial kingdom—that highest level of Mormon heaven. *She deserves the highest level*—thought Remi, in her dream going to get the cigarettes out of a vending machine; she had no recourse for the priest.

When Remi woke up again, she knew her mother was gone. Or going. Either way, gone. The woman in the corner was a social worker—guessing by the sensible shoes and the Peter Pan collars. Why was she biting her lips?

Remi tried on a new word, remembering when Paula was in her Word a Day phase with the kids: orphan. Had that ever been on Paula's list?

A policeman came toward her, all glinty, little pieces of him—his gun, his badge, his Polaroids hanging from his pocket. The social worker ("I'm Rachel," she said to Remi) got him to sit down in the chair next to the bed. Less threatening. Rachel sat down too. The officer pulled out his silver pen, his little metal spiral-bound flip book of paper.

"I'm sorry for your loss," he said. Officer Carpenter, Remi read his name.

"Losses," Remi whispered, or maybe just said in her head.

"Do you like your family?" Carpenter asked.

Rachel sat up, alarmed.

"Do I like them?" Remi was astounded by the question.

"Why were you jumping on the trampoline?" Carpenter switched his question.

"She isn't Nero playing the fiddle while Rome burned," inserted Rachel, outrage blooming across her face.

"Why didn't you try to break a window?" Carpenter didn't even look at Rachel. He was working up to a direct accusation; Rachel felt it. He wanted to know if the fire was started on purpose. The insurance company wanted to know too. Rachel would stop this interview, this jerk cop.

Remi's eyes dilated. *Oh my dear God, why didn't I break the window?*

Rachel saw the girl turning to stone, knew that she could help her to understand the very human response of doing nothing in the face of extreme danger and trauma. Not many people run into a burning house.

"Did you start the fire?" Carpenter pushed before Rachel could intervene.

Rachel stood up, trying to interrupt, to stop Remi from saying anything at all, but Remi said, "Our Lady of Guadalupe started the fire."

And then both adults in the room thought she was crazy; even the social worker thought the poor girl might be crazy.

Remi stopped looking at them; they left. She thought about when her father would read to her from the Children's Bible, alternating between the horror stories of the Old Testament and the Jesus miracles of the New. The little lamb stories were nice, but Remi loved the idea of living inside the rib cage of a whale, locust, sliced throats of baby boys. She thought now she was the locust and the knife.

Remi had fallen so far from grace, so far from turning into a cobalt-and-gold-leafed holy card, that she gravely considered running away and turning into a portrait on the back of a milk carton. Would she never walk again with her father through slot canyons in hopes of bees that burrow holes in sandstone cliffs? Never drink chunky date milkshakes at China Ranch with her mother, who loved them so? Remi closed her eyes.

Paula came into the room. Her daughter looked as if she were wearing Jacob's coat of many colors, such was the rainbow-bruising beneath the cloth of her skin. Remi felt a presence and opened her spindrift eyes. She thought she was still asleep. "I got the cigarettes, but I couldn't find a priest," she said to her suddenly nonplussed mother.

Morphine is a Cheshire cat.

It took some effort to explain that Paula was alive, and that the bandages on her arms and face, with the glossy smears of ointment, were from cuts from the palm fronds and not burns. She hadn't been in the house! *You look like a mummy, Mommy.* Oh, to hear her daughter joke! To put her arms around her daughter! But then Paula had to tell Remi about her dad and pulverize Remi's relief, her joy. "But it wasn't your fault," she assured her again and again.

Paula didn't want Remi to imagine George's crushed body. The white lie to her children was that he got a quick hit on the head. Grace backed her up, ever-and-a-day.

Grief is the *blind men and an elephant*—something different to everyone who touches it.

Addie missed the father who put necklaces under her pillow, puka shells and Nevada turquoise, who always wanted to watch her dance and helped her apply to Juilliard—*Ballerina trained at the Amargosa Opera House in Death Valley? Face like yours? You're dancing on a street of gold!*

Blue was a bright kaleidoscope, tumbling, too young to settle. Love was a blood amethyst in his heart. He just missed his daddy.

On each wedding anniversary, Paula put on her he-loves-me daisy dress while George pushed back the furniture. When Remi was old enough, it became her job to place the stylus on the record of Sonny King singing "If I Didn't Care." Paula and George would dance. Remi felt she could capture the love of her parents in the up-swoop of the very first note of that scratchy record, and in the step of her mother's wedding shoes on their hardwood floor. What would they do, when the anniversary came around this year?

Remi decided, but told no one, that her dad wasn't gone, just now over at the Oasis, skimming ponds to watch the water patterns through the net. And she believed it. When she went looking for him, she avoided the six telltale, graying stumps, stayed higher in the grove, followed the rills of Travertine Spring. He was always just a bit ahead of her. The best time was in the afternoon when the slanting light poured gold. Sometimes Remi picked a date up off the ground, brown and shiny-skinned. She ate it, pretended it was her dad, and it wasn't strange at all, but comforting.

Grace missed the man who never struggled with religion or theology. Nature was God, God nature. You need look no farther than a feather. Forgiveness is rain in a long summer. In a way, she felt that George had succumbed to the thing he loved. Would that we could all do that.

Paula, well, she touched every side of that elephant. She remembered George's water-blue eyes, how they looked at her. How she felt on their wedding night, how proud she felt to hold George's hand. His wide shoulders, the way he shouldered the world for her. The way his body felt over hers. If she could count the saddest things on five fingers, one of them would be that, for the life of her, she couldn't specifically remember the last time they made love.

They had left Neon City for a place where you could walk on salt. Raised their children in the dust. Paula knew it was a good life, she was grateful. She just didn't want it to be over.

Francine came up right away to help with the emotional and physical overload. She organized everything right down to buying extra Kleenex. The Carrolls moved into a nearby house, bolstered by a general potlach to get the new household started. Not everything was destroyed, but most of what survived was smoke-infused, so the whole family smelled like pioneers for quite some time. The new kitchen was bigger, with yellow-check tile countertops, and Remi and Grace got twin beds instead of bunk. The holy candle was not replaced.

About three weeks later, those who had lived a long time at Furnace Creek got together at the suddenly appropriately named Last Kind Word Saloon for the wake. Then just the family headed out for the long drive to the St. Thérèse Mission on the Old Spanish Trail, where George was to be interned. During the short service, Addie sang "Nearer My God to Thee" in a voice that covered them in petals. On the way back, the family took a detour, followed the dirt road of the slot canyon to the China Ranch Date Farm for date milkshakes. Remi thought about the irony of George ending up in the Our Lady of Guadalupe mausoleum, within the St. Thérèse Mission. Honestly, it made her laugh.

On the first night after George's service, Remi slept with her mother. Francine slept in the room with Grace. Near dawn, (old habits) Francine got up for a smoke, went out to catch the Panamint range flare amethyst. Returning to the bedroom, something made Francine perch on the edge of Grace's bed.

The heaviness on the mattress pulled Grace to semiconsciousness. She thought she saw a glowy angel at the foot of her bed. Nope, it was her mom. But still she asked, "Are there angels, do you think, Mom?"

Francine lit up another cigarette, right in the room. "You thinking about George?" she asked.

Grace was. "And Twentieth Century."

"I think so," Francine said. "But kind of just a shadow of light. Positive energy, that's it. You can block it or receive it; it's up to you. But mostly I think those who have died have to work on their own paths. Twentieth Century is probably a koala by now, and George's negotiating coming back as a sequoia. Mostly we are on our own."

The morning light coming in the window lit the dust motes gold. Francine shifted and the motes swirled. Angel dust. "Here's what I have come to think," said Francine. "God's God. That's it. Don't worry too much about it. All the prophets, He likes them all. No favorite. Well, except maybe Joseph Smith. Paula says that opportunist wears a baloney suit."

"What about L. Ron Hubbard?

"I think Ron actually is an alien. With a brain injury so he doesn't count. But here's the point: God likes all the names. No favorite. Doesn't care which path you take."

"You told me I could only go to the Catholic Church. I wanted to eat that Baptist chicken."

"What did I know! I was young when you were young. I know better now. Eat the chicken." Francine's skin, her light hair, shone alabaster. Nothing matches a desert light. Grace looked as if she might start to cry. "Okay, I'm going to tell you the Secret now," her mother said.

Grace leaned forward, sunburnt hair falling over her shoulders. She really wanted to pay attention to the Secret. Francine leaned toward her and said most earnestly, "Super-califragilisticexpialidocious."

"Oh, Mom, come on, are you shitting me?!" She had shared the smart-alecky theology shortcut with her mom long ago.

Francine held out her hands and there was blue light within the veins of her wrists. "You girls had it right! Be kind, have joy in other people's joy, help the needy. Decrease your personal desires. Meditation and prayer are the best paths to God. That's it. That's all you have to remember. The world flows from God's endless energy. Say your prayers."

Francine had been doing some studying on her own. That and dating the nicest ex-priest, Roger Ward. Oh, the theological wrestling matches those two had over pizza and beer at Tony's in Washington Square, drinking Irish coffees at the Buena Vista.

The little magic time ended. Here-and-now returned. "Grace," asked Francine, "have you given any thought to going back to a school?"

"Yep. I've been thinking about it."

"The scholarship is still in an account for you . . ." Francine watched Grace's eyes, her shoulders, her body sizzle just a little bit as the idea ran through her. "UC Berkeley—"

"I don't want to go back to Berkeley," Grace interrupted. "I want to go to Dreaming of Pastry in Las Vegas"—Paula's culinary school, where Paula had mastered all things marzipan.

For one minute, Francine had envisioned her daughter returning with her to the Bay Area, only to see it shimmer and pop in the same instant. Was she sad? Yes, but—*Joy in other people's joy.*

"Do you think my scholarship money would pay for that?" asked Grace.

"I do. It will."

Two months later, Grace moved to Las Vegas.

The night before Grace was to leave, she and Remi were in bed, moonlight like mercury on their spreads. Grace reached a disembodied hand across the space of their two beds. "These are for you." She dangled the rose velvet bag, tasseled drawstring frayed, some cards still inside. Neither of them had looked at the holy cards in a couple of years.

"Thank you," said Remi, reaching over. She ran her fingers over the fabric like it was a baby blanket. Remi's head suddenly popped up. "Are there any good ones left?"

LAURA NEWMAN

"You are the good one left."

Addie took her sister's hand; everyone understood. Paula flanked Remi as the truck drove away and turned to a shimmer. The goodbye was hard on everyone, but Remi felt like she was standing at the bottom of the Grand Canyon with no donkey. How to climb out of this feeling? She started to cry. But then Addie said, "You're being over-dramatic. She's coming home, like every weekend. Her apartment is a shithole."

Bright lights, big city. Jimmy Reed sang it in 1961 and now Grace was living it. Well, she wasn't such a cowpoke as to be overawed; she grew up in the San Francisco Bay Area after all. Grace knew a faux city when she saw one. But, oh, the fun! All her Madonna clothes came out of the closet.

Maurice was long gone from Dreaming of Pastry, replaced by Célestine Chalamet in her sharp pencil skirt and no-nonsense white apron. Well, her last name means "blowtorch" so she had better be good with the crème brûlée. Célestine hoisted that propane canister, with its sci-fi gun pointed at Grace. "You know, *chérie*, all that tulle, I could burn you like steak!" Grace loved her!

Grace did go home to Death Valley on most weekends, and Paula pored over her assignments with her. *Half the salt, I'm telling you; otherwise the dough will be too tight! Fondant? I'll show you fondant!*

How long does it take to fall in love? About the time it takes to bake a cake. Everyone knows it. It starts with the tension of stirring the batter in the bowl. Then the aroma coming out of the oven, almonds and vanilla. Orange zest. Then it's the way it feels when you push down on the center of the cooling round, the texture and the *push-back*. Frosting on top, but-

244

tercream and ginger. Next, of course, the way the knife slides through. Seal the deal with the first bite.

That's how Grace felt about her cooking partner, Rowan O'Conner.

Rowan's family sailed from Dun Laoghaire to San Francisco two generations ago and Rowan was as American as corned beef and cabbage, egg rolls, and tacos. He melted in the pot. His parents migrated to Virginia City, Nevada, same as many an Irish family before them. His old countrymen were in search of their share of the Comstock Silver Lode, and so were his parents, just with a different plan for mining it. They opened a bar. Rowan lived in a high mountain ghost town. He grew up in saloons with barmaids as babysitters; his bedtime stories were about the spirits of the Comstock. It was understood that one was likely to meet those very spirits on a street corner under a dim moon, the shadow lighting up a cheroot, or cleaning the horse dung from the heel of his boot. Or walking into his parents' pub.

Rowan was a transplant to the high desert. Grace to the low desert. He grew up in a bar—Grace's bootlegging grandfather owned one! It felt a good start of common ground. That and baking. Hot crossed buns and sugar, sugar everywhere.

And Rowan had just a shimmer of red below his thick brown hair, didn't he now?

When Grace and Rowan eventually got married at the oasis in Death Valley, Paula made the cake, Prinsesstarta—white sponge with raspberry cream filling, draped in almondy marzipan. Addie came home from her teaching job at the Cornish College of the Arts in Seattle and sang Madonna's "Like a Prayer" a cappella while Francine walked Grace down a twisting aisle of palms. Blue served the best prickly pear margaritas—before the service. Roger officiated with his online license from the Universal Life Church. Remi stood maid of honor, and cried.

Grace's silk slip dress poured over her in a long run of heavy cream. Veil held in place by a single gardenia in her garnet hair. Her freckles were outstanding. Rowan wore a Black Watch kilt, commando.

It was so hot a day, all the bouquet roses just went *poof* and sighed into perfume.

Before Rowan and Grace left for their honeymoon—Paris!—Grace and Remi visited the Unofficial Our Lady of Cake Carmelite Chapel-lite. Much of the stone had fallen, but the turnstile was still there, yellowed and warped by the heat. The ladders remained, looking like bones. The women ran their fingers over the carvings on the sandstone wall, touched their past. Then let it be.

Remi was a student at UC Berkeley on an anonymously funded, full-ride scholarship. She was studying architecture, with an emphasis on the West. That girl would grow up to champion the lowly adobe, specializing in ceilings of mosaic stars set in desert midnight blue. She might become famous.

Francine and Roger were moving to Las Vegas!

Eventually Rowan and Grace got a concession from the National Park System to open up a dessert bar—One More Bite—on the Ranch at Death Valley. If you go there now, you can try Carrageen Moss Pudding, or Irish Whiskey Truffles. Their kids—Clare, named for the Claremont Hotel that stands so stately in the Berkeley Hills, and Fox, named after his sister who died at Big Sur—sometimes work at the Bite. Or they can be found with their grandmother, Paula. Right now she is teaching them about seed banks of the world— wait until they hear about the botanists who starved to save the seeds in World War II St. Petersburg!

But mostly Grace and Rowan's kids are left to be raised by the desert. *Just be home by the time the sun sets or you might die out there and we won't even know where to look for ya bones.*

Death Valley looks the lonely place. But it isn't.

Laika the Soviet Space Dog

ACKNOWLEDGMENTS

ABOUT THE AUTHOR

Laura Newman s the author of the short story collection, *The Franklin Avenue Rookery for Wayward Babies*. Her stories have been printed in *The Saturday Evening Post*, *Literary Hub*, *Failbetter*, *Apricity Magazine*, *New Plains Review*, and the *Reno News & Review*. Newman is the 2024 recipient of the University of Nevada Libraries Nevada Writer's Silver Pen Award.

Printed in the USA
CPSIA information can be obtained
at www.ICGtesting.com
JSHW021452031124
72871JS00002B/59